AS LA VISTA TURNS

KRIS RIPPER

Riptide Publishing
PO Box 1537
Burnsville, NC 28714
www.riptidepublishing.com

This is a work of fiction. Names, characters, places, and incidents are either the product of the author's imagination or are used fictitiously. Any resemblance to actual persons living or dead, business establishments, events, or locales is entirely coincidental. All person(s) depicted on the cover are model(s) used for illustrative purposes only.

Cover art: L.C. Chase, lcchase.com/design.htm
Editor: May Peterson
Layout: L.C. Chase, lcchase.com/design.htm

ISBN: 978-1-62649-442-8

First edition
February, 2017

Also available in ebook:
ISBN: 978-1-62649-441-1

AS LA VISTA TURNS

KRIS RIPPER

For my community of queers and freaks and outcasts. May we feel joy even in the jaws of grief. May we never forget the road we've traveled. May we, more than anything else, remember to love one another even when it seems our goals are not shared, even when it feels like more divides us than unites us. Let us stand our ground together.

TABLE OF

CONTENTS

I didn't mean to kiss Dred. It was an accident.

I was a little hungover after the wedding, and the sunlight was, like, *glaring* through my windshield, and when she got in the car I was happy to see her, so I kissed her. Okay, so "kiss Dred" wasn't on my list of things to do, but it was an accident. And we were grown-ups. It was no big deal.

Except for the way neither of us pulled back.

Except for the way I really wanted to kiss her more.

Except for the look in her eyes—all open and warm and eager—when she started to say, "Whoa, Z, that was—"

Then: "Fuck!" She glared over my shoulder. "Damn it, Emerson. Z, will you roll down your window for a minute?"

"Okay . . ."

I hadn't noticed Emerson calling her, but she'd heard him, so he must have been. I was in "accidentally kissing Dred" land. No external forces need apply.

Also, what had she been about to say? *Whoa, Z, that was*—what?

Emerson was wheezing and leaning on his cane when he got to the car. "Swatches. Jesus, that's a long haul when my leg's being a bitch. Obie wants to know which one of these they want to buy." A manila envelope landed on Dred's lap.

"Do I look like his errand boy to you?"

Emerson offered one of his crooked smiles. "Pretty much, yeah. You girls have fun now."

"Don't think I won't beat you with that cane."

"I'm pretty sure you won't. Bye, Zane."

"See ya, Emerson." I pulled away from the curb, trying to decide if the silence in the car was awkward, or I was imagining things. Not that it mattered. "So I'm not pregnant."

"BFN?"

"Big fuckin' negative, yep. Yesterday, before the wedding."

"Wow, and then you spent all day smiling and making nice with people. It's like God really hates you or something."

"Shut up. I actually enjoy smiling and making nice with people. Plus, it's better than sitting in my condo staring at the walls wondering why I'm such a failure." I couldn't talk this way to everyone. But I could to Dred, even after accidentally kissing her and crossing all the made-up lines we'd drawn around fake-dating.

Fake-dating had seemed like a good idea to get my best friend off my back about "getting out there" and "staying open to relationships." And it had done its job. Dred and I had fun, no one got hurt, and for six months I'd been free of friendly nudges toward any lady with a pulse.

Damn it. I shouldn't have kissed her. No. I should kiss her again. All the time. Or never. Hell. I blushed even thinking about kissing her again. If she saw the blush, she'd probably kill me; I made sure I kept my face pointed away, and turned up the radio. "I haven't heard this song in months! Clean Bandit and Jess Glynne. Listen to her voice, it's amazing."

Jesus. *Way to compound the awkward, Zane.* I'd just drawn our attention to a song all about how there was no place the singer would rather be than with whoever she was singing to.

I turned it down again and tried to come up with a distraction. "You want to hear the other thing that happened at the wedding? Or no, after it. I may have cried all over the grooms."

"Poor you." Her voice wasn't exactly sympathetic.

"They, uh, offered me sperm." I repeated it in my head, but no, that was the correct sentence. "Tom's sperm."

"No fucking way." She shifted, and even though I didn't look over, I could tell she was facing me now. "No way."

"Yeah."

"Shit, Zane. You gonna take them up on that? I mean, it'd be cheaper, but then you're stuck with . . . men."

She knew from being stuck with men. Her ex had every other weekend with Baby James, after skipping out on the first five months of his life. Shit was complicated.

"They know I'm not looking for co-parents. But I don't know. There's a lot to think about."

"Genetics-wise, it'd be a solid match. Tom's all kinds of perfect specimen of blond, blue-eyed Aryan man."

"Okay, thanks, now I'm totally creeped out. I'm not trying to have baby Hitler!"

She laughed. Dred's laugh was low and sharp, like if you got too close it'd make you bleed.

"You're so mean." I may have huffed.

"You're the one who wants to have baby Hitler with Tom of Finland."

"Oh my *god,* stop it, Mildred!"

Her hand ghosted over my knee and withdrew. Would she have done that pre-accidental-kiss? I didn't think so. Did that mean the kiss had been good for her, too? How could I tell? A sentence that starts with *Whoa, Z* could be going anywhere.

"Well?" This time she poked me. That was definitely the usual way of things. "Are you going to think about it?"

"Of course I'm going to think about it. It's been twelve cycles. Twelve BFNs. And I'm supposedly healthy. And all of those donors I tried had other positives, so it's not them." I blinked a few times to keep my emotions from taking over. The thing about trying to get pregnant is that it's a constant pressure, a weight on your skin, and even if your awareness of it drops for a few minutes, the smallest thing can remind you that you're compressed on all sides by an inability to do this very basic thing.

I cleared my throat. "Anyway." I pulled the car into a parking spot that may or may not still be a red zone from back when the drop-in center was a warehouse of some kind. "Hey, that's interesting."

"What is?"

I gestured to the car in front of us. "Cam Rheingold's car. He's been down here a lot lately."

"I thought you were only allowed to make people into a soap opera at Club Fred's."

"What? I'm not! I'm just saying, you know, that's interesting."

She poked me again, and when I turned she was smirking. "I know exactly what you're saying, gutter brain."

"Shut up, I'm so not. I'm *not.*"

The smirk. Oh jeez. I wanted to kiss her smirking face.

"Let's off-load all this junk," I mumbled, and got out of the car.

Cam and Keith were in the kitchen when we walked into the center, standing at closer-than-regulation distance. Not that I inferred anything from their apparent intimacy. Except that they were . . . close. Physically. In the kitchen.

Keith waved. "Please tell me you come bearing food and I can eat something other than peanut butter and banana today."

I gestured to the car. "So much food. You guys want to help unload?"

"Definitely." Oh look, he casually touched Cam's arm. Because they were close. Physically. "If you can tempt Josh away from the computer, I'd appreciate it. He's gonna go blind if he keeps staring at that spreadsheet, willing it to tell him something different."

"Sure." Cam smiled at us. "I'll be right back to help."

I shrugged. "Oh, three of us is enough, don't worry about it."

Dred kicked my ankle, which I took as: *Stop making them into a soap opera.* Which I wasn't, kind of, though what Cam was going to do to tempt Josh away from the computer was intriguing.

My brain tried to tag that thought like I was entering it in my notebook app: *blowjob, kissing, massage.* I could go into the temptation business. That was a list I could keep going with: *dirty talk, handjob, kissing.*

Why was I thinking about kissing?

I performed a forced shut down on my mental processes and led the way to the car.

Donating all the leftover reception food to the Queer Youth Project's drop-in center was Carlos's brilliant idea ("I mean, the last fucking thing we want is to start married life with half a ton of goddamn catered food"). I'd volunteered to do it as my final wedding-planning-job duty, and man, I was glad to see the last of it emptying out of my car.

"Good riddance to bad rubbish." I shut the hatch with a flourish.

"That bad?" Keith carefully balanced huge portions of cake in each hand.

"No. Well, yes, though I'd do it again. For Carlos, not for just anyone."

He batted his eyelashes at me suggestively.

I pointed at him. "I'm not going to trip you out of respect for the cake. Why, are you guys getting married?"

"No way. Well, maybe someday, but not anytime soon."

Dred poked her head out the sliding door. "We good?"

"We are so good." I did not stare at her lips. Or, okay, I made myself stop staring at her lips.

"Does that mean it's time to eat cake?"

Gah, stop making me think about lips. I swept an arm through the air and called, "Let them eat cake!"

"You're such a nerd." She grabbed half of Keith's armload. "But we're going to eat this now, right? You better not be teasing me, Zane."

"Are you sure you don't like it when she teases you?" Keith slid past her, evading a clumsy kick in his direction. He laughed (and didn't see her getting ready to kick him again). "The lady doth protest too— Oof!"

He managed—barely—to not drop the cake. My heart was pounding like crazy until all the cake was safely on the counter.

That cake was wildly expensive. It'd be like dropping a Fabergé egg or something.

Keith shook out his arms and spun around. "Totally uncalled for, Mildred! Plus, you know it basically proves my point, right?"

She glared at him. "Are you having sex with Cameron?"

His jaw dropped.

"What are we interrupting?" a new voice asked.

I turned to Josh with relief. Despite being a mere twenty-four years old, the boy had the kind of calm control that immediately soothed a room.

Keith shook his head, still looking flummoxed. "Uh, I pissed off Mildred. Or something. And hell yes, I'm having sex with Cameron. It's not a secret."

Poor Cam. His face was crimson and he had busied himself picking through food, maybe trying to sort it, or just trying to pretend he was somewhere else.

"It's definitely not a secret," Josh agreed.

"Sorry." Dred glanced at me. "Anyway, can you guys take all this?"

"As long as it was at food-safe temperatures between last night and right now." Keith started picking through. "We probably can't serve the hot food."

Josh grabbed a stack of plates. "More for us."

"Josh! It hasn't been at temp. It's not safe to eat."

"It was refrigerated and I'm reheating it. It's no different than if we made it at home and then—"

"Except that like a hundred people breathed on it and it sat out for hours."

"Seriously?"

Keith rolled his eyes. "Fine. You get salmonella. I'm sticking with things that are safe to eat."

Since I wasn't pregnant, I went ahead and joined Josh and Dred in eating potentially toxic leftovers. So that was a perk. Kind of.

Cam notably stuck with Keith in avoiding potentially toxic leftovers, even leaning next to him against the counter. At least his blush had calmed down a few threat levels.

"Where's Mister James today?" Josh asked, when our initial feeding frenzy had died down.

"With Obie and Emerson." Dred felt around in her pockets. "Oh, and Obie sent you swatches."

Keith and Josh exchanged a glance. Keith shoved the manila envelope in a drawer. "Thanks, we'll, uh, get back to him later."

"Swatches?" Cam asked.

"Nothing. Um."

Josh waved a fork. "We're commissioning a piece. It's no big deal."

Oops. I caught Dred's eye and mouthed, *Oops.*

"A piece." Cam studied the two of them. "That's interesting."

"It's not that interesting," Keith said quickly. "Anyway. Um. Let's talk about something totally unrelated. How's the baby thing going, Zane?"

Everyone winced.

"Er, sorry, never mind."

"It's fine." I executed an oh-so-casual one-shoulder shrug. "Future Kid continues to be elusive. There is one development, though, which is that a friend recently offered to donate sperm."

"*Whoa.*" There was something charming about Keith's excitement. "That's really cool, right? I mean, is that a thing people do? Should we have done that?" He appealed to Josh, who answered by kissing him. Keith accepted the kiss, but not as an answer. "No, but seriously, should we have?"

"No, babe."

Dred tossed her plate and went to open one of the cake boxes. "Plus, you'd want to be daddies. Zane doesn't want daddies."

"We wouldn't *have* to be." He paused. "Actually, that's probably a lie. I think if a kid was running around with my genes—or Josh's—I'd probably, you know, want to kind of be involved."

"Me too." Josh smiled at me apologetically. "Sorry, Zane."

"Hey, I'm right there with you. I couldn't be totally detached from a kid who was part me."

"Oh, I could." Dred deposited the cake and a handful of forks on the table. "As long as I didn't have to give birth to it. I don't think I could be a surrogate. Pregnancy was way too much of a pain in the ass. But if I could just jerk off and fill a cup with eggs—" She shrugged. "I'd give them away to whoever the hell wanted them."

Cameron cleared his throat. "I think I could as well. I don't feel any instinctive need to father a child. But if someone needed sperm, I think I could contribute my own without being emotionally attached to the outcome."

"That's a difference between us, Cam." Keith grinned. "I would *totally* be attached to a kid with your DNA."

And poor Cam was blushing again.

"Anyway," I said, taking the spotlight off his bright-red cheeks. "There are a lot of things to think about. And it's not quite as easy as just jerking off in a cup. Like, for best results he'd have to not come for a day or two before, which is kind of an awkward thing to ask someone." Though Carlos would probably make it into some kind of chastity game and they'd both get off on it. I turned my mind away from . . . that.

"But consider yourself added to the list, Cam." Dred smiled a little maliciously.

I elbowed her. And grabbed a fork. "Family-style cake. You people better not have germs."

"So many germs." Keith dug into the cake. "Oh my god. *Oh my god.* This is the greatest cake that has ever been baked. Is this . . . salted caramel that I'm tasting?"

"It really is. Salted caramel filling with a chocolate ganache frosting. And it cost a fortune, so enjoy."

Keith made a sound, something between a moan and a sigh. "I am *so* enjoying."

Josh quirked an eyebrow at him. "We might have to take some of this home. It's obscene watching you eat cake, babe."

"Don't listen to him," Dred advised, closing her eyes to better appreciate the bite she was chewing. "Be one with the cake, Keith."

"I am so *completely* one with the cake right now."

We left sometime later, full of cake, with some to take back to the farmhouse for Obie and Emerson and Baby James.

We were quiet for most of the trip. When I made the turn onto her street, Dred asked, "You want to come in?"

I couldn't read her tone. I usually went in. If this had happened two days ago, I wouldn't even be thinking about it.

But for that damn accidental kiss. I wanted to kiss her again, but I couldn't say that. Fake-dating worked for me because it got my friend Jaq off my back. It worked for Dred because it got her out without actually requiring she *date* people. My whole role was to not be pressure. I couldn't switch it up now.

"Did you start your new quilt yet?" *Give me a reason to come in.*

"Started sewing it, started ripping it out."

I parked the car. "But, jeez, you've been planning it for months."

"That's quilting. Plan for a million years, sew for five minutes, rip for five hours."

I wanted to go in. Was there any reason not to go in? Maybe we could accidentally kiss again. No. Bad idea, Suzanne. "So . . . can I see what you're ripping out?"

"If you want to see my crap, sure. When're you gonna bring over some fabric so you can get started on your quilt?"

"When I grow some ovaries. I still don't think I can actually make a quilt, Dred."

"Of course you can make a quilt. Everyone can make a quilt. Not everyone can make a *show quilt*, but everyone can make a quilt." She sat back in the seat. "Take us to the fabric store. We'll work on it today."

I restarted my car, trying to tell myself that this was only a volunteer job to her, that it had nothing to do with wanting to spend more time with me. It definitely had nothing to do with that kiss. I wanted to ask her what she'd been about to say, earlier, when Emerson interrupted, but it wasn't the kind of thing I could bring up randomly.

Maybe if I accidentally kissed her again . . .

No. *Bad idea, Zane.*

Distraction time. "You're just procrastinating about your own project."

"Yeah. I am."

"I'm good with that."

The moment stretched. We were idling at the curb. The car was in park.

I wanted to lean across the console and kiss her. But I didn't.

CHAPTER 2

Dinner on the third Sunday was always at my sister Andi's, ever since she married her childhood best friend when they were twenty. Fast-forward sixteen years and here we were, sitting at her dining room table, me checking my phone every five minutes because I desperately needed the Andi-and-Jimmy show to be over.

She poured herself another generous glass of wine, and when she leaned forward I could see the professional lowlights in her hair. It was a nice job. Didn't compare to my half-shaved purple, but hey, not everyone can be me. "You don't understand the legal ramifications of this. You think you do, but you don't."

You think you understand, but you don't should be on Andi's tombstone. She forever believed she had the only relevant take on any given situation.

"We're not being alarmist," Jimmy said. The additional *as usual* went unspoken, but his furrowed brows communicated it clearly enough. "Really, Zane. I've done some research. There are some pretty gnarly outcomes."

"Did you see any of the good outcomes, or were you only looking for the freaky stuff?"

"I'm sure there are good outcomes, but is this where you want to take a chance? An anonymous donor offers so much more protection for your family—"

"I don't have a family. Big fuckin' negative. No baby. Anonymous donors might well be the cat's meow, but right now they're just a huge money pit and I keep not getting pregnant." Shit. Mayday, mayday. *Do not cry, Suzanne. Do. Not. Cry.* I checked my phone again. Quarter after 7 p.m. Also, a message from Jaq: *You can come by here after you escape. We have chocolate mousse.*

Oh, *we*, was it? So that was a *here* in the sense of *at my girlfriend's*, which was interesting. They'd been together for seven months or something? I did math on my fingers and tried to tune out the grating sound of my sister warming up to an argument.

Both Andi and Jimmy were lawyers, a matching set, so cute you could put them on the cover of a magazine: Andi's pale skin and long, brown hair; arm in arm with Jimmy, who was slightly taller with dark skin and short hair. In complementary business casual, of course.

They were trained in arguing. Me? I'd gone into real estate. I was trained in negotiation and gently, subtly nudging people to the thing that was best for them. I was no match for Andi and Jimmy when they really sank their teeth into something, and wow, I should not have told them about Tom's potential donation to Team Future Kid.

Or at least I shouldn't have told them until I decided what I was going to do. The thing with my sister was that you couldn't convince her you knew better than she did, but you could convince her there was no point in arguing about it. But only if it was true. And at the moment I couldn't figure out if the risk was worth the potential reward.

If I got a kid out of the thing, it was probably worth anything. I'd be willing to put up with an ugly custody battle and a dissolution of my friendship with Carlos and Tom. I didn't think it would come to that, but I really wanted to be a mom. And I was getting more desperate with every cycle, which of course Andi knew.

Andi wanted a partner and a stable, monogamous relationship—but no kids. Ever. I wanted a kid, maybe two, but I wasn't really invested in the idea of a stable relationship to go with it. That wasn't part of my whole picture of the future. *Have a kid* was on my list. *Find a stable partner* was not. Between Andi and me, you could make one stereotypical woman, who wanted a family. Instead of two half-credit women who wanted such different things we could only understand one another intellectually.

"—aside from the not inconsiderable danger of the child itself discovering that you asked someone you barely know—"

"I don't 'barely know' Tom! He's been with Carlos for years!"

"Zane, do you really know anything about him? Or his family?"

"He's from the Midwest. He came out here for school. What's there to know?"

"His medical history for one! Is he estranged from his parents? If he is, I'd like to know why."

"If he is, it's probably because they wanted a nice, normal, straight boy and they got Tom!" I pushed back my chair. "I'm pretty much done with this conversation."

"You're not done until you make a decision, and I want you to have all the information you need to make an *informed* one!"

Jimmy shifted in his chair. He didn't get off on the Jaffe family dramatics. Well, he must've gotten off on it a little, since he'd been around long enough to know who he was marrying. In his customary role as peacemaker, he said, "Okay, okay, come on now."

"Come on now nothing." I stood up. "Control your wife!"

As I walked out the front door I could hear Andi sputtering in rage, which didn't make me feel nearly as good as it should have.

The bitch of it was . . . they were right. There were a lot of risks. Starting with all the basic risks of having unprotected sex with someone, since you were shooting their jizz in your vag. And continuing to the real legal danger that they might not sign a paper relinquishing their parental rights when the time came. And they couldn't do that until after the kid was born, which was messy on all sides.

Technically if I got pregnant I could sue Tom for child support. How shitty would that be?

I lingered on the front steps of their narrow row house until Jimmy came out to smoke.

"Thanks a lot, asshat." He offered me a cigarette, which I took. "Happy BFN."

It was our monthly ritual. Andi pretended she didn't know. I was pretty sure she pretended not to know that he was still smoking at all, and I really didn't smoke, except for this one time each month.

I took a drag and offered a totally insincere apology. "Sorry, pal. That's what you get for marrying into this family. You have no excuse."

"She's taking a bath. So I'm off the hook for processing."

"You're lucky she's not a lesbian."

He waved his glowing cigarette in my direction. "Excuse me, unnecessary stereotype? And the lesbian I know best in the world never processes anything with anyone, so I have reason to doubt that one."

"Oh, it's true. So true."

"Come on, kid. What's really going on? I thought you were just as against known donors as we are."

I blew smoke into the air and shivered into my hoodie. "What's going on is I'm tired, Jimmy. I'm tired of doing this every month for over a year. I'm sick of taking my temperature and checking my cervix and looking at my cervical mucus."

He shuddered.

"Looking at my *cervical mucus*, and waiting for it to go stretchy like egg whites so I know I'm fertile."

"That's gross, FYI."

"You don't have to tell me."

"I hear all that, Zanie. I do. I get this is a fucking endless thing right now. And I know why you keep trying." Unspoken: *Unlike Andi, who thinks you should adopt already and save your money for the kid's college fund.* "But I don't want you to make a rash decision because you're starting to freak out, then regret it later."

"I'm not starting to freak out, Jimmy." I waited a beat before adding, "I'm so far into freak-out I'm numb."

He shook his head, stubbing the cigarette butt out on the steps, then absently brushing away the ash. "You keep acting like it's all fine."

"What else am I gonna do?"

"At a guess—maybe indulge in a moment of honesty and actually tell me how you are for once?"

I'd always liked Jimmy. Most of the time I liked him a whole lot more than I liked Andi. But there was no way he could relate to how deeply my need to be a mother went, or how utterly inevitable it felt, that all I needed to do was keep trying and it would happen.

"I'm fine. I have a good job. I have a place to live in a safe neighborhood, good food to eat, excellent health care, and an extended chosen family. Oh, and a pain in the ass for a sister. You're okay, though."

"Jeez, thanks."

I modulated my tone. "I know you're worried about me, but I'm fine. I just wish this would happen already so I could move on with my life."

"I wish you would see all the other paths you could take to get to where you want to go." He kissed my cheek. "You coming back in?"

"Nah. Tell her I forgive her for being a butthead. That oughta help."

"I'll tell her you were willing to prostrate yourself in abject apology, but I told you it would only disturb her bath, so I finally convinced you to go home."

"Actually, I'm going to Hannah's."

His eyes narrowed. "Oh. Jaq's new girlfriend?"

"I did the math on that. Apparently they've been dating for like seven months."

"Wow. That practically makes her family."

"For real. Also, I'm gonna tell Jaq you said that and next time she sees you, she's gonna kick your ass."

"You just like promoting drama so you can feel like the only sane girl in La Vista."

"You know that's right, big brother." I stubbed out my cigarette and stood up. "Thanks for the smoke."

"Hopefully it'll be the last one."

"Yeah. Hopefully." I kissed his cheek. "See ya, Jimmy."

"Bye, kid."

I got in my car and started to text Jaq that I was on my way. But stopped.

It wasn't that late, but Andi had the right idea; I didn't want to go to Hannah's and eat mousse right now (well, okay, I kind of wanted to do that). What sounded even better than chocolate mousse was a bath, a book, and candlelight. Thank all the gods for the invention of self-lit ebook readers.

I texted, *Maybe next time. Gonna go home and wallow in my own filth.*

The car was still warming up when she replied: *Have a good bath. XO.*

Couldn't beat old friends to understand your dumb jokes, right?

I tried really hard to relax in my bath, but I ended up spending most of it thinking about Tom, and what it would be like if I decided to use his sperm. It did feel like a risk, no matter how well I knew him. On the other hand, the idea of it—of trying something new—actually felt exciting. In a way that nothing related to trying to conceive had felt exciting in a long time.

Jaq and I went to the gym on Mondays, Wednesdays, and Fridays. The only exception was that I didn't go the day after I ovulated on an insemination cycle out of a totally superstitious belief that I might somehow, during vigorous treadmilling, jolt the egg and ruin everything.

It's not a real thing. Obviously. The human race wouldn't continue if reproduction were that fragile. But when you'd worked as long and as hard as I had to get pregnant, you didn't take chances. And anyway, it was a good excuse not to go to the gym. Even Jaq didn't argue with it.

Before she'd hooked up with Hannah, we'd always done *something* after the gym. We'd get tacos, or smoothies, or we'd head to Club Fred's for a drink or four. Nothing says *healthy* like liquor and women, am I right? In the post-Hannah world, sometimes she'd meet up with us somewhere, or sometimes we'd cut our thing short so Jaq could get home.

Sometimes, like today, Jaq said, "My girlfriend's sending me sexy text messages, I gotta go," and kissed my cheek on her way out of the locker room.

It's not like you could really be bitter at a moment like that. At least someone was gonna get laid.

I made my way to Fred's all by my lonesome and took the stool next to Cameron's. "'Sup?"

"Hmm? Oh, hi, Zane." He looked up from his phone, and it took him a moment to focus on me. "I'm reading this historical romance. It's weirdly captivating."

"Why weirdly?"

"I don't know. I suppose I didn't think I'd be all that interested in Regency England, but I've been doing some Google searches—and apparently I am. The whole thing is fascinating." He shook his head. "How are you?"

"Went to the gym, so I'm ready to drink all the calories I burned. Fredi! Give a thirsty woman a beer, would you?"

Fredi shot me a vicious glare, which had been my goal. "I'll serve you when I feel like it, Jaffe! Hold your horses!"

"She hates me," I confided to Cam. "Tried to sneak in one time and she's hated me ever since."

"You wouldn't think she'd be able to keep track of everyone who'd ever tried to sneak in here."

"What can I say? I'm just that memorable." I nudged him. "So. Josh and Keith, huh?"

"They're here somewhere. Dancing, I think." Cam could usually get away with pretending he hadn't caught the nuances of whatever was going on around him, but the way he was looking anywhere but at me blew his cover.

"You don't want to dance with them?"

"I don't dance."

Nudge, nudge. "So. Keith and Josh, huh?"

He sighed. "Yes. That is the answer to your not-question. Yes. Me and them."

"Good."

"Good? What does that mean, 'good'?"

I studied him, thinking about how many times I'd seen him on this particular stool, how easily I could picture him in the Rhein's ticket booth. "Good for you. Way to change things up, Cam."

"I don't even know what that means."

"I really think you do, and it's okay. Seriously."

He cleared his throat. "How's it going with Mildred?"

A beer landed in front of me on the counter, accompanied by another patented Fredi glare. At close range Fredi's glare was unsettling, almost physical.

To say nothing of her growl. "You running a tab tonight?"

"I—"

"I'll get Zane's," Cam said smoothly, pulling out his wallet.

"Why thank you, kind sir." I tipped an imaginary hat to him.

Fredi grunted, took his money, and walked away.

"How's it going with Mildred?" he asked again.

"So you bought my beer and now I have to answer your questions?"

He opened his mouth, shut it, and paused. "Actually, yes. I think that's exactly correct. You owe me."

"Listen, Dred and I aren't really *dating*. We're pretend dating. Fake-dating, if you will."

"Uh-huh."

"I know it sounds ridiculous, but it's a mutually beneficial thing where she gets out of the house and spends time vaguely 'in the world' and I get Jaq to stop making online dating profiles in my name."

"I can see all that. I guess my question is . . . why aren't you actually dating? Since it's so mutually beneficial? You aren't attracted to each other?"

"Uh—I—I wouldn't say that—" I came up short. "Wait, what do you mean?"

"What's stopping you from asking Mildred on a real date?"

"I don't think she's interested."

He blinked. "Really."

I was still waiting for a follow-up to "really" when Josh came from behind Cam and draped an arm around his shoulders. A warm, very nearly beautiful smile lit Cam's face as he twisted a bit to look up.

Josh returned the look. "Keith wants you to dance with us."

"I don't dance."

"He's pouting."

"He knows I don't dance."

"Fine." Josh sighed dramatically. "What if we put on music back at the apartment? Would you dance with him then?"

"I don't dance. It's not a question of venue." But the smile teased up at the corners.

"Cam, c'mon, do me a solid and dance with him. I hate it when he pouts."

Cam considered this for a long moment. Clearly they'd forgotten about me, but I wasn't complaining; I'd been watching Cam go through the world alone since he started showing up at Fred's. Before then I'd known him as "the Rheingold kid, who's always reading in the ticket booth." It was a little bit glorious watching him . . . play.

"So I'd be doing both of you a service," he finally said.

Josh grinned. "You saying you'd want to negotiate terms?"

"I'm ready to go if you two are."

"Hell yes." Josh waved to me. "How's it going, Zane?"

"My night's not looking as good as yours is, but it's still pretty good."

"Man, you don't even *know*." He kissed Cam's cheek and melted back into the crowd.

I leveled a look at him. "So."

Cam blushed appropriately. "Hmm?"

"Don't 'hmm' me, buddy."

"Anyway. I've been thinking about it, and if you trust Tom and Carlos, I think it's an intriguing idea, you know. The thing you told us about the other day."

"Oh yeah?"

"Yeah. Like—" He paused, eyes narrowing. "I think about how families are built a lot lately. The different ways it happens, and how it's not always the way people think it will be. So anyway, not that I have an opinion to register really, but I think it's an interesting idea."

"Thanks, kid." I socked his arm. "You're gonna dance with Keith when you get home, aren't you?"

"Not my home. Actually. I, uh, stay a lot of the time at their apartment. Not because, you know—even if we weren't, they'd let me sleep on the sofa. My place is . . . difficult. Right now."

It took me thirty seconds of staring dumbly at him to figure out what he meant. "Oh shit. Because of the attack?"

"I still think about it a lot, even though it turned out fine. And the case—the case against him is good. I can't imagine how people feel when the perpetrator gets out, or isn't arrested at all. That must be horrible."

Even just watching him in Fred's, I could see his rising discomfort, the sweat at his temples, the way his fingers tapped lightly on the edge of his phone.

"I was sitting here, before you came in, thinking about how it affected everyone." He gestured to the bar. "Club Fred's is made up of two groups now: the people who are oblivious, and the people who are . . . wary. The people who were afraid before and aren't quite sure if they can stop being afraid yet."

"It's definitely more depressing around here than it used to be."

"I think it's fear. But I might be projecting." He offered a tired smile. "You think?"

"No." I swiveled around to see more of the room. The changes were almost imperceptible. Business had gone down—I knew only because Tom had mentioned it—but not noticeably. I couldn't tell by all the empty chairs or anything like that. But Cam was right. Club Fred's used to be . . . open. People flitted from group to group, socializing like honeybees, or joined conversations at the high tables without being invited. I hadn't noticed a change as it happened, but now, looking around, I could see its stamp. Chairs drawn more tightly together, heads down, conversations lower than they would have been before. I knew a whole lot of people, but only a few I could have approached unannounced without feeling like a suspicious presence.

"You used to be able to walk up to anyone and feel welcomed," I said.

"Well. Maybe *you* used to be able to do that."

I smiled. "I did. Now I'd feel like I was intruding. How do you notice it, Cam?"

"People used to linger at the bar, talk to strangers. Sometimes me, sometimes just whomever was around. Now there are fewer people on their own. They move in small packs, even the ones who seem most oblivious. It's interesting. But I miss the way it was before." He shrugged. "I used to feel like sitting here reading was normal. Now it feels like an imposition, or—"

Keith tumbled into his arms. "Josh said you're gonna dance with me when we get home."

"I didn't commit."

"Oh, you're committed. Sorry, Zane, Cam's got a date with me and some music."

I pretended annoyance. "Oh, sure, fine. I'll sit here and philosophize to myself, then."

"Glad you understand." He shot me an impish grin and slid out of Cam's lap. "C'mon. Plus, I can tell you're thinking about him again, so stop."

"Not him." Cam tucked his phone away in the inner pocket of his coat. "We were talking about how Club Fred's has changed."

"Yeah, it's morose everywhere but the dance floor." Keith tugged Cam's hands like a little kid. "C'mon."

"Good night, Zane."

"See ya, boys. Have fun."

"We totally will."

As they were walking away I heard Cam ask where Josh was. I turned in time to see his body stiffen when Keith airily replied that Josh was getting the car.

It's so weird what you can see when no one knows you're watching. Keith put an arm around his shoulders and whispered something in his ear, something that made Cam take a deep breath.

Then they were gone, out the door, and I was left by myself at the bar, thinking about how happy I was for Cam. And maybe a tiny bit bitter that no one was around to whisper calming things in my ear. Which was stupid, because for most of my life, the last thing I wanted was that kind of intimacy. Getting laid was one thing. People grabbing my hand and acting giddy about being with me was fun for about five minutes before I found it exhausting.

I had so much to do. With my life. I had my career, which I intended to make an awful lot of money at, and a social schedule that let me hang out with a lot of different people every week, and I had good friends. I wanted to have a kid. I didn't need to add a girlfriend to that mix; where would I find time for a girlfriend?

Good. Settled. I didn't want a girlfriend.

A text message came in from Dred. *Emerson made apple pie. Get ice cream on your way over. He says vanilla, and don't cheap out.*

I finished my beer, bemoaned my lack of diet, and made my way to my car.

Apple pie and ice cream at the farmhouse was better than sitting at the bar, thinking about how not-lonely I was.

Wednesday's after-gym treat was dinner at Hannah's. Her ex was some kind of low-level celebrity chef, so I never knew if Hannah was overcompensating, or if they got together because both of them really liked food, or what. But eating at Hannah's was always delicious and casual-fancy. Dress code: relaxed; food: came in courses.

Somewhere during the entrée, Jaq stopped freaking out about Tom offering his sperm. "Why didn't you *tell me*? This is too fucking weird."

"It's too weird that someone would want to mate with me? Thanks a lot, Jaqs."

"Oh my god, *mate with you*?" She exploded into laughter. "You just made yourself into livestock!"

I tried not to laugh and ended up giggling in an undignified manner. "Shut up!"

"You did, though!"

Hannah waved both of her hands. "All right, all right. But the real question is, what are you going to do?"

"I don't know!" I let myself whine, because Jaq was my best friend, and I needed a whine. "The attorney twins are going to disown me if I do this."

"They'll be fine," Jaq countered immediately. "Uncle Jimmy will back whatever play you make when Andi's not around."

"Yeah, but Andi's a bitch."

She shrugged. "Always has been. No use crying about it now."

Hannah refilled our wine and Jaq's sparkling water. "Your sister and brother-in-law are attorneys?"

"More's the pity. Is thinking you always know the right answer to everything some kind of lawyer trait, Hannah?"

"I'd think it was more that a higher-than-average number of know-it-alls go into law as a profession." She grinned. "Obviously, *I* really do have all the answers."

"Hit me up, Obi-Wan."

"Do you want to use a known donor?"

"Uh. I don't know."

Hannah shook her head and Jaq rolled her eyes. Classic.

"I mean it! I've been fine with using frozen, but it hasn't worked. Maybe it's time to switch it up."

"Did you ask about diseases?" Hannah's lawyer voice was a lot like Jimmy's, actually.

"I was . . . really drunk. At the time. When we . . . had that conversation."

Jaq raised a hand. "Do you even know if this really happened? It might have been a drunken fantasy."

I threw a dinner roll at her.

"I'm just saying."

Hannah moved the rolls out of my reach. "Let's assume it really happened, for the sake of debate. You obviously have to talk to Tom and Carlos again and hash out the details. But the question is, do you want to do that, Zane?"

"I . . ." I swirled wine around in my glass. "Yeah. I think I do. You don't think it's a crazy risk to take?"

"Oh, it's full of risk. Legal, medical, psychological. He might decide once he sees a kid that he wants to parent, or Carlos might. He might not be fertile. It might be impossible to raise a child in close contact with their donor without making that person part of your family."

Jaq raised her glass. "Which he already is. He has been since Carlos got serious about him."

I toasted her, thinking about how much we'd ragged on Carlos about his gorgeous statuesque conquest, and how weirdly fitting it was when his conquest turned into more than just a guy who let him do whatever he wanted.

"It's complicated," Hannah said. "But I don't believe in only making the safest decisions. Boring."

"I'm ovulating next week. I don't know what to do about this right now. I think I want to go through with it, but that's really fast." I still had a vial stored away, but what if this was *the* cycle? What if doing this crazy spontaneous thing was exactly right and I was totally overthinking it?

Jaq tipped her chair back with the bowl of pasta in her lap so she could pick the olives out. "You can always do it next month. Or the month after. Not like Tom's gonna run out of sperm."

My breath caught in my throat. *Next month. Or the month after.* Oh god. Trying to conceive was like a lifestyle now. I'd made it into a . . . hobby, or something. The kind of thing my friends could casually refer to as ongoing.

"Hon." Hannah glanced at me. "I'm not sure that's what Zane needs to hear right now."

Jaq frowned. Then her expression cleared and the chair came down on all four legs. "Oh fuck. Sorry. I didn't mean— I didn't mean— Uh—"

"That I'd be shooting up with sperm every cycle for the rest of my life? Yeah, you did. But it's okay. I get it. Sometimes it feels that way." I sat at Hannah's dinner table and felt all those cycles, those weeks and months and now over a year weighing down on me. I felt like I was in that scene in whichever Star Wars it was where Han Solo was stuck in the Death Star's trash compactor. And even though I knew it wasn't going to kill me, even though I knew there was no real danger (except to my bank account), suddenly it felt like those failed cycles were crushing me on all sides.

Hannah's hand touched my arm. "Redirect, sugar. Let's talk about something else."

"Yeah, okay. Right. So, have you guys noticed Club Fred's has been super depressing lately?"

"Right?" Jaq's voice went high-pitched with her eagerness to veer away from the awkwardness of a moment before. "I thought everyone would be relieved and happy and ready to party, but not so much."

"Cam said people are either oblivious or wary."

Jaq nodded. "I've noticed that." She raised her eyebrows at Hannah.

"Oh, I wasn't around that long before it all went to hell, but I wonder if you're expecting a bit too much."

"In what way?"

She shook her head, her hair coming loose from the knot she'd bound it up in. Jaq's eyes locked on, and I could practically see her drool. She'd always loved a woman who kept everything tightly coiled until she decided to really let go.

"I think you haven't mourned." Hannah absently tugged the clips out of her hair. "You guys need a wake. A celebration of the lives you lost, of the attitude you lost, the space where you felt . . . safe, happy, whatever it was you felt before people started dying."

"A wake." It was genius. It was so genius I couldn't believe I hadn't thought of it myself.

"Or something like that."

I snapped to drag Jaq's attention away from her lady's hair. "What do you think about that?"

"About what?"

"Oh my god, focus, woman. What do you think about a wake?"

"At Fred's?"

Wait. No. Dred couldn't go if it was at Fred's because of Baby James. "Maybe not at Fred's. Maybe at QYP?"

"I don't understand what the point is."

"Try to stop thinking about Hannah's hair for like five seconds."

Hannah swung around; Jaq blushed. "Shut up," she mumbled.

"Aw, am I distracting you?" Hannah reached back to shake her hair out more fully. "Like what you see, Jaq?"

"For the record, I despise you both."

"Noted, hon. Noted."

"You two disgust me." I pulled out my phone and opened my note-taking app. "So I'd need a venue, probably either QYP or Club Fred's."

"Then you'd have to talk to Fredi. Is that why you want to do it at QYP instead?" Jaq lowered her voice to explain to Hannah. "Did I tell you that Zane thinks Fredi hates her?"

"And food," I continued, ignoring her. "And how to invite everyone, or how to limit it, though I'd rather not limit it. Wouldn't it be amazing if a whole lot of people showed up? Seriously. Hannah's right. We haven't really commemorated anything that happened. We have to like . . . face it all, before we can move on."

"Uh-huh." Jaq leaned forward in her chair to tug Hannah's hair. "So, not to kick you out, but you're leaving soon, right?"

"She can't leave before dessert."

"But—but— You're . . . teasing me?"

Hannah laughed.

"You're awful and should be ashamed of yourself, Hannah. You're a truly repulsive human being."

"Thanks, sugar."

Dessert was berries in some kind of pastry with a dollop of whipped coconut cream on top. It was delicious. Especially because it allowed me to linger and cockblock Jaq more.

Hannah, in full cahoots, also dragged out her dessert. She offered me coffee with an evil gleam in her eye, and I pretended to consider it while Jaq freaked the fuck out across the table.

I demurred and took my leave, though I didn't feel like she fully appreciated my mercy. Then again, Hannah was way less merciful, so she probably had other things on her mind.

I resolutely did not wonder what my best friend and her girlfriend got up to after I left, and spent the drive home composing mental notes I'd need to enter into my app, pre-tagging them with an event-specific taxonomy.

A wake. It was perfect.

I stopped by the drop-in center on Thursday to see what Josh and Keith had to say about holding a wake at QYP.

"Is this really the right place for a thing like that?" Keith and their assistant, Merin, were collating massive stacks of papers into folders.

"I don't know. I guess I was thinking... what if people wanted to bring their kids?"

He tilted his head to the side. "Their kids?"

Merin snorted. "You really want to have little kids running around here? Anything with food's gonna draw a bunch of lowlifes and drug addicts. Is that who you want around your kids?"

I didn't correct him. He meant *your kids* in a general sense, so I substituted Baby James. Maybe I didn't really want him crawling around on the floor amid lowlifes and drug addicts. Or maybe as long as we stuck close to him it wouldn't be a big deal. Except he did put pretty much everything in his mouth...

Keith shuffled a stack, then stopped. "Wait. You don't mean random people. You mean Mildred."

"Um."

"Zane!"

"I take the Fifth."

"Because having the hots for the woman you're dating is incriminating?"

"Fake-dating! We're fake-dating."

"You keep pretending it's fake. We won't tell. Right, Merin?"

Merin rolled his eyes. "Are all adults this dumb? I'm just wondering."

Keith smacked the back of his head, but I could tell it was gentle. "Don't be rude to people when they're desperately in denial."

"What am I supposed to be, then?"

"More subtle than that. So Zane, what's the downside to having this wake thing at Club Fred's?"

"Um." I tried to come up with something non-Dred-related. "Well, I'd have to ask Fredi. That's pretty scary."

"Granted. Anything else?"

I sighed. Heavily. "Is it really that wrong that I want Dred to be able to come to this thing, if I pull it off?"

"Hello! No, it's not wrong. Because you have the hots for her and you want to spend time with her and you want to touch her and kiss her and—"

This time Merin got Keith in the back of the head. Keith laughed.

Merin shuddered. "Ew. Stop. You're gross."

"Thanks, Merin," I said.

He grunted. I took it as *I didn't hit Keith for you, dummy.*

"It's not that I have the hots for her. It's . . . I like spending time with her. I don't think they're the same thing."

Both of them looked up. Keith's expression was sort of bland, but Merin's was pitying. "Seriously, it's embarrassing that you can't even ask a woman out because you like her too much."

"Amen, brother," Keith added.

Merin elbowed him. He grinned unrepentantly.

Jerks. I tried to get them back on track. "For that matter, if we have it at Club Fred's, Merin can't go. So there."

Merin shook his head. "Like I'd go to your little funeral anyway."

"Okay, okay." Keith brushed his hands off. "You want coffee?"

"Ugh. What kind?"

"It came out of a Sobrantes bag."

I narrowed my eyes at him.

"It wasn't Sobrantes when it went into the bag, but I find the psychological benefit of seeing a high-quality coffee bag is high."

"Hell. Yeah, I'll take coffee."

The QYP kitchen was gorgeous. Straight out of an Ikea showroom, all clean lines and smooth surfaces in grays and blues. Wear was beginning to show up after the five or six months they'd been open—the floors were scuffed and the sink had a dent in the side—but it was still about a hundred times better than the kitchen at my last crummy apartment before I bought my condo.

"Your target demographic for this wake is Club Fred's." Keith handed me a cup of coffee and pushed a basket of coffee additions across the counter. "Merin wouldn't go because Merin wouldn't care. You're trying to get to the folks who actually felt something, you know? Because they were afraid, or they knew one of the people who died, or because they danced with Joey once."

I glanced up from stirring my coffee. "First-name basis, huh?"

"When a guy pistol-whips you while talking about how he's going to torture your boyfriend until he prays for death, you get close." This smile was a little ill. "Sorry."

"Don't apologize. I don't think anyone has a clue what actually happened, except that it ended with him in jail and you guys at the hospital." And I'd heard some pretty strange rumors about that too. Apparently Josh and Keith were into some kinky shenanigans the police misunderstood as domestic violence. That must have been fucking awkward. I dropped my eyes back to my coffee so I wasn't thinking about Josh. And Keith. And kinky shenanigans.

"It was awful. Which I guess you probably assumed. My point is that I wouldn't mind a wake. In some ways, Club Fred's is the scene of the crime for a lot of people. And I wasn't super afraid before, but I am now. A lot. Of everything. I don't think it's as bad for Josh, and I can't speak for Cam, but I wouldn't mind a symbolic putting-to-rest, Zane."

"I'm really sorry." I couldn't help saying it. "I know that's totally meaningless and basically making it about you comforting me because I feel bad you got caught up in the whole thing, but I'm really, really sorry, Keith."

"It's okay. I mean, it's terrible and not okay, but I'll live. Let me know if you need help planning, or if you want to make flyers or something. I'm pretty good at that. And we can get the word out, though Merin's right; anything advertising free food isn't going to bring in exactly the crowd you're looking for."

The door at the back of the room opened, and both of us looked over. Josh had a ready smile for Keith, a wave for me, and even though

Merin didn't look up, Josh checked his presence in the room with a glance.

"I am done battling the demons of our budgeting software."

"It's not *budgeting* software. It's money management software."

Josh kissed Keith's forehead. "Sorry. It all looks the same to me, babe."

"Except that *budgeting* is when you tell your money what to do, and the thing you're looking at is telling us where our money already went. Fundamentally different."

"Can I say I balanced our checkbooks? Because that's really how it feels."

Keith sighed. "Yes. Fine. You balanced our checkbooks. Even though I've never had a checkbook in my life."

I laughed. "Damn. Youth today. Checkbooks are going the way of the dinosaur. Hey, Josh, what do you think of having a wake?"

"Did someone die?"

Before I could reply, Keith said, "Six people died."

"Oh. A wake for Togg and Honey and that kid Cam met for a minute?" He put his arm around Keith's shoulders. "I think that's an interesting idea. You mean for the sake of closure or something?"

"I guess so." Closure was as good as any other reason. "Or for the sake of making Club Fred's less depressing."

He nodded. "Fredi's okay with this?"

I made a face. "God. I guess I have to talk to her, which is annoying. But let's say she agrees." I couldn't think of why she wouldn't, but then again, Fredi moved in mysterious ways. "Is that the kind of thing you'd go to?"

He looked at Keith. "Yeah, I think so."

Keith tugged on his hand, pulling himself closer in the half embrace. "The question is, can we get Cam to go? Because I think that'd be good."

"His process isn't necessarily our process."

"As long as he has one, which I'm not convinced of."

I sipped my coffee to avoid feeling like an intruder, but I could hardly miss their concern. What was up with Cam?

"Anyway." Josh turned back to me. "Keep us posted. I'm intrigued."

"Will do. I should get back to work."

I surrendered my mug and told Merin good-bye as I was leaving. He grunted.

Keith was right, of course. The thing had to be at Club Fred's. Which meant I'd have to talk to Fredi.

No matter how I badgered Carlos and Jaq, I couldn't get either one of them to be my backup to talk to Fredi on Friday night. In fact, they conveniently went and found a table so they weren't even at the bar when I tried to talk to her.

With friends like these. Jeez.

I led with an apology. People love apologies, right?

"Hey, Fredi. I, uh, wanted to say sorry for sneaking in here that time."

She looked at me, squinting a little, leather vest tight around her chest, some kind of braided choker thing around her neck. Eyes dark and ruthless.

I swallowed.

"What the hell are you talking about, sneaking in here?"

"Uh. You know. That time you kicked Jaq and me out. When we were kids."

"You tried to sneak in here when you were underage?" Her eyes got even smaller. "You think I remember kicking you out of here fifteen years ago? I don't even remember the punk kids I kicked out last week."

"Uh— Oh. But—" I tried to regroup. "But then why are you always on me like I did something wrong?"

"Jaffe, I give you a hard time because you're a damn nuisance. But that's not your fault, it's your nature. Like mine is giving people a hard time. Now what the fuck did you want?"

I was suddenly glad my friends weren't there to hear that I'd been harboring a totally baseless persecution complex ever since I was legal to enter Club Fred's. "I have an idea. For an event. That I'd like to have here, if you're okay with it."

"You want to pay to rent the place out, I'll get the paperwork."

"No— It wouldn't be that, exactly. Though I'm not saying I wouldn't pay." It hadn't even occurred to me that there was a way to rent out Club Fred's. Not that I wanted to.

Fredi made an impatient motion with her hand. "Spit it out."

"I want to hold a wake. For all of us, actually. But also for Honey, and Philpott, and Felipe, and the rest of the people who died. Who came here and died after. To celebrate their lives. And I guess also to celebrate that we don't have to be afraid all the time the way we were for a while."

"Huh."

I had no idea how to interpret that.

"Tom!"

Tom smiled at me as he walked up. It was weird. A guy you'd known for years offered you sperm and all of a sudden you were looking at him differently, like he was made up of component parts. Eyes, and shoulders, and hands. Pieces of his DNA. Pieces he might pass down to a kid, if his DNA ended up in one.

"Jaffe wants to hold a wake at the bar. What do you have to say about that?"

He blinked. "Who died?"

Fredi did the hand thing. "Everyone, no one, all of us, blah, blah, blah, new-age bullshit. The point is moving on, if I'm catching her bleeding-heart drift."

"You mean, since that guy was arrested? The actual guy."

Not to be confused with that one time when Tom—*not* the actual guy—had spent the weekend in jail.

I nodded. "Yeah. Well, and it feels kind of—" My hand motion was sort of floppy and ill-defined. "It feels unresolved in a way. Here. You know?"

He nodded and looked at Fredi. "I think Zane has a point. As long as we're not giving away food or booze, I'm down with it."

"Bite your tongue, boy. Get back to work."

Tom flashed me another smile before walking back down to the far end of the bar. I'd never really thought about the management structure of Club Fred's, but Tom had just given his opinion as if he was part of it. Huh. I surveyed Fredi a little differently. Not that she was doddering on the brink of senility or anything, but she probably didn't want to be standing at the bar until she keeled over, either.

Which made Tom the heir apparent.

"All right, Jaffe. Here's what we're doing. You're writing up one page of exactly what you plan to do, how many people you think it'll bring in, and when you want to do it. I'll read that and quote you a price for using my bar during business hours, which I assume is what you're asking."

I nodded.

"Fine. Get it to me soon. If you wait, the usefulness of this 'wake' as a hippie exercise will be wasted."

"So in other words, do my homework?"

She grinned. Not in a friendly way. In a *Don't mind my wolf's teeth, Little Red Riding Hood* kind of way. "Yeah. Do your homework. I look forward to seeing it. Now scram."

"Yes, ma'am!" I fled to the safety of my friends, who were already laughing at me when I sat down.

"You survived an encounter with the wicked witch!" Jaq cried.

"In my head she was the wolf in 'Little Red Riding Hood.'" I stole Carlos's beer and drank, since I'd left mine on the bar. "Oh my god, I'm nervous-sweating into my clothes right now. She is so scary."

"Wuss." He took back his beer.

"Hey, is Tom gonna take over Fred's when she retires?"

Carlos shrugged. "I'll be shocked to shit if she ever manages to retire, but she's talked to him about it."

"Damn." Jaq looked around with slightly wide eyes. "Seriously, that would be really weird. Anyway, what'd she say?"

I took a long drag off her soda. "She gave me homework. I'm supposed to come up with a page telling her what I plan."

"Plan to clean." She ran a finger along the chair rail behind the table. "Can you do that? Because this place is fucking disgusting."

"Oh, yeah. I bet that'll really endear me to Fredi. 'First: clean the bar, because it's fucking disgusting.'" I cleared my throat. "By the way, she doesn't remember that time we tried to sneak in."

Both of them erupted into laughter.

"You guys are such jerks," I muttered.

"This moment is the culmination of years of anticipation!" Jaq wiped tears out of her eyes. "I knew she couldn't remember us from that long ago!"

"Jerk."

They stopped laughing at me. Eventually.

CHAPTER 6

Saturday morning breakfast at the farmhouse was one of those things I'd sort of... stumbled into, not knowing it was an actual thing until I'd showed up a few weeks in a row. The farmhouse was smack-dab on the line where the decent part of the La Vista suburbs became the dangerous part of the La Vista suburbs. It was still in the decent area, but you could tell there was encroachment. Fewer houses were selling, more were bank owned, sitting there for months while lawns died and fences crumbled and paint chipped.

Sometimes I wish I were a developer. Those neighborhoods used to be kind of grand when I was growing up. Jaq's dad said when he was a kid, this was the fancy side of town. That was only, what, sixty years ago? And now look at it: dead grass, sagging roofs, a general air of having once been pretty. It was so sad.

Also, it reminded me why I switched to commercial. I couldn't take residential, man. Too many feelings.

The farmhouse where Dred and James (and Obie and Emerson) lived wasn't really a farmhouse. It was a three-bedroom craftsman-style house with a big kitchen, a screened-in back porch partially converted into a pantry and laundry room, and a huge, incredible garden in the backyard.

But my favorite part of the house was a mix of the entryway and the kitchen. You stepped into this foyer with wood floors, and straight ahead was a big staircase heading up and to the left, and if you went through the archway slightly back from the stairs on the right, you got the kitchen.

If you enjoy any aspect of food, you'll love the farmhouse's kitchen. That side of the house is cut with the front quarter sectioned into a little sitting room (which Emerson and Obie attempted to turn into a sewing room for Dred as a Christmas gift, mainly by adding a pair of those crummy accordion wood slat doors), and the entire rest of that side of the house is the kitchen. Small breakfast nook in the far corner, with built-in bench seats and windows overlooking the garden. Long counter, deep sink, plenty of cabinets.

I could sell the farmhouse and make a ridiculous amount of money. But I didn't do residential and the farmhouse wasn't for sale.

Up the broad front steps, courtesy knock on the door before trying the handle, inner conflict about how nice it was not to have to disturb someone to come unlock it but how dumb it was for them to leave it unlocked, pushing it open when—

Dred, all flowing skirt and brightly colored headband—accentuating as opposed to containing her natural hair—raised her eyebrows at me from the kitchen doorway. "You coming inside or just trying to heat the neighborhood?"

Oh my *god*, I wanted to kiss her.

"Hey," I said.

One eyebrow arched a little bit higher. "Mm-hmm."

"Good morning," I tried again.

"Hi, Zane!" Obie called.

"Hi, Obie!"

Dred gave me another look.

"What?" I patted down my blouse. "Do I have food on me or something?"

"Nope." She turned and walked into the kitchen.

What does that MEAN? I valiantly tried not to wail out loud and followed her.

Emerson stood at the stove, as he did every Saturday morning. In this crowd, dour Emerson was the only one who could put a meal together. "Hey, Zane."

"Hey, boy. How's it going?"

"Two of my eggs were cracked, the bacon was green when I pulled it out, and I have three people taking the GED right now." He glanced at his watch. "For the next six hours. Sorry, you weren't really asking. Everything's fine, Zane. How's it going with you?"

"I'm not pregnant, and Tom and Carlos offered me sperm. Also, I'm thinking about holding a wake at Club Fred's. You know, the usual."

He blinked. "Whoa. Sperm. That *is not* 'the usual.'"

I laughed and snagged a bit of red pepper on my way to the table.

I really liked Emerson. He was one of the last people I helped find a place to live before I took over the commercial side of the business from my boss. He was prickly and hard to get to know, but if you could dig below the surface, he had a good sense of humor and was the kind of guy who'd help you out and never make you feel lousy for it.

He didn't have his cane handy, so it was probably an okay day on the multiple sclerosis front.

I kissed Obie's cheek and sat down beside the high chair where James was holding court. "What's up, man?"

He chattered at me and offered a slice of his avocado, mushed between his fingers.

"Oh, no thanks, I think I'll have whatever Emerson's making."

Emerson snorted. James protested. Dred and Obie resumed what they were doing at the counter.

"So, guys," I said. "Should I have Tom's baby, or what?"

"That's still a little weird to me." Dred waved an exceedingly sharp knife around. "I mean, Tom's always been a good guy, but still—did you ask them?"

"No. At least, I don't think so. Though . . . I was so drunk. So, so drunk." I replayed what I'd said and felt compelled to add, "I mean, obviously I wouldn't be *having Tom's baby*."

"Obviously," Emerson muttered. "Where the hell is my cheese?"

"Here." Obie kissed him. "These smell kind of spectacular."

"'Kind of spectacular' is what I'm going for."

He could make his tone as dry as he wanted, but I saw him smile. Aw. Cute.

Emerson delivered my eggs with a flourish.

"Thank you, thank you, thank you." I picked up my fork, debating where to dig in.

James started, uh, talking again. I guess that was probably what it was called when a kid was making a bunch of noises.

"Ha." Obie grinned, tugging James's shirt. "I think he's pissed at you for taking Emerson's food, but not his."

"Um. Sorry, James. I sort of prefer . . . nonmashed foods. At the moment."

He didn't seem all that pleased with my apology, and raised his voice.

"Zane didn't mean to offend you." Dred slid into the seat next to mine and held her hand up to her son. "High five, baby."

Great distraction. James immediately grinned. Unfortunately, I didn't duck in time and took a little avocado to the face. "Shit!"

"Nice manners there, Jaffe. Way to teach the kid."

"Oh, like you're any better." I glared at Emerson across the table. He smirked back.

"Okay, okay." Obie took the bench seat across from Dred's chair. "I think we've had enough of messing with Zane, though admittedly when she shows up at breakfast talking about sperm, it's hard to resist—"

Emerson raised his fork. "Did they offer you Tom specifically? I mean, not that—not that Carlos's would be bad—" His face twisted. "Aw, fuck, I'm a dick."

"Yes, Tom's specifically. Carlos said I should have 'the bigger man's seed.'"

"Ha!" Obie handed around glasses of orange juice, carefully out of James's reach. "Actually I have no idea how, like, little person genetics work. But I'd guess it's pretty strongly genetic."

"Yeah. Not that I'd be all 'Oh, no, I can't have a dwarf kid' or anything."

"I don't think it's about that," Emerson said. "It's more about general health than dwarfism specifically. As long as you're genetically engineering your kid, you might as well go for as uncomplicatedly healthy as possible."

Dred sat back from dangling sweet potato fries in front of James, arm brushing mine. (I didn't blush or anything. That would give me away.) "I'm done with the Tom's sperm topic. What the hell are you talking about with this wake thing?"

"Oh. Uh. Well, I think Club Fred's has been . . . depressing lately. Like, we should be happy that the killer is caught and the mystery's solved, but people still seem afraid."

Obie shook his head. "Oh. Damn. I forgot. We don't have to worry about dying anymore."

Emerson nudged him. "Speak for yourself."

"Nah, it's different for you." Mildred paused, like she was giving this some serious thought. "Possibly dying is kind of your hobby, Emerson. Everyone else wasn't so much into it. Isn't that guy rotting in a jail cell right now?"

"I think so," I said. "According to the *Times-Record*."

"And Ed. We talked to him . . . sometime this week?" Obie glanced at Emerson, who shrugged. "I think it was sometime this week. He said we might all have to give depositions."

"Not me," Dred countered. "I never saw the guy."

Emerson shuddered. "I tried to do him in the bathroom at Club Fred's. Remember, Zane?"

"How would I remember you doing some guy— Wait, you tried to have sex with the La Vista Killer? No, I don't remember that!"

"Yeah, the kid who looked like DJ Rixx. You told me to go get laid." He smiled, but it was clearly forced. "I didn't recognize him until Ed called him 'Joey,' because the papers all refer to him by his full name, but that's him. Joey. The DJ Rixx look-alike."

I remembered. It was, what, almost a year ago? We'd been sitting at the bar and the kid had been eyeing Emerson from across the room. "Oh my god."

"Sorry, Aunt Florence," Emerson added automatically. "You know, I bet he wanted to kill me. If his thing was purifying the gays. I'm definitely not pure. You think he had his eye on my diseased ass that night? He offered to walk me to my car."

Obie buried his face against Emerson's neck for a minute. "Don't even fucking think about that."

"Why not? It happened. And you know, I'm not social. I'm no drag king, or what's-her-name, Honey. They really liked being around people. But he could have gotten me just by offering to walk me to my car, and my leg was all fucked up that night, you know? I wouldn't have had any defense."

"Except your cane." Dred reached over to pick a bit of caramelized onion off his plate. "You should learn how to cut a mother with that thing."

"You think I should get one with a blade inside?"

"Hell yes. Why wouldn't you? Maybe we should get a family set." She tweaked James's nose. "Not for you, though. You're too young for a blade, baby."

"Anyway," I said, hung up on the word *family*, and a little jealous that I wasn't part of it, which was weird for me. *Acquire family* was not on my list. *Have a kid* didn't seem like quite the same vibe. "So Hannah said we needed a wake. A celebration, you know?"

Emerson made a stab at Dred's wandering fingers with his fork. "Isn't a wake the thing where you sit around staring at a dead body? Oh my god, Mildred, I made you a whole plate!" He winced. "Sorry, Aunt Florence."

"Yours tastes better because you don't want me to have it."

"What're you, five?"

Dred grinned.

I resolutely turned away. "An Irish-style wake, with food and booze. And anyway, it's not like we're really mourning the people, though kind of. It's more that we're mourning how we used to not worry about someone walking us to our car at the end of the night. That's the body in the room. So to speak."

"This is a dark-ass conversation." Obie picked a chunk of cheese out of his omelet and put it in front of James, who immediately grabbed it and shoved it in his mouth.

"It's not supposed to be dark! It's supposed to be celebratory. Or something."

"Yeah, but—" Dread shoved her chair back. "What's the fucking point? To make everyone feel better about partying with a murderer for months?"

I was still marshaling some kind of explanation when Emerson cleared his throat. "The point is we survived. And for some of us it was a kind of close thing, so I think we get to celebrate. I'll come, Zane."

"Thanks." Wow. Talk about support from unexpected places. I figured Obie would have to strong-arm Emerson into coming to the wake, if he came at all.

"Did you talk to Cameron and whatever-their-names are, the kids with the drop-in center?"

"Josh and Keith, and only a little."

"Well, they had a closer shave than anyone else, so you should maybe make sure they're either happy about your wake, or they know when it is so they can avoid Club Fred's that night."

Huh. Maybe that's what Keith had meant, about getting Cam to go. "You think they might want to avoid it?"

Emerson picked at his food, not eating so much as mining. "I think that I had Joey's hands on me for a split second and I feel gross thinking about it. I'm not sure I'd want to celebrate much of anything if he'd gotten as close to me as he did to them."

What had Cam said? He'd rather sleep on Josh and Keith's couch than go home? "Okay, good note." I tapped *Talk to Cam* into my phone's notebook app as a task with a due date and hit Save, tagging it *to-do* and *urgent.* "I'll talk to them."

Dred began gathering our plates. (Well. Their plates. I wasn't done poking at my omelet.) "I still don't get why you'd bother."

"Because it matters," Obie said. "I think it's a great idea, Zane. If you need any help, let us know."

"Thanks, Obie."

They cleaned around me while I finished breakfast and chatted with James, who managed to get me with sweet potato before Obie hauled him up to be mopped off at the sink. It was pleasant and domestic, listening to the bustle of the farmhouse. Dred was bitching about her quilt, Obie was telling her to just keep piecing it together already and stop tearing it out, and Emerson was talking—to himself or James—about what he needed to buy at the store.

And I sat there at the kitchen table, thinking about something else Cam had said. Families were built in different ways. I wanted to kiss Dred again. The idea of her kissing anyone else made me *slightly* homicidal. But I also wanted this: the farmhouse, breakfast on Saturday mornings, the simple bliss of other people's voices.

Could you fall in love with a family? With a house full of people? With the different ways you could imagine fitting into their lives, and fitting them into yours? I'd always been happy on my own, but somewhere along the line that had changed, shifted, and I hadn't noticed.

I was supposed to stay for more quilting lessons, but instead I ran away like a scaredy-cat and promised to come back tomorrow.

I couldn't deal with how secretly hungry I was to be there. How easy it would be to stay until dinner, to kiss James good night, to linger, in Dred's makeshift sewing room, with the lamps lit, talking about quilts when we were really talking about our lives.

I had to get my shit together. So I went to the place I had gone to get my shit together for years: Jaq's house.

Not her apartment, or Hannah's condo. Her childhood home. Where her dad still lived.

Jaq's dad was a way better parent than either of mine. When I was about twelve, eating dinner at the Cummingses' house because no one bothered to cook dinner at my house, Richard had told me I was welcome whenever I wanted to come over. Which I, being twelve, actually had taken literally. Andi had eventually pointed out that he'd probably said it to be polite, but by then I was eating over there five nights out of seven and he was treating me just like he treated Jaq and her siblings.

More than once when we'd gotten in fights as teenagers, I'd forgiven Jaq out of a desire to keep her dad in my life. I knocked on his door Saturday afternoon already crafting a pitch for maybe building a chicken coop, or tackling the back raised beds.

He opened the door. "Thank goodness you're here. We have a plumbing problem, Zane. Roll up your sleeves. Or no, go find one of the girls' old shirts. It's gonna be messy."

I tracked down a shirt and followed the sound of the local oldies station out to the yard, where Richard had pulled an entire sheet of siding off the exterior wall.

"Um." I made my voice cheerful. "I've never taken a house apart before, so you'll have to show me how it's done."

"Quiet, you. We're having a plumbing problem."

"Yes. All right. But don't you usually autopsy plumbing from the inside of a house?"

"If you're an *amateur*. Come over here."

I obliged and stared into the wall, where, yeah, there it was. Pipes. And water. How much water was supposed to be, like, all over the place? Not this much, I didn't think. "It's looking a bit waterlogged in there, Dad."

"That is the problem we're addressing, thank you for paying attention, dear." He took a deep breath. "We're gonna need to go to the Home Depot. Wait, no, I'll just send your sister."

Like that. He didn't mean my sister. He meant Jaq. Thirty seconds later he had her on the phone and he was cajoling her into coming over, and "stopping by" Home Depot on the way.

"It *is* on the way, Jaqueline! It is between your apartment and my— I see." He caught my eye. "You're not at your apartment. You're at Hannah's. All becomes clear. Well, if you don't have time for your old dad and his old man problems—"

I rolled my eyes at him.

"And you can pick lunch up, too. Get enough for Zane." He hung up. "*That* was interesting. Did you know she'd been spending a lot of time over at Hannah's?"

I know they spent the night together the first time they hooked up and she's been a big lovesick baby ever since. "No comment. And yeah, they had me over to dinner the other night. At the condo."

"Now *that's* a nice place. I like the layout of your place better, but you can't beat a Harbor District view of La Vista and walking distance to the pier."

"Yep. If that building had existed when I was looking to buy, I'd've probably moved there. Wait, you've been to Hannah's?"

"You think you're the only one who gets dinner invites? I'm insulted, missy. Now let me show you what's going on in here. It all started when Ducky noticed the doors were no longer closing . . ."

I listened to the curious tale of the senile, incontinent dog in the kitchen, who was not necessarily responsible for a puddle simply because he was sitting in one. How that ended up with part of the siding removed from the exterior wall remained something of a mystery, but I didn't need to understand to hand over a pipe wrench and dump the bucket when it filled up.

"What brings you over here, by the way? Things going all right with that young lady Jaq says you've been seeing?"

"Sure. Except we aren't really *seeing* each other."

He shot me a look. "No? Way Jaq talks, it sure seems like you are."

"Well. I kind of. Um."

"Out with it. They'll be here soon, since the mandatory allotted time for foot-dragging is over, and Home Depot doesn't take that long."

"It does when Jaq's involved."

"Yeah, but I'm calculating for Hannah. Girl knows her way around the Home Depot." He made an alarming circular motion with the pipe wrench. "Talk, Suzanne."

I gave in—as we'd both known I was going to do—and sat down on the overturned bucket, which had been replaced by a lower-profile container for ease of plumbing. "I sort of pretended we were dating to make Jaq shut up. And because it was fun."

"Uh-huh."

"And now I kind of wish I hadn't done that."

"It stopped being fun?"

"No. But I wish it was . . . more than pretend."

"And she doesn't?" His tone implied I was being painfully dense.

"Everyone acts like it's so obvious she wants it, too. But you don't know Dred. She's not like that."

"Exactly how many people have you been pouring out your troubles to, Zanie?"

"Uh. Not that many?"

He shook his head. "This is that thing you girls do, where you think if you talk to enough people, you won't have to talk to the person you need to talk to, and the group will do all the talking for you. Not to be a pigheaded misogynist, but man up, kid. Talk to this Dred if that's what you want."

"I don't know what I want," I whined.

"Yeah, you do. You always show up here when you've already decided what to do and need that extra boost. Same as Jaq. Consider this your swift kick in the pants. Now hand me that plumber's tape. We might not need all that stuff I sent her out for."

We didn't need it—a fact Jaq repeated no fewer than four times—but food was definitely welcome. And Richard didn't say anything else until we were all leaving later that night, after beer and a fire in his fireplace.

"Bring that young lady around one of these days, Zane. I want to meet her."

"And her son," Jaq added, smirking at me.

"Oh, well, then. A son?" Richard looked around. "It'd be good to have some little ones around again, I think."

I tried to picture Dred in the house and failed, though I thought James would be climbing all over everything, and Richard would be a great pretend grandfather.

God. What the hell was I thinking? "I hate both of you."

Hannah took my arm. "I got your back, hon. You don't have to marry Dred just because Jaq thinks the two of you would look real cute on top of a cake."

"We'd— She thinks— *Cake—*"

She laughed. "Oh, she's got the wedding planned already."

"True." Jaq, behind us, lowered her voice. "You're good for the reception, right, Dad?"

"Unless they want more people than can fit in the yard. It'd be a good excuse to finally do the landscaping I've been meaning to get around to since before you graduated from high school."

"I can't hear you!" I called while Hannah led me away.

CHAPTER 8

Dred was ripping out her quilt. Again. She was hunched over on her bed, single panel gripped hard in one fist, and was angrily swiping at it with the sharp little tool that cut through the stitches.

"I can't make it work. I have this idea in my head, but this—" She brandished the stitch-ripping weapon at me. "It won't work."

"Okay. But you're not gonna hurt me with that thing, right?"

"I might. Don't tempt me."

The baby monitor crackled and an indistinct James sound came from it. Both of us went silent and listened, but he settled again.

"I spend all my time ripping this damn thing out. I hate it."

I didn't say anything. It wouldn't matter that I thought it looked beautiful, that the green fabrics she'd chosen were different enough to be distinct and similar enough to all work together. It wasn't what she wanted.

Instead of arguing, I poked around in her "sewing closet," which was her only closet. It was half-empty now, since she'd moved some stuff downstairs. The sewing machine was in its place of honor, on a wall-mounted table she'd probably built herself. The shelves were lightly dusted, with outlines where bins had been, but there were a few left. One of them caught my eye. It was deeper and wider than the others. I couldn't see inside.

She was still hard at work, so I risked sliding it out and lifting the lid. Most of Dred's bins didn't have lids; they were organizational, not protective. But this one had one of those snap-down lids, the not-totally-cheap kind.

More scraps. All kinds of different scraps. From all kinds of different fabrics. These weren't odds and ends from Obie's projects. I touched a long, odd-shaped piece, with fraying ends.

These were scraps from her life. One felt like a thin blanket, another a sheet. As I picked through, I saw other things—logos that must have been salvaged from old shirts, a leg from an old pair of jeans with a cut-off cuff, a pocket with no matching pair of pants. This *was* Dred's life, all packaged carefully away in a bin with a lid.

"Don't even bother with that. I'll never be good enough to make the thing I want to make with all those."

I turned toward her, offering the bin. "What's this?"

For a long moment I thought she was going to put it back on the shelf, but instead she took it out to the bed and started sorting the scraps into piles.

"Aunt Florence has this quilt she made when she was seventeen. An actual genuine crazy quilt. She was about to go off on her first missionary trip and she knew she couldn't take hardly anything with her, but she wanted to make something that would remind her of home, of her memories. So she pieced together all these bits from everything she owned. She went into her grandmother's boxes and found baby clothes, old dresses from when she was a little girl. And she made this—" Dred paused, smoothing her hands over the jeans leg. "It's so beautiful, Zane. This quilt she made out of all these different pieces, sizes, shapes. You can feel how much it meant to her, how much she cared about every single stitch. And it's not— Sometimes people make meaningful quilts that don't actually look that good. But hers is gorgeous. From far away it looks like a show quilt because of the composition, but when you get up close you can see that these bits are real, that they've been worn, and lived in. That's what I want to make."

I risked taking a seat across from her on the bed. Damn, she was so fucking beautiful. Her eyes were dark underneath from exhaustion, and her shoulders hunched, but I loved the way she moved, the way she took up space in a room. I loved watching her hands work, even when she seemed to think it was hopeless.

"What's the obstacle to you making that?"

"I'm not good enough. I'll never be good enough. I mean, I can follow patterns, but you've seen what happens when I try not to follow a pattern—I can't even get a good start on something before I have to rip it out."

I still didn't know what was wrong with her earlier attempts. "And they don't have patterns for that kind of quilt?"

"Aunt Florence didn't use one. I guess it's kind of a stupid dream, to think I could follow in her footsteps, but I always thought that one day I'd suddenly figure out how all these scraps fit together. Then I'd be able to make it."

"You don't want to . . . try, though?"

She narrowed her eyes at me, and I liked that, too. Even when she decided she was pissed in my direction, I still wanted to kiss her. "You can't just *try* things. If I cut wrong, that's it."

"But if you never cut at all—isn't that also it?"

"You don't get what I'm saying." She started playing with one of the piles, fitting pieces together in different configurations. "Maybe if I started with a block . . . I could applique it. Blanket stitch the edges so they don't look dumb. I'm not sure I could piece all this together, but applique would work, and that way I could tie them in with something neutral. It wouldn't be quite the same, but . . . "

I held my breath while she mumbled and played with her scraps, turning them and swapping them out for other scraps. She dragged over a pillow and used that instead of the duvet.

"I think I have batting somewhere. I could kind of quilt-as-you-go, except then I'd be committed, and I'm not sure . . ." The scraps took on the appearance, vaguely, of a rectangle. She pulled one in tighter and pressed another farther out, playing with the negative space in between them. "I don't think . . ."

It was working. I could feel it working. She was making something, even if it was only in her mind. That was where everything started, right? At least, everything except babies. I wanted Dred to start making this quilt, this special, perfect quilt, but part of me was envious that it was something she could choose to do.

Or not.

"Fuck it. I'm not good enough. Why'd you drag this stupid shit out anyway?"

Just like that, it was over. She shoved all of the scraps back into the box—taking none of the care I'd seen when I opened it—and pushed it away from her.

"The problem is I suck at quilting. So fine. I'm done." She stood up and headed for the hallway. "You want lunch? I'm making something."

I listened to her footsteps down the stairs and sat there, in her bedroom full of golden light, with the scraps of her entire life at my fingertips. I replaced the pillow, stacked the patches she'd ripped out, and put the bin carefully away in the closet.

It should have been downstairs in her sewing room.

Hell. The thing about being friends with Dred was you knew she was gonna be pissed at you about roughly half the things you did or said, so it sort of freed you up. No need to fear; Dred's annoyance was inevitable, like the rising sun.

I quietly carried the bin down to the sewing room at the front of the house and put it with the other bins on a bookshelf Obie had cleared of books and movies. There. That was way better. I sort of hoped I'd be long gone by the time she saw I'd done it, though.

Maintaining a breezy air of devil-may-care, I casually wandered into the kitchen. "What're you making?"

"Egg salad. Good? Emerson boiled all the eggs so it can't be screwed up. For the most part. Though he'll probably decide I used too much yellow mustard."

"Can I help?"

"Yeah. Track down the chopped black olives? We have a can around here somewhere."

I hunted for black olives. The sandwiches ended up pretty delicious and Dred turned quilting back on me, asking why I hadn't even started a quilt with my bundles of perfect squares yet.

"I don't know. I guess I got distracted by this wake idea. I've been doing research and making notes."

"Oh yeah? I guess I never thought of a wake as a research project. You gonna have a ceremonial fire or something? Some kind of hippie deal where people write down their deepest fears and ritualistically burn them before they're ceremonially reborn through some kind of cushy satin vagina?"

"That's genius!" I pulled out my phone and pretended to type that into a note. "We're totally doing that. Do you think Fredi would let us burn some of the stuff she's got on the walls? I swear it's older than you are."

She snorted. “Good luck with that.”

“Anyway, smart aleck, no, that’s not the kind of research I’ve been doing. I looked into fire codes for Club Fred’s, and I asked her about attendance at theme nights. I did some brainstorming with Keith about the best ways to raise awareness about the event. I’ve been working very hard.”

“Since yesterday.”

Technically since last night, after I left Richard’s. After he told me to be honest with her about how I felt.

“Since yesterday. Listen, uh, Dred . . .”

“You don’t like your lunch? I told you I always put too much mustard.”

“No, I like it. It’s really good.” I pushed the plate away. “It’s not about lunch.”

“Mm-hmm.”

Shit, shit, she had her bland expression on. The one that meant she was planning not to respond to whatever I was going to say. Usually she got that look with Obie. I fiddled with the edge of the tablecloth. “So you know how I asked you if you’d . . . pretend to be into me? For fun?”

“Fake-dating. It’s not like it slipped my mind.”

“Yeah, fake-dating. Um.”

She stared at me, giving absolutely nothing away. If I could get a hint from her, the slightest nudge in the right direction, everything would be easier.

“Um. So. I was wondering if—if you kind of—” I should have led with, *Remember that time I accidentally kissed you in the car? Could we do that again, only not on accident?*

My mouth dried up around the words.

The doorbell shattered my concentration. Or, alternately, saved me from making a bigger fool out of myself, depending on her response. Before either of us could get up, the door opened.

I looked around the kitchen for a weapon (the fire extinguisher would work), but I didn’t end up needing it.

“Mildred?” a voice I’d never heard before called through the house. “Obadiah? Hello!”

"Oh my god," Dred whispered. "Auntie? *Auntie*?" She scrambled out from behind the table, and Dred was not a skinny lady. I'd never seen her actually scramble before.

"Here you are! I thought I might have to search the house. Hello, darling."

First: Aunt Florence was white. I'd always wondered, because Dred's mom was white and her dad was black and I'd never been able to work out which one was related to Aunt Florence.

Second: she was shorter than I expected; Dred was both taller and bigger. When they hugged, Aunt Florence got a little lost in Dred's embrace.

"What are you *doing here*? Shouldn't you be preaching to pagans in Paraguay right now?"

Aunt Florence arched an eyebrow, a move that echoed Dred so perfectly I had to swallow and look away. "Should I take the alliterative offensive to mean I'm not welcome?"

"You'd've been more welcome if you'd given us some warning! Auntie, this is Zane. Zane, this is Aunt Florence."

I stood to shake her hand, and maybe I was taller, but her handshake held just enough *please let go* to make me think Aunt Florence could hold her own in a fistfight. *Gulp*. "Really good to meet you. Dred and Obie talk about you all the time."

"Nice to meet you, dear. I've heard a lot from Obadiah. Not so much from Mildred." She turned away before I had to reply, which was good, because I had no idea what to say to that. "Where is my great-nephew?"

"He should be waking up soon." Dred touched Aunt Florence's arm, brushing long fingers over her cool Ann Taylor-looking linen shirt. "I can't believe you're here. Obie is going to lose it."

"I certainly hope he doesn't. In lieu of seeing James, I'll settle for the garden."

Dred went out with her, and I stayed in the kitchen, a little shocked by the enormity of Aunt Florence walking in without warning. Hadn't they said it had been fifteen years since she'd been in the States? How was it even possible that she just showed up on a Sunday afternoon?

I heard, distantly, the sound of James crying. And the even more distant crackle of the baby monitor we'd forgotten in Dred's bedroom. A glance made it clear that the two women now slowly touring through the garden hadn't heard either of those things. I made my way upstairs and into his bedroom, where he was sitting in his crib.

"Hey, kiddo. How's it hanging? Did your nap go all right?"

He babbled something at me. God, it was gonna be so much easier when the kid was understandable.

"Uh, are you looking for Emerson? He's also taking a nap, but you can come downstairs with me and we'll find your mom. Can I pick you up?"

He lifted his arms.

"C'mon, mister man. You won't even believe what just happened. Your mom's Aunt Florence is here. That's nuts, right?"

More babbling. I really needed to not call it "babbling" since he was clearly talking. Just, sort of incomprehensible-to-me talking.

"Let's go, kid." I settled him on my hip and started down the stairs.

Aunt Florence wasted exactly no time before taking over the household—while emphatically stating in no uncertain terms that she was not moving in, that she'd be staying with her sister and that was final.

"Do you forget what living with Mom is like?" Dred finally asked, having failed to talk her aunt into moving in to the farmhouse.

"I will give up my suffering for the souls in purgatory. Now, about this young man's sense of himself as a child . . ."

According to Aunt Florence, Baby James (whom she would not hear referred to as "baby" anything because he was eight months old) should be in childcare because without the presence of other children he wouldn't have a feel for his identity as a kid. Which I thought was kind of weird until I considered it like the way Jaq and I had banded together when we were eleven, never to be separated, because at least when we were with each other we knew we weren't the only gay girls on earth.

Maybe James *did* need other kids around. I didn't know. But I hadn't factored in "childhood" as "identity" before, so I made a note to look into it later (tagged *to-research, parenting, early childhood development*).

"Auntie, we don't have the money for that—"

"I will give you the money if it comes down to it, but I don't think it will. You remember Wanda Reed? From church?"

"Yes, but—"

"Wanda's running the daycare at St. Patrick's these days, and she says there's always room for my great-nephew. She also said they have a sliding scale and the folks down at the community action agency can help you with your portion, so that's handled."

"Handled? It's not even— I don't even know if I want him in daycare at St. Patrick's—"

Emerson, uncomfortably witnessing the scene beside me on the back steps, stretched out his legs. He was never happy and relaxed after he'd been lying down, and discovering Aunt Florence in the house had definitely not helped him wake up any more smoothly. He reached out to graze his hand over James's soft baby curls.

James squawked and pushed himself all the way up until he could sit.

"You'll go down there in the morning." Aunt Florence turned away to pluck at some dead leaves on the vine beside the porch.

"Who's gonna watch James while I sit in an office filling out forms I don't care about for a service I'm not interested in?"

"You'll bring him with you, Mildred. Like women do all over the world when they have a child."

"You bully women all over the world? No wonder you were gone so long. That must take ages."

I could see what Dred, standing directly behind her aunt, couldn't: Florence smiled.

"It did take *ages*. Now, moving on. When will Obadiah be home?"

"He's off at eleven."

"Far too late. I'll be long asleep by then, so I'll have to see him in the morning. Give me my bag, please."

Dred obeyed, and was that an actual carpet bag? It was definitely the kind of handbag that might just have a lamp in it, even without Mary Poppins's magic.

"Thank you, dear." From its depths she pulled a battered paperback. To our collective surprise, she handed it to Emerson.

I bit my lip. If she was going to try to convert Emerson right now, Obie was gonna be down one boyfriend by the time he got home.

"This is your assignment. It will seem unreasonable to you and I welcome your complaints, but I still expect you to follow through."

"*Full Catastrophe Living*? This isn't— Is this a religious thing? Because no offense, Miss, um—"

"You may call me 'Aunt Florence' or 'Florence' like the rest of the kids. No, it's not religious, and if it were, it would be more closely aligned to Buddhism than Catholicism. It's a program, with an audio component." She took a seat on the step right below ours, but not too close. Emerson pulled his legs in anyway. "I have heard a rumor that you aren't managing your multiple sclerosis very well, Emerson. While I understand your reservations, I've seen people suffer with later stages than yours, and for Obadiah's sake—and James's—I would sooner you avoid that as long as possible. Tell me you'll do what the crazy lady says, if only for a few weeks."

He gulped. Audibly. "How long is 'a few weeks'?"

"Eight. Technically."

"That's two months."

"It's really only a few minutes a day. You can make it work."

"How long is 'a few minutes'?"

She smiled. "Oh, you'll work that out fast enough. But how long is too long when it means being active for James? And I promise you, if you do this, you will be happy that you did."

"That's the pitch for every scam ever pitched."

Aunt Florence nodded. "Then do it because if you don't, I'll tell Obadiah, and he'll want to know exactly why you won't."

He sighed. "You drive a hard bargain, Aunt Florence."

"And you're unequal to my deviousness, so you know I'll win." She tapped the book. "Start tonight. If you like, he can do it with you. But for you, Emerson, this is very vital. You must stop ignoring your body."

Emerson looked up, and I caught Dred's eye, transmitting *Oh my god, he's gonna blow up right now*. But he didn't.

He shook his head slightly. "I'm not ignoring it. I can't."

"I'm glad we agree. Start tonight."

"You said there's an audio thing?"

"Cassette tapes, but lucky you—now there's an app. Download series one, and if you want me to cover the cost, I'm happy to."

"I'm sure it's fine." He lowered his head and began flipping through the book.

"Good. I'll check in with you later." Aunt Florence glanced at me, then stood up. "I'm looking forward to a home-cooked meal after a few days' traveling."

"I hope you don't think you're getting that at Mom's house."

"Dear girl, of course I meant here. Now tell me—do we need to go out, or do you have enough for a spontaneous guest?"

"We have enough." Emerson's fingers played along the binding of the book he still held as if he couldn't bring himself to put it down. "Zane, you staying?"

"Uh, sure. If it doesn't mess up your meal plan?"

"We're making lasagna either way, but I could use some help with prep."

Florence clapped. "Excellent. That gives us time to go for a walk around the block. Mildred, get your coat. And a blanket for James."

"A walk around the block?" Dred echoed.

"James should know his neighbors."

"Auntie, things have changed since the last time you lived here."

"You no longer have neighbors?"

"No, but—"

"It's the perfect time of day for a walk, Mildred. Come on. Are the Hernandezes still next door?"

"Yeah, but—"

"Good. I'd love to call in on them. Then while we walk, you can tell me more about this Brian person Obadiah has no positive things to say about."

Dred's shoulders slumped. "Ugh. Don't ask. James was supposed to go over there this weekend, but Bri had something come up at the last minute. As usual."

"That is not acceptable. A child needs reliable adults in his life." She patted Emerson's back as she passed him on the way up the stairs to the kitchen. "This Brian boy can decide to grow up or he can come back in a few years."

Dred scooped James into her arms and followed. "Auntie, that's really *not* how shared custody works . . ."

We sat on the porch until their voices faded completely and the front door opened and shut.

"Okay." I sat back, trying to catch as much of the sun as I could on my skin. "That was wild."

"I feel like I just got run over by a semi."

"Is it wrong that I'm relieved I wasn't invited on their walk?"

"Are you joking? I would have cried."

I smiled up at him. "Yeah, but that thing at the end there—you're a reliable adult for James. That was cute."

"That was— I don't even know." He pulled out his phone and held it to his mouth in the position that meant he was catching the microphone so he could send Obie a voice message. "So basically Aunt Florence is a huge control freak, but I think I just agreed to do what she said because—because—I don't know why, except I couldn't *not* agree. Please advise." He put away his phone. "I need another nap now."

"Yeah. Me too. Except then she'd get back and dinner wouldn't be done and we'd get in trouble or something."

He began an organized set of stretches. "I do not envy the poor heathens on the other end of her missionary shtick. They probably convert in sheer self-defense."

"On the other hand, that's kind of exactly as I'd imagine Aunt Florence being."

"True. A force of nature."

"Yep."

"We should get dinner going."

"Yep. What do you want me to prep?"

He carefully levered himself upright. "Everything, Zane. I want you to prep all the things. Let's see what we've got."

Dinner turned out well, and I snuck a peek at Emerson's book later. It was hard to imagine him meditating, let alone doing yoga, but then again, Aunt Florence really was a force of nature. It was even harder to imagine him explaining that he hadn't followed through.

And damn. I'd been kind of in the middle of maybe possibly telling Dred how I felt. Ish. Now what?

CHAPTER 9

The application process at the action agency was apparently grueling. But not so grueling Dred couldn't send down-to-the-minute text message updates.

I've been sitting in this room for ten minutes. This broad is still inputting my application. I COULD HAVE JUST FILLED IT OUT ONLINE, FOR FUCK'S SAKE. >:-(

Application: entered. For her next trick, this lady will try to do math.

Okay, I'm a jerk. She said her kid was up all night and apologized for being slow.

I'm a super jerk. Her kid has Down's syndrome. Maybe I'm the same amount of jerk? I can't decide if it's ableist of me to feel more jerky about shitting all over a mom with a Down's kid than I'd feel about shitting all over a mom with a kid who doesn't have Down's.

A minute and a half later:

Nah, fuck that. If James had DS I wouldn't want people feeling sorry for me because of it. I'm the usual amount of jerk.

But for real, this broad types with one finger of each hand and keeps staring at the keyboard like the letters have changed position since the last word.

How does someone get to her age (like, she's gotta be forty, it's not like she's ninety and only ever used a typewriter) without figuring out computers?

Z, I am DYING, send help.

I should have brought James. At least he would have entertained me. O offered to keep him at the house, but at this point I might be here FOR-FUCKING-EVER.

She wants proof of my income. I showed her. I explained the business. I explained the profit and loss. She said, "So do you receive a paycheck once a week, once every other week, or once a month?" SERIOUSLY, WOMAN, WAKE THE FUCK UP.

I wish I had coffee.

She just said, "You're so fast on your phone! It takes me a long time to send one of those messages!" Uh-huh. I believe it, lady.

She's confounded by my unstable income. "But this can't be right. This says your net for November was $235. But for December it was over a thousand!" I'm seriously going to wig the fuck out and start breaking shit right now, Zane, no joke.

Sorry, now you'll probably be subpoenaed because they'll confiscate my phone and find I texted you in advance of my crime.

They'll want to know how many times I threatened violence and if it was a new thing.

What did that dumb kid say? He was purifying the gays?

No. I can't think of anything here to purify. It'll just look like some black bitch freaked out on some people.

Damn it. I can't go out like that. Like an angry black woman stereotype. I guess I can't break anything.

JESUS. She's really stumped trying to average my earnings. THIS IS ENDLESS.

You there? Showing a house? Breathing air? Drinking coffee? If I never leave this office, you'll help the boys raise James, right?

Text messages are legally binding, I'm pretty sure.

I finally turned my phone on silent-silent instead of vibrate-silent, but it was too late. My boss, Steph, had come out to lean against the doorjamb.

"Hey." Her eyes drifted down to my phone.

"Hey."

"Someone special?"

"It's my friend Dred. She's filling out paperwork somewhere."

"It sounds more like she's messaging you incessantly somewhere."

Since she'd been particularly touchy of late, I didn't tease her like I usually would have. "Yeah. I guess she's waiting to see if some organization will help her pay for daycare."

"Ugh." Steph elegantly draped herself into one of the chairs on the other side of my desk. I'd been front office help until recently, and since our new front office help had the week off, I was splitting time between his job and mine. Which was probably why Steph objected to my text messages; she wasn't normally a micromanager. "*Daycare.* You'll be doing that soon enough, Zane, and good luck to you."

"Future Kid doesn't even exist yet, so they definitely don't need daycare."

"Oh, you'll find a kid."

"You make it sound like I'll find one in an alley or something."

"We hope not. And no, I don't mean *find* like you'll stumble upon one. I mean find in the sense that you don't necessarily know how it'll happen, but it will."

The hairs on the back of my neck rose. She didn't know about Carlos and Tom's offer of sperm. But that had most definitely been unexpected.

"Anyway, will you try the Schlotts again? I know she's kind of a—" She twirled a hand beside her head. "But I still need to talk to her."

I sighed. "Sure thing, boss."

"You are planning to keep working after you've become a parent, aren't you, Zane? I mean, I assumed."

"Well, yeah. Unless you want to give me the kind of severance package that would mean I'd be set for life."

She stood up. "*Not* likely."

"Then obviously I'll keep working. Jeez, Steph, what's up your butt?"

She paused, all long limbs and business casual with just a hint of sex. "Nothing." Away she glided, back to her own desk. I heard her start typing.

I waited until she seemed into her email or whatever, then loaded Dred's messages.

Free at last. I'm so fucking poor they're paying for him to go to daycare. Like almost all of it.

Not that I even wanted him in daycare. And like, with who? That place down the street where you can look in the window and see kids freaking the fuck out all day long, and you can always hear the TV blaring? Going home.

Aunt Florence already has an "interview" set up for us at St. Pat's tomorrow morning. I'm so tired already. E said it's leftover lasagna if you want to come for dinner.

Sure, I wanted to go over for dinner. I texted that I'd be over after the gym and went back to work.

CHAPTER 10

I loved my midwife. She was the hottest lady regularly playing with my cervix. After she finished depositing the last of my prepurchased vials of frozen spunk into my uterus, we sat down at her desk for a post-insemination chat. In the beginning she'd had me do a visualization thing after, like I'd close my eyes and imagine the sperm swimming their way through my fallopian tubes, to my ovaries, finding eggs.

After about cycle six, we gave up on all that. I'd pull my clothes back on and sit in one of her chairs with my feet up on the other, waiting for her to be done with her notes in my chart.

"All right, fess up." She looked at me over her glasses. "You tossed a Peet's cup in my waiting room trash, didn't you?"

"Aw, c'mon, Jane! You said—"

"I *said* you could have the occasional cup of coffee, as long as it wasn't chemically decaffeinated and you didn't pour a lot of poisonous flavoring into it." She looked over her glasses at me. "You wanna tell me that coffee cup you just threw away had mother's milk in it?"

"Hey, does Peet's sell mother's milk? That would solve all my problems! 'Hi, can I get a medium-dark roast for me and a small mother's milk for the baby?' It's a great idea, Jane!"

She rolled her eyes at me. And you wouldn't think that could be quite so effective coming from a five-foot-tall, blue-haired old lady, but it was. "Give me your nutrition journal."

"Yes, ma'am. You sure I can't do it on my phone and email—"

She held out her hand. "The way we're doing it is fine. Hand it over."

I sighed.

Jane read through my notebook, making the odd noise, and I did what I always did at Jane's place: I studied the big bulletin board behind her desk, with all the snapshots of babies and children and families. Obviously it was there to give you faith that Jane would eventually pin your picture up there with all the others, the picture of you and your future kid(s). And even though I knew I was being played, every time I sat in Jane's office I totally regained my faith in the face of all those giggling children.

"What kind of cake?"

"Hmm?" I asked, bringing myself back into the moment.

"What kind of cake did you have on—um—the Friday before last? And that Saturday."

I blinked. "Vanilla. With salted caramel filling and chocolate ganache frosting. You trying to say I'm fat, Jane?"

She laughed out loud. "No, darlin', and a little extra weight on your bones wouldn't kill you. But I'm glad you're eating more." She handed me back the notebook and folded her hands. "So? What's shaking, Zane?"

"Lucky cycle number thirteen. That's what's shaking. Or maybe what's not." I usually tried to hide how each day a tiny bit of hope sort of melted away. But I let Jane see, because she'd had a lot of women in her midwife fertility assistance practice, and she'd seen a lot of them get pregnant. "Am I wasting my time? Should I adopt? I don't know what to do."

Jane leaned back in her chair and crossed her legs. "You're healthy, you're only thirty-five, your charts indicate ovulation, you eat well, and you know damn well your timing was off on at least four of the twelve cycles you've inseminated, not including today." She shrugged. "I think you need to concentrate on all the things your body is capable of, and you should remind yourself that as far as we know conception and a successful pregnancy are on that list. You're probably just as able to get pregnant as you are to drive your car down the street safely. And even that, once upon a time, seemed impossible."

I swallowed. It sounded pretty stupid. And pretty true, too. "You ever notice our names rhyme? Jane, Zane. Funny, right?"

"You say that at least once an appointment."

"So . . . what should I do?"

She smiled. "Keep doing what you're doing. Go to the gym. Do not smoke. Don't drink to excess. Limit your caffeine. Maybe consider inseminating at home again, now that you know what you're doing. The stats are lower, but I've seen it work in women who tried a lot of rounds in the office."

"Actually, I kind of . . . a friend of mine—a couple, really—offered to donate. Well, one of them. Not both of them. You know what I mean." I waited to see how she'd take it, almost expecting a repeat of the attorney twins.

"Known donor?" She nodded and started rustling around in a drawer. "Have him tested for everything, iron out your parenting agreements before you even think about starting, if he doesn't currently have kids, you should think about having his sperm analyzed for motility, and—most importantly—trust your gut, Zane. If something feels bad to you, take a step back." She tossed a folder across the desk. "And take this. It has every question you need to ask him, sample donor agreements, a list of things he should consider, and a few other goodies. Saves you from saying, 'Hey, could you try not to ejaculate in the thirty-six hours before I ovulate?'"

"Whoa. You totally said 'ejaculate.'"

Jane grinned. "It *is* a relatively regular part of the process, you know."

"Sure. Sure. Yeah. Ejaculation. I'm an adult. I can deal with this." I tried to remember what an erection looked like. I'd had sex with a boy or two. In college. Gay boys. You know, for fun. It was all pretty vague. "Um . . . right." I shoved the folder in my bag. "Thanks for that. I'm not sure yet. I'm still thinking about it, and my-sister-the-lawyer is dead against."

She waved her hand. "Let me put it this way: Sometimes known donor relationships end with hurt feelings. Sometimes they end in court, though not as often as people fear. But sometimes marriages end up in all those ways, too, and no one thinks that's a good reason not to get married."

"Well . . ."

I'd meant it as a joke, but Jane zeroed in on me. "Is there a lady on your horizon? Do tell."

"There is no— That doesn't even make sense."

"I'll take that as a yes."

Blushing did not help my denial. "I might be kind of seeing someone. Casually. *Very* casually. Do not get excited."

"I'll get excited when you do. The important thing to do with known donors is talk about everything. There's a whole list of questions in that packet, and you should go over all of them with him and his partner. Possibly with a bottle of wine. It's a long list."

"Oh great. 'Thanks for offering your sperm. Now for your pop quiz.'"

"Better to talk now than later. If they react in any way uncomfortably, you can still back out with no hurt feelings. There's actually some suggested language in there for a few different scenarios. And can I float another idea?"

"Shoot."

"Obviously the risk of inseminating at home with donor sperm from someone who hasn't been cleared through a cryobank or a clinic is that you might pick up a sexually transmitted infection. However. If you talk with him, if he's been monogamous with his partner in terms of fluid transfer, if he's willing to be tested for everything, if all of his answers feel right to you—you might think of taking it easy for a cycle. Inseminate once or twice or three times, if that works in both of your schedules, but keep it laid-back. Consider it a shot in the dark. Maybe don't temp after you inseminate. Give your body a chance to just *be* for a couple of weeks. High levels of anxiety are anathema to conception."

"If that's true, then I'll never get pregnant."

She shot me an unimpressed look. "Well, keep me posted. Eat salmon, Zane. And seriously, keep the coffee in moderation. I've seen a lot of coffee-drinkers conceive, but think about what will happen when you're passing everything through to the baby. Think about your own milk, okay? All things in moderation."

"Yeah, okay, okay. I give up. I give in. Whatever you say, oh wise midwife of the north."

She wrinkled her nose in a gesture way too cute for someone in her seventies. "Give me a call if you decide to skip next cycle."

"I will. Thanks, Jane."

"My pleasure. Take care of yourself."

"You too."

I waved good-bye to the girls at the front and got in my car. I could do this, with Carlos and Tom. I could bring over homework and a bottle of wine and shoot the shit and talk about this whole thing like a serious adult. Like all of us were serious adults. Maybe it'd seem like a good idea. Maybe it wouldn't. But either way, now that it was an assignment, I could get it done.

Before I pulled out of my parking space, I added a new task to my list: *Dinner and homework with C&T.*

CHAPTER 11

If you've never been trying to conceive—that's TTC in the lingo—then I don't know how to explain the two-week wait to you.

Well, first, the luteal phase isn't necessarily two weeks. My luteal phase—that's the part of the cycle between ovulation and either getting your period or testing pregnant—is twelve or thirteen days long. It's been fourteen a few times since I've been tracking my fertility, occasionally longer. Once it was twenty days long, but thankfully that happened before I was actively trying to get pregnant. If it happened after an insemination I'd have been certain I was having a baby. If I was having sex with a person of the sperm-ejaculatory persuasion (and not trying to conceive) I probably would have had a heart attack.

Every TTC cycle is its own little circle of hell, and the two-week wait is when someone who's trying to get knocked up almost loses their mind. Every single month. Every month you try to get pregnant, if you understand how it works and you've been intentional, the two-week wait does you in.

For over a year my whole universe had been divided into pre-ovulation and post-insemination, two or so weeks on one side and almost exactly two weeks on the other.

And here's the thing about early pregnancy symptoms, in case you're wildly curious: every single one of them can also be a PMS indicator. Even if you never in your life had sore breasts before your period, the minute you read it might mean you're pregnant you get them every month. And every time you think, *Maybe that means I conceived!* Then your goddamn period comes and screws everything up.

The downward spiral after that is so fucking intense it takes your breath away. You can't believe in anything good. You have no hope. And after twelve cycles you try not to talk about it with anyone because as sick as you are of not being pregnant, everyone in your life is even more sick of it. Jaq and Carlos used to take me out to dinner after every big fuckin' negative. That stopped after about the third cycle. Then it was just me and Jaq drinking—or me drinking and crying, and Jaq soberly trying to tell me that it would happen, probably sooner than I expected. That lasted until the fifth cycle. My luteal phase ran fifteen days and I thought—I swore—I was pregnant. I was so sure of it I even told Jaq it might be true.

I didn't want to get drunk and cry after that. I sat in my condo and stared into space. I lost hours. I called in sick to work and did . . . nothing. At all.

That was when Jaq started pushing me about finding a girlfriend. A month or two later I asked Dred if she'd pretend we were dating for the sake of appearances.

It was when I had started wondering if it would have been easier if I'd decided to do all this with someone. For months I had been glad to be single. I liked falling asleep by myself, thinking I might have conceived. But at some point it turned, folding in on itself, and more than I wanted to be alone, I wanted someone to hold me while I cried, again, because this thing that other people seemed to do so easily was a thing I might not be able to do at all.

This time I took the gym off, like I usually do after an insemination. But I should have gone to play pool with the team, since that can't really be considered "risky."

I didn't do that either.

It was too early for any actual signs of pregnancy, which was almost enough to stop me from obsessing over them. So I did the only thing I knew would distract me.

I went to the farmhouse to bother Dred.

Preparations were being made for either the apocalypse, or James's first day at daycare. Standing in the doorway to the kitchen, it was hard to tell which.

Only Emerson and James were in the kitchen. I heard Dred's voice before I located her out on the back porch, phone clutched to her ear.

"He is *your son*, this is *your weekend—*" She broke off, and I could see her shoulders go stiff. "That's the funny thing about babies, Bri. They don't always do what's convenient for you."

I made a face at Emerson. "The famous Bri, huh?"

"Yeah. It's like he has exactly the worst timing." He gestured to the table, cluttered with what looked like a bunch of James's clothes. "She's decided to mend and get the stains out of all his stuff so he doesn't look like a poor kid at preschool."

Oh. Damn.

Outside, Dred's voice rose. "Brian, it's your weekend, and you're taking your son. Stop being a child and try being a father."

Emerson winced. "And cue Mildred hangs up, puts her phone on silent, and acts like nothing's wrong."

She came in a minute later and collapsed on the floor beside James, absently picking up his blocks and starting a wall. Her eyes caught mine, lingered, then settled on Emerson. "You're not still trying to make him a lunch, are you? They'll feed him, I told you."

"He might get hungry. Shouldn't he have a snack from home? What if they don't give him anything he likes?"

"Well, I'm sending him with formula, so he'll drink that."

Emerson didn't look convinced, but I thought he might be playing along to distract her from Brian. "I feel like he should have comfort foods with him. What if he gets nervous? What if he misses you? He misses Obie when he goes to work every day, and he's still here with you, or with both of us."

"He misses you when you go to work every day, too. He'll survive."

"But . . . he won't have anyone. He'll be with strangers. *How are you okay with this*?" All right. So maybe he really was freaked out. Emerson stepped back. "I don't understand how people, they just—they drop their kids off and then . . . you don't even know what's happening when you aren't there. How is that okay?"

Dred sighed. "I wasn't going to tell you this. But you're clearly freaking the fuck out, so I will. Listen, there's an app you can download that'll let you watch a nanny cam in their main classroom. I guess it doesn't cover the playground or anything, but the main classroom is big, and that's where they eat and do activities and stuff, so if you want—"

"Of course I want, oh my god. Sorry, Aunt—" He paused. "Do we still say 'Sorry, Aunt Florence' when she's actually . . . here?"

"She's not here right now."

"You know what I mean."

She shrugged and hid James's favorite brown bear behind her back. "I don't know. Maybe we should just try not to be blasphemous."

"Bite your tongue. And tell me the name of this app or whatever. I need it."

They worked out the app, and the school code, and the parent password or something that let Emerson finally access the correct feed. Which . . . was a little creepy. Not that I objected to the idea of the thing, but that there was a company that had made an app that solely existed so that schools could transmit live streams of kids over the internet so people could watch them. Sure, there was security, but still. Tad bit creepy.

Since I had nothing better to do, I took over the game of hide-the-bear, to James's delighted giggles, and Dred went to help Emerson with dinner prep.

I wanted to kiss her hello. No. I wanted her to kiss me hello. So badly I almost asked for it, for something, for some small token of affection or interest.

For Dred's lips to keep me from shattering. It was going to be a bad two-week wait. Usually I could keep myself on the level until I hit day eight or so. That was when I had *every pregnancy symptom anyone has ever had*, even the ones that conflict with each other. But slightly over twenty-four hours out from the insem, here I was, about to crack into a thousand jagged shards.

Dred brought a block of cheese down to the table to grate. "You do okay at the midwife's yesterday?"

"Here I sit before you, spermed up and ready to conceive."

"Spermed up," she repeated. Both she and Emerson wrinkled their noses. "Gross."

"Okay, you know what, my pansexual and homosexual friends, you two have both been spermed up way more than I have in life, so I don't think you should act like it's really all that gross." I said to James,

"Sperm's not gross, buddy. I mean, okay, sometimes it's a little gross, if you aren't into it, but I don't want you thinking that *your* sperm is gross—"

"Jeez, stop." Emerson swooped down to cover James's ears, which James obviously thought was hilarious. "Don't talk about the kid's sperm. He's eight months old. He, like, barely has balls."

Dred burst out laughing. "He has balls, Emerson! That's my boy you're talking about."

"You know what I mean." He uncovered James's ears, and caught him when James craned his neck to look backward and almost landed on his head. "Listen, technically Zane is right, but I don't think you should be thinking about sperm for like . . . years. Okay? Years, James. Ignore Zane."

"I'm gonna tell Future Kid all about sperm." I sat back, now that James was preoccupied by feeling Emerson's face. "Sperm and eggs and what pregnancy is and how babies are born. All of it. No secrets."

Emerson frowned. "You don't think some of that stuff isn't really appropriate for—you know. Kids?"

"Why wouldn't it be appropriate?"

"Because. You know what I'm saying. It's all . . . sex stuff. Which so isn't appropriate for kids."

"Oh damn." Dred shook her head and brushed bits of cheese off her hands. "I can't even believe you just said that to Zane. Man, Emerson. You're dumb sometimes."

"What? How am I dumb?" He looked at me, genuinely stumped. "Did I say something dumb?"

"You implied that babies exclusively come from sex." I stared at him and waited.

Since Emerson actually wasn't dumb, it didn't take that long.

"Oh. Oh *shit*. You're having a baby without sex. It never even occurred to me. And I've known all along." He smiled—actually smiled. "Zane, your kid's gonna be kind of a miracle."

"Well, whatever kid I end up having, even if I adopt one of those sex-derived kids, is gonna be a miracle. But yeah. Took you long enough to catch on. So no, for me it's not about sex. And really, for you it shouldn't be either. If you and Obie decided to have a kid, you wouldn't be having sex with one another to make that happen.

So sex might be involved for someone, somewhere along the line, but for you it'd be a whole other process, right?"

"We *are not* having a kid," Emerson said, exaggerating his tone and facial expressions to make James laugh again. "Right, James? No babies!"

James made really emphatic noises of agreement.

"Exactly."

"Mm-hmm," Dred observed from the table. "Zane and I can tell you hate children."

"I never said I— Oh shut up and grate your cheese. I gotta go work on dinner, James."

James let loose a long string of . . . words? Something.

"I didn't catch all of that, but I can tell you that we're having chicken and rice with lots of cheese. I gotta get back to it." Emerson made certain James was sitting stably on his own before moving away.

I made my voice innocent and unassuming. "How's the meditation going, Emerson?"

"Bite me, Zane."

I laughed.

"Well. I'm doing it. That's all I can say. It's a pain in the ass and I feel like an idiot lying there while some guy tells me to breathe into my toes, but whatever, I'm doing it." After a brief hesitation, he added, "Obie really likes it. He said he sees his breath like it's a light, like it lights up every part of his body as the guy talks. Whatever."

"Lights?" I thought about it. "That could be kind of cool, actually."

"Feel free to download the app and try it for yourself."

"I might." Would it make me feel more like my body was a whole thing, and whether it was going to conceive this cycle, or next cycle, or the one after was irrelevant? I definitely needed to stop acting like if I couldn't conceive, I was a failure. That . . . was not a recipe for success. And not what I'd think about anyone else. If Jaq had fertility issues, I'd be supportive as hell. I definitely wouldn't think she was anything less than totally okay.

James started talking to me, and not the usual rootless babbling, but right *to me*, straight in the eyes. Talking so seriously, so earnestly, that I couldn't help but nod and smile and hold his gaze like I had some clue what he was saying.

Out of the corner of my mouth I said, "Hints? Anyone?"

Dred came around to sit with me. Us. Beside me. Knee brushing mine. "Basically, we just make it up."

"Maybe he's telling her about the sewing machine of doom." Emerson glanced over his shoulder. "Huh, James?"

James waved his arms, still babbling, but I looked at Dred. "Sewing machine of doom?"

"Obie has a bee in his bonnet."

"About his sewing machine?"

Dred snorted. "Oh, not *his* machine. Mine. And it's fine where it is." She stood up and dusted off her pants. "I'll be back."

I watched her retreat up the stairs before saying, "Um. Okay."

"Yeah, don't get between Mildred, Obie, and their sewing machines. She keeps saying her machine is fine in her room, he keeps saying he made the front room into a sewing room so why wouldn't she put it there, and whatever they're actually fighting about?" He shook his head. "I have no idea, but it's got fucking nothing to do with that sewing machine."

"But . . . why won't she move her machine into the sewing room?"

Emerson deposited his chicken into a roasting dish and washed his hands. "Not that I know anything about it, but I think she likes feeling like quilting is this little nothing hobby she doesn't take seriously. The second she starts acting like it means something—which it does—then she might fail at it. But what the hell do I know about being a cynical asshole who doesn't dare hope for good things because hope makes you vulnerable to despair?" He shot a somewhat wry smile at me. "Anyway. They've been feuding since Christmas."

"I wondered why only some of her stuff was downstairs," I mused. James had flopped onto his belly and was now playing with the fringe on the big kitchen rag rug. She'd probably want to be alone. Right? "So . . . I'm kind of thinking of going up there."

"Go ahead. But don't come crying to me when she bites your head off. And will you lift James into his chair for me first?"

"Sure thing." I'd seen Emerson hold James, but he didn't like relying on his ability to get to the ground, pick James up, and stand again with a wiggling kid in his arms.

When the kid was secure in his seat, and Emerson was camped out next to him with an array of thick crayons and a lined notebook, I hesitated.

"This is a dumb idea, right?"

"Yep." He waved his hand. "Go on. If you don't do it, you'll wish you had. Soothe the tiger, Zane."

"She's not a tiger."

"She really is, but that's not an insult. It's what I like about her. All right, James, I'm going to draw a red pepper. What're you gonna draw?"

James babbled something incoherent.

"You're gonna draw the sewing machine of doom? Sounds good."

Make it up. Right. If you don't know what someone's saying, make it up. Sure. Sounds good.

Wait, that might only work with babies.

Dred was lying back on her bed. My mouth went dry when I saw her, all stretched out, hands over her belly.

"Hey."

"Hey." She didn't look up.

If we were dating, but early dating, pre-making-out dating, I wouldn't sit on her bed. But we'd been fake-dating for months and months. I'd sat on her bed before. I was probably overthinking this.

I sat down. Next to her. And kicked my shoes off so I could pull my legs up.

The two of us, sitting on top of her made bed, on a quilt that was all reds and maroons and magentas.

She sighed. "Would you think it was weird if I said I never wanted to have sex again?"

I blinked and looked over, but she was staring out the window. "Um. I don't know. Maybe. Why? Is that— I mean do you—" I ran out of words to leave trailing.

"No. No, it's not that, not really. But I think about what it used to be like. Going out, going to Club Fred's, meeting people, maybe just seeing people I already knew, and that whole dance where maybe you kissed a little, got close, touched their arm, they touched your arm, you leaned in . . ." Another sigh. "I think about that and I'm so exhausted already. I don't know where I'd find the energy to do even half of it. And then, god, bad sex is like the worst. I think maybe I had it dialed in before, I had some kind of . . . radio waves or something that told me how to talk to people, how to flirt, how to initiate. And now all that's sort of white noise. And I'm so *tired*."

I risked reaching over to brush my fingers across hers. "You're totally not allowed to date people while you're fake-dating me. I demand fake-dating exclusivity."

"You know I'd date you for real, right? Like, I assume if that's what you wanted, you'd say something."

I shriveled up into a ball and said nothing. Or maybe I only *felt* shriveled, but I still said nothing.

"Sorry, I know you're not interested."

"Oh my *god*. Shit, sorry, Aunt Florence." I turned. "I am *so* interested. Are you kidding me? I obsess over kissing you. I mean, not obsess in a creepy way, but it was a genuine accident the one time and ever since I've—"

She pulled me in and kissed, hard.

Ohhh, yes, everything was Dred: her lips, soft and warm and so right, and she tumbled me back until she could kneel over me and look down. She opened her mouth like she was going to say something and then decided against it, leaning down to kiss me again.

I couldn't breathe but to inhale her breath, her scent, and my hands found her sides. I was careful, not sure how to take what she'd been saying, not sure if she was too exhausted for anything more than kissing, or if she wanted to control the flow of it.

She groaned and pushed up just enough to speak. "You always talk about being a single mom, how that's on your list. I didn't want you to think I was giving you an ultimatum or anything, but that kiss, girl. Damn. Then you went back to normal like nothing happened."

"I thought *you* were pretending nothing happened!"

"Zane." She kissed me again. "Why didn't we do this months ago?"

I moved to touch her hair, then converted it into a light caress down her neck. Her eyes fluttered. "I figured you weren't interested in hooking up with some broad who wanted to get pregnant."

Then, because that was totally incomplete, I added, "And you're right. This isn't on my list. I wasn't supposed to fall for you like this, and it's really inconvenient. I have a list, Dred."

"Okay, I'll come back to how *inconvenient* I am, but did you just say you were falling for me?"

"Shhh. No one heard that." I played like I was gonna get up, and she shoved me back down. "Did you mean it before, about not wanting to have sex? Because that's not a deal-breaker, but I'd like to hear more."

"No. Well, sometimes, but no. It's less that I'm not interested in sex, and more that it's a lower priority than it used to be." She stretched out over me, letting her weight come down on one of her legs and sliding the other between mine. Not in a foreplay kind of way. In a "tangle our legs because it's comfortable and fun to cuddle" kind of way. "Like it used to matter so much to me. I almost can't believe it. I blame Jaq, by the way. She got me hooked on consistently available high-quality sex, and I've never been able to recover. And Brian—for his many, many fucking faults—was a decent sex partner."

I tried not to smirk, but come on. "Uh . . . that's a very nice compliment. 'Decent sex partner.' Maybe that'll go on his headstone."

She glared down at me. "Shut up."

"I hope everyone I've ever had sex with describes me in such glowing terms."

"You want to keep talking shit?"

"No." I let my hands trail down her back. "Why are you thinking about this right now?"

"Because. Because he's suddenly back in my life—or in James's life—and every time I look at him I think about this dumb fantasy I had for the future, where we were a family, and did everything better than my parents." She let her forehead fall against my neck. "I know that's dumb."

"It's not. It's what most people want, so why do you think it's dumb?"

"Because I'm not 'most people.' And I didn't know I wanted that until—" Her eyelashes fluttered against my skin. "And he left. He fucking disappeared. So fine, that sucked, but I dealt, and it's like the second I got my shit together, oh look, Bri's back, Bri wants to be a good dad now, but it's like he's fake-parenting, you know? Like he's trying it on to see if it fits. And I don't have a choice. I'm stuck with him. Hell, I don't know. I was thinking about how the sex was good and he had a job and he wasn't stupid, and I'd put all that together like it meant maybe we could build a life. But that's not how it works."

"You must have loved him, though. I kind of think maybe that's how it works."

"Sure. I did love him. And I think he loved me. And none of that mattered. Anyway, then I was thinking about how I'm never having sex again in my life and I can't even care."

Yikes, *never having sex again in my life* sounded sort of bad, if you were into sex. "I haven't been laid since before Christmas," I offered.

"Oh man." She fell back some, looking at me from under her eyelashes. "Zane, I haven't fucked anyone since like two months before James was born. It's been almost a year. I probably forget how to do it. Also, what the hell do you mean, you got laid before Christmas? I thought this was an exclusive fake relationship! You pig!"

"Baby, it wasn't like that!" I made my voice wheedling. "Come on, baby, you know you're the only one for me. She didn't mean anything! She was just a body!"

"Uh-huh. Whose body? Now I gotta know so the next time she comes up on you I can rip her hair out or something."

I rolled my eyes. "Yeah right. You'd punch someone before you'd touch their hair."

"Ha. True. Like I want my fingers in some bitch's gnarly weave."

"For your information, she doesn't have a weave. She has a very nice high top. And I don't think she'd appreciate you messing it up."

"Oh damn! You fucked the librarian!"

"Guilty as charged." I smugly polished my nails on my shirt. "And yes, she was every inch as hot as she looks." Mel-the-librarian was thirty-nine, cute as a button, and able to wear the kinds of clothing combinations that normal people shouldn't be able to wear (like converted prom dresses with jeans, and suit coats with frilly skirts).

"You like black girls."

My mouth dropped open. "I—I do not— Not that I *don't*, but it's not like I do— Because— Oh my—"

She threw her head back, that smoky sharp laugh making me smile, helplessly, because it sounded so real.

"Mildred, I do not have a racial preference for black women! Not that there's anything wrong with that, but I don't, and you're trying to mess with my head right now, which by the way *is not* attractive!"

Dred laid her head back, one leg still between mine. "What if I started falling off the bed? Would you catch me?"

"I'd point and laugh."

She twisted toward the edge. "Really?"

"Dred—"

I tried to catch her, but we were too tangled and I ended up almost coming down on top of her, both of us gasping and laughing and rolling to avoid collision.

"You just tumbled us off the bed, you loon." This time I knelt over her and pinned one of her arms over her head. "You're fucking nuts."

"You love it, don't you?"

I leaned down. I hadn't had the chance to control a kiss, and this time she let me. This time I tasted her, but not too much, slipping my tongue between her lips so she'd understand I was a supplicant, not a thief.

Her nonpinned hand came around my head, holding me tightly.

We broke for air minutes later.

"I might be all fucked up in the sexy bits," she murmured, the purple gleam from my hair casting her skin darker than usual.

"I'm not worried about that."

"I'm not *worried* about it, either. I'm just saying. No one's seen all that in a long damn time. It might no longer resemble the map."

I touched her face, her cheek, her jaw. Maybe she wasn't worried about it. Maybe she was. I couldn't decide yet. And it didn't matter. "The thing you said about the sex itself not being a priority? That's true for me, too. It's like . . . this was always my plan. I thought I could do it alone. But I didn't really prepare for it to take this long, you know? I've read all the stats, but I thought it'd happen faster. Now that it hasn't, now that it might never happen . . . I guess I wish I had someone to hold my hand, even if I never get pregnant, even if I don't get to check that off my list."

She hummed a few bars of "I Want to Hold Your Hand."

"You gonna sing the Beatles to me?"

"If you want me to? Hell yeah. But we should probably go downstairs and see how it's going."

"Sounds good."

"You gonna get off me?"

I kissed her one more time. "If I must."

"We should kiss a lot more often."

"Agreed. I'm adding it to my list."

"Oh damn. On the list now. No backing out."

We walked downstairs together. Emerson looked up at us, narrowed his eyes, and didn't say anything.

Dred waved a hand at him. "FYI, Zane and I are allowed to kiss now. So you can shut your trap about it."

He grinned. And Emerson, not a grinner, looked about five years younger when he grinned. "Sweet. I'll text Obie so he knows to shut his trap."

"Oh, he won't. Asshole. Anyway, let's do dinner and shit. What's next?"

We did dinner. And I kissed Dred good-bye before I left. Because now we were allowed to kiss.

I took the boys to the San Marcos Grill for our "so you wanna be a known donor" intensive. We got all the way to dessert and still had barely cracked Jane's big folder.

Carlos eventually pulled the papers out of my hands and shuffled them back into some semblance of order. "We'll take it home."

"But shouldn't we—shouldn't we all, like—"

"We will do it." He patted my arm. "Why are you so nervous? We did research before we offered. Tom went and got all the tests run, and all of them were clean, which we knew. Nothing we've said so far has been different than we read before we talked to you." He looked up at Tom for confirmation.

"The only sticking point for us was the hot tub." Tom grinned at me. "You know how he likes to get me into the hot tub."

"But I can hold back for a few days for the good of the little swimmers." Carlos made a sperm-swimming motion with the fingers on his right hand. "Swim to Mama, little sperm. Make a baby."

I laughed out loud. "Oh my god. It's like Carlos is some kind of sinister magician conjuring a child into existence!"

"You think I can't conjure humans? I'm fuckin' Zeus, children. I will fuck you up with my fecundity!"

"I'm not sure that follows." I shot a conspiratorial look at Tom. "Didn't Zeus only personally birth Athena?"

"Zeus was everyone's big daddy!"

Now we were laughing way too loudly, drawing stares from around the room.

"Crap," I mumbled, attempting to muffle myself. "We're gonna get our asses booted out of here. It'll be like college all over again."

"You're conveniently forgetting that time at Taco Junction when we were in high school."

Tom shook his head. "No way you two got kicked out of Taco Junction. Between the frat boys and the linebackers, no one gets kicked out of Taco Junction."

"Ah, well." Carlos relaxed back in his chair. "It was the three of us. Jaq was there too. And technically, dear boy, we were *lifetime-banned* from Taco Junction."

"Which didn't apply to me and Jaq because we looked like every other average-sized white broad," I said. "They could never keep track."

"But, Carlos, I've seen you at Taco Junction."

"True. The old owner—a rotten sonofabitch who liked to hire young illegal girls so he could pay them on the basis of 'whenever the fuck he felt like it'—keeled over one day out in the back. They said he had a massive heart attack, but I like to think of it as his just deserts for a life poorly lived."

Tom shook his head, smile playing around his lips. "It's weird that there are still stories I haven't heard before."

"Look." I started scraping ice cream out of my bowl. "We only got lifetime-banned from Taco Junction once. That means it barely even happened at all."

"And was null and void when new owners took over. Though the food was better under the old regime."

"Dude had like thirty little Mexican fourteen-year-olds in the back making tacos. But you're right, they were pretty fucking delicious."

Carlos picked up his wineglass and tipped it toward mine. "We are horrible people. Cheers, Zane."

"Cheers."

"As for everything else." He looked at Tom, who shrugged. "Let us take this home and look over it. But darlin'—we didn't go into this on a whim. We have no idea if this would even work, but Tom and I know what kind of family you're thinking of having, and we can support that."

Tom cleared his throat. "I don't want kids, Zane. I never did. I think it'll be cool when you have one, or Jaq if she decides to go that way, but it's not something I want. You wouldn't have to worry about that from me."

"And even if he thought about it, I'd—"

"Don't joke," Tom murmured.

Carlos nodded once. "Yeah, you're right. Well, we don't want any babies. We'll leave that to you and Mildred."

"What do you know about Mildred?"

They did a comical *Who, us?* Carlos glanced at Tom. "I heard Richard's hosting the reception. Didn't you hear that?"

Tom laughed.

I glared across the table. "You know, if your legs were longer, it'd be a lot easier for me to kick them under the table."

"Oh, hating on dwarfs, that's classy, Suzanne."

"Don't you *Suzanne* me, Carlos!"

Tom started looking for a server. "Check, please!" He lowered his voice. "I'm getting us out of here before you two get us ejected."

Something about the word *ejected* was too much. Carlos and I laughed.

"I can't take you guys anywhere!"

Tom's deep respect for the service industry got us out of the San Marcos Grill without any disciplinary actions against us. I kissed them good-bye and sat for a long moment in my car with my hand over my stomach.

"Are you in there, Future Kid?" I sent my awareness deep in my body, and for the first time ever during the two-week wait, I didn't feel a damn thing. Instead of the usual cascade of "might be pregnant" alarms ringing, my body said . . . nothing at all.

"No, huh?" Maybe that wasn't all bad. Maybe this thing with Carlos and Tom could be interesting. Maybe it might even work.

Or maybe not. But if they looked over Jane's novel-length summary of all the information we should talk about and were cool with it, this could be . . . yeah, interesting. For a cycle. Maybe a few cycles, if it worked out.

A small, tentative voice in the back of my head whispered, *If you need a few cycles.*

Emerson was right. Hope was goddamn dangerous. I started the car and drove home.

I'd only been to Saturday breakfast without James once before, but that had been Before Aunt Florence. Like so many things BAF, this, too, was irrevocably marked by her presence.

And not always in obvious ways.

"Are you going out of your mind yet?" She was washing as Obie and I prepped, talking to Emerson at the stove. "The first week of meditation was the worst for me. The first two weeks. That was true all three times I tried to follow that book before I finally stuck with it."

Obie and I raised eyebrows at each other.

Emerson shifted, not quite looking over. "You tried three times?"

"Four. I failed the first three."

He didn't say anything for a long moment. "I feel pretty stupid. I mean, I'm doing it. And I usually stay awake for the whole thing, but it still doesn't feel like it's doing anything for me."

"This is your seventh day?"

"Guess so."

She nodded. "It might feel that way for a while longer. Or it might start feeling like you're getting somewhere. I quit where you are the first time, and I quit at the third week twice after that."

Dred, lounging on the built-in corner bench, whistled. "I can't imagine you quitting anything, Auntie."

"Oh, I've quit a lot of things in my time. This book came to me from a woman I admired greatly, but I thought at the time that it was—" She broke off, hands no longer moving in the soapy water. "Well. Heathenistic, I suppose. With all its talk of finding wholeness in the self, not in God."

"Then what happened?" Emerson asked.

"I quit it the first time, and my mentor smiled and told me that was all right, but I should keep the book just in case. I quit it the second and third times, and didn't even tell her I'd tried it. And then a very dark period fell upon us—upon all of us. We'd had those terrible plane attacks back east. People embraced vengeance and violence over clarity. The voice of God seemed ever more distant."

We didn't speak. For a moment the kitchen only held sounds of running water and knives on cutting boards.

"I wouldn't say I lost my faith, but that's as close as I ever want to come. My mentor asked me if I still had my tapes, if I still had that book. And I suppose everything seemed so dark that I was numb even to the things that had made me uncomfortable before. I wanted to heal. I wanted to be an instrument of God, to heal others, to help."

Obie put his knife aside and looked over at her. "That's when you went on your first trip. You left a year after September eleventh."

"You two were going into your senior year and you didn't need my supervision. I'd set aside that account so I could send money for the mortgage until you could afford it on your own." She laughed. "People thought I was crazy, you know. 'You left two seventeen-year-olds in your house, with access to your bank account!'"

I didn't think that was actually legal, when it came down to it, but I wasn't about to say that. Plus, it was Dred's and Obie's parents who should have been looking after them. Not Aunt Florence.

Dred shook her head sadly. "And all those signed checks. Damn, Obe, we should have cashed them."

"I made them out to the bank, if I recall correctly," Aunt Florence said, voice prim. After a minute, she turned to her niece. "It wouldn't have mattered. I would have left you cash if I hadn't thought that would be far more suspicious. You two were more trustworthy at seventeen than most people are at thirty. And you've fulfilled every expectation I had of you, so my trust was well-founded."

She turned back to the dishes and Dred directed her face toward the window, but not before I saw her blink a few times.

"What I was going to say, Emerson, was at a certain point, when I finally kept at it long enough, the sensation of wasting my time that I'd felt before eased off. I still couldn't necessarily hold my focus for an entire sitting meditation without wandering, but I realized that wasn't the point."

"Then what's the point?"

"You'll figure it out on your own, I'm sure. The point might be different for you than it is for me. But if you stick with it, you'll find *something*." She flicked water off her hands into the sink and dried them. "I've been meaning to look into your workshop, Obadiah, but you have hardly been here. Show me around in the few minutes before breakfast?"

"Sure, Aunt Florence. I love your pictures on Instagram, by the way."

Dred gasped. Like actually gasped. "You *are not* on Instagram, Auntie!"

"Of course I'm on Instagram! How do you think I keep up with all of James's growth? Though I applaud you, Obadiah, for not taking pictures of his face. I really don't know about some of these people, parading their children all over everything as if they were accessories . . ."

Their voices faded as they went into the next room, and I began pulling together this week's omelet fillings. Mushrooms, peppers, two kinds of cheese, ham.

"Anyway," Emerson said, as if he'd been talking. "It's forty-five minutes a day. I guess I can keep doing it if it makes Florence happy."

"I can't even *believe* all that." Dred drifted over, lowering her voice. "I had no idea she ever wavered in her faith. That's crazy."

I dumped the mushrooms and peppers on a plate and handed them to her. "I think it's probably pretty normal. I mean, among people of faith. Doubts and stuff like that."

"Hold up." She narrowed her eyes at me. "You aren't— Do you believe in God?"

"No. I mean, I used to, when I was a kid. Do you?"

"I'm totally agnostic. I have no idea, and I don't really care. I know that I'm not gonna live my life based on what some god judges, or fears, or thinks."

I nodded. "Exactly. But I find it hard to believe there's an actual . . . being. It feels too much like Santa Claus. But for people who *do* believe, past the Santa Claus stage, I think having doubts makes a lot of sense. And I think it's brave when they keep trucking with the whole faith thing despite their doubts."

"I can see that." She leaned back against the sink and nudged Emerson. "What about you?"

"Atheist to the bone. No idea why anyone wants to spend time thinking about all that when I barely have the energy to get through the day I'm actually living. We're at the 'request your fillings' stage, if one of you wants to get them."

Dred shoved away. "I will."

I watched her leave the room, wondering if I'd be able to finagle lingering for a while after breakfast.

Emerson cleared his throat. "Don't hurt her, okay? Or I'll take my cane to you."

Since the defensive big brother act was pretty foreign to Emerson—he didn't even sound right saying it, as if his own vocal cords weren't certain he was actually delivering that line—I raised my eyebrows at him. "Is this the cane with or without the blade?"

"Don't need it. I can do some pretty fucked-up things with a cane." Uncertainty bled away to a smirk. "Just ask Obie."

"TMI. And it's not like I'd try to hurt her. Obviously I would try *not* to do that."

"Well, it's all cute right now, but I remember pregnancy, and if you wake up and decide you're not into it, you'll really mess her up. So don't."

"I'm not pregnant."

"Yet." He started on the first omelet. "You want everything?"

"Yeah. Thanks."

Dred, Obie, and Aunt Florence came back into the kitchen. We didn't say anything else.

The time for quilting was upon us. Sort of.

Dred's sewing machine was in her sewing room.

"I'm going to kill him!" But even as she said it, she caressed the machine, like maybe she was happy to see it there.

I decided to take that as a sign, and proffered the couple of squares I'd pinned together. "Before you kill him, though, will you show me what I'm supposed to be doing?"

She took them, already shaking her head. "Don't pin longways. I know that makes sense, but when you're machine-sewing, you want to be able to slide the pins out easily, so it's better if they're actually stuck in like this." She pulled out and repinned so the plastic bit on the end went up to the edge of the fabric. "And you'll be able to use the presser foot on the machine to keep your seams consistent, so don't put too much time into pinning. The real question is design. Did you lay it all out?"

I pulled out my phone. "I laid it out and took pictures so I'd remember where everything went."

It was set to be a twin-sized quilt. I'd arranged the squares in vaguely rainbow-ish stripes from left to right, though each square had a different pattern. The colors were, I thought, strong enough to pull off the rainbow.

Dred blew up the zoom and went down each row. "This isn't bad. Do you have them all here?"

"In the car." Packed at the last minute, just in case. And because I thought I'd basically exhausted my sewing-machine-less ability to progress further.

"Okay, go get it. We're gonna lay everything out and see what it looks like. Bring it upstairs."

"Okay."

Upstairs, meaning her bedroom. Of course. Right.

As in: place where kissing happens. And tumbling off the bed.

And quilting.

Dred's grabby hands were no match for my control issues. I shooed her away and laid out the whole quilt from my carefully put-together stacks, row by row, taking the pins out of the column I'd pinned so as to better lay them out. I'd studied it, and taken the picture, and studied the picture, but even as I was putting it all on display, I saw things I hadn't seen before, places where I could rearrange.

The second I stepped back, she stepped up.

"Swap these two. And these two. And I don't know about this green, babe. Swap this one with that one. Yeah, let's see what that looks like."

I finished her revisions and stood beside her, feeling the word *babe* weasel under my skin. She used it with Obie, with James. With Jaq. I couldn't decide if I liked the effect of it for me. "I see what you're saying. All the rest have the same level of brightness, but the green has an almost gray tone."

"It's not gray, I don't think. You've got a nice progression, where a few of these incorporate some grays and low tones. The green is *muddled*. That's why it's not working. Hold up." She disappeared into her closet, made some noise of irritation, and left the room.

I wandered the three sides of the bed, looking at it from all angles. It could be a good quilt. Something I'd be happy to have, to have made.

"Oh damn," Obie said from the doorway. "Is that yours, Zane?"

I wasn't so sure I was ready for the whole critique process, but Obie would probably be kinder than Dred anyway. "I guess so. It's my first attempt."

"It's fantastic for a first attempt. You're just winging this, right? Or did you find a pattern?"

"No. No pattern. I looked at a lot of pictures and knew I wanted to play with the idea of a rainbow, so I kind of made it up."

He nodded, also touring around the bed. "Hot. I can't wait until it's done. Who's it for?"

I didn't know what to say.

Dred's voice, from the hallway, saved me the trouble. "It's for Future Kid, obviously. Obe, pull that green square."

He went directly to the one she'd pointed out before. "Oh good. I wasn't sure if I should say anything or not. That's a perfect swap."

The fabric Dred had brought up from her own stash *was* perfect. Green swirls and whorls, different shades of grass and leaf, almost exactly transitioning between the square above and the square below. It wasn't the right size, but she tucked it under the pieces around it so we could see the effect.

"Wow." I stepped back again. "That made the entire quilt better."

"Quilt top," she corrected. "It's not a quilt until you've got the whole thing put together with batting and backing."

I didn't care about the terminology. I cared that I could picture it on a twin bed, with a kid fast asleep beneath it.

Obie put his arm around my shoulders. "Art is fucking hard-core sometimes, Zane. This looks really good. You should definitely start piecing it together."

"I'm afraid to sew. Dred seems to spend most of her time ripping stitches out."

"Yeah, well, she's trying to force fabric she doesn't love to become a quilt she does. Never works. Don't force your fabric." He squeezed me once and let go. "I gotta nap before work. This is ready. Be brave."

I smiled to show I got the joke. Except he didn't give me a jokey smile. He gave me a real one.

Oh. Okay.

"You're a passive-aggressive jerk sometimes," Dred mumbled to him.

"I love you, too." He kissed her cheek. "Aunt Florence made me move your machine. She took one look around and demanded I bring it to her. Sorry."

"My forgiveness ain't cheap."

"I'll bring you a burrito on my way home."

"You're forgiven."

He kissed her other cheek and waved on his way out.

I glanced over. "How did you know it was for the kid?"

"Because you talk about it differently when you get a BFN. You talk about the quilt like it's an obligation. Not like today."

"No. It doesn't feel like an obligation today. I, uh, talked to Carlos and Tom. I think I'm gonna do it."

"Good."

I laughed. "You really want me to have the perfect Aryan kid, don't you?"

She pressed her hand flat on the center of the squares, a green patch a few rows up from the one she'd swapped out. "Moving forward is good. Get these picked up and I'll show you how to start piecing them together on the machine. Don't worry about the pins."

"When are we gonna do this for your quilt?" I asked as I stacked.

"My quilt's a fucking lost cause. But I'll show you what I've been working on later."

That was good. I hoped.

"Let's get you sewing. In the *sewing room*." She sighed. "I love my Aunt Florence, but she's a meddling bitch sometimes."

"How's daycare going?"

"Honestly? It's great. It's only been two days, but I've gotten more done in those two days than I got done in the week before that. I cleaned the refrigerator. I invoiced everyone who owes us money, sent out some 'final warning' letters we can't actually back up, and got bored enough to do Obie's books, too. But I feel shitty because I don't feel guilty enough. Emerson checks the nanny cam every chance he gets." She looked at me, eyes dark, wary. "I don't even look. I'm probably a horrible mother, but I drop James off at daycare and I drive home and I—I think about him, obviously, all day long. But I don't *long* for him. I don't wish he was here."

"You think that makes you a horrible mother?"

"Yeah. The only way you win at motherhood is by feeling worse about yourself than everyone else does. You should find a way to circumvent that, by the way."

"I'll add it to my list." Last week I couldn't have done anything but tell her I didn't think she was a horrible mother. Not that it would have helped.

I put down my stacks, so carefully, and turned to her.

"I don't need you to—" she started to say.

I kissed her, letting my hands drift down her arms, gently intertwining our fingers.

She didn't sigh, not with her mouth, her lips. Her lips were busy. But it was almost like a full-body sigh. I could feel it where our breasts pressed against each other, where our bellies touched. Her body released something into that kiss, something that was more than breath.

I wanted to say all the things. But I didn't.

"I'm gonna teach your sorry ass to sew now." Her lips brushed my ear. "Okay?"

"It's a pretty sorry ass."

"I'd tell you I like it, but I don't want that to go to your head. Come on."

We went. Dred whistled "I Want to Hold Your Hand" as we walked down the stairs.

CHAPTER 13

I shoe-horned wake planning in with pool the following week. I considered the pool team a solid part of my promotional plan.

What blew me away was how emotional a few people got.

"This is *so* necessary." Alisha was winding her braids into a knot at the back of her head. "For real, Zane, I'll tell everyone. We gotta do something to shake off the heebie-jeebies."

A woman named Sally raised her hand, like I was a teacher. "Can we— Is there some way we can honor the people who died?"

"Sure." I paused. "Within reason. I was thinking about maybe having a table set up with pictures and note cards people could write on." I didn't mention burning them in a ceremonial fire, but I hadn't ruled it out yet.

"I'd like that," she said.

Mario and Anthony, a couple who'd just joined the team together and seemed to spend about half their time fighting and half making up, were standing uncharacteristically close to each other, so I figured they were on the upswing tonight. Mario looked around, as if waiting for someone else to speak. When no one did, he said, "Has anyone heard what's going on with the case?"

"They're still building it." Alisha sucked down what looked like a mai tai. "But from all reports I've heard, it sounds like it's pretty solid."

"If it's so solid, why couldn't they find this guy before he killed six people?"

She shot him a *look*. "Because he hadn't screwed up enough yet. Can we play pool now?"

Two hours later Alisha and I retired to the bar and toasted each other with our winnings. Or rather, with a pocketbook advance on our winnings.

"Where's your boy?" I poked her.

"He's around somewhere. Tell me everything about this wake, Zane. I'm so with you."

I was halfway through telling her "everything" when Ed showed up and wanted me to start over again.

"This could be really good," he said when I'd finished. "I definitely think you're onto something where healing comes into it. It feels like we're waiting for that wound to reopen, because for a while that's all it did. We'd get a few weeks out and it would happen again." He slid his arm into Alisha's. "It's still my first thought when my phone rings in the middle of the night: who's dead this time?"

My stomach clenched. "That's awful."

"I guess it's a good reminder that we don't have to worry about it. Until . . . you know. Until someone else decides to start killing people."

Alisha banged his arm. "Oh my god, *stop*."

"Sorry. But it's someone. It's always someone. The next victim, the next crime, the next killer."

"Morbid, boyfriend. Very morbid. Should we dance?"

Ed shook his head. "I gotta process more death for a minute."

"Okay. You'll come find me in a bit?"

"Definitely."

They kissed, and Alisha was already starting to dance as she made her way through the crowd.

"So the wake will be a party?"

I focused back on Ed. "Right. A big party, as big as I can make it staying inside fire codes."

"You don't think it'll have more impact if it's smaller?"

"It depends on the impact. I want to go wide, you know? There are people who won't feel welcome if it's too small. But ideally it can be both. I—" I paused to put my thoughts in order. "I want to create a space for the people who lost friends, who feared for their lives. And I also want to create a space for the people who barely knew what was happening, who maybe don't even know how much they're missing out because Club Fred's has changed now. And I want both of those spaces to be the same space. So to speak."

He smiled. "So . . . simple, right?"

"Yeah. Simple. Easy as pie. Seriously, though. Do you think that's possible?"

"For most people? Hell no. But you'll probably pull it off. I can't wait to see."

"Thanks for the vote of confidence."

"Anytime. And you should get in touch with Star Everett. She's the social media director for the *Times-Record*. She's got a ton of contacts, and while I think she'll actually be happy enough to send a couple of tweets or something to support the event, I don't think that's the kind of range you want. You might see who she thinks would hit the Club Fred's demographic, and talk to those people."

"I'm kind of shocked the *Times-Record* even has a social media director, to be honest."

"I think they forget they hired her, judging by how she sits in her office with her headphones on for eight hours a day and I'm the only one who works with her. But she's really nice, and I know she'd love to do more community-based stuff." He downed the rest of his beer. "And get Obie to promote. Have him post the flyers to his Instagram and Twitter accounts. *That's* your demo, right there."

"Keith promised to help with flyers and posters."

"Perfect. He's great. And I'd also suggest something subtle for Cam to put up at the Rhein, or for anyone else who wants to post one. You don't want to get *everyone* to come to this thing. But if you word it cleverly, you can attract only the eyes of people who should actually pay attention."

"Thanks, Ed."

"And seriously, tell me if you need anything."

"I will."

"I'm gonna go dance with my lady now."

"Have a good one." We kissed good-bye.

This was the moment when at the old Club Fred's I would have tried to find a table, a group, or a handful of people to entertain me. I didn't really feel like hitting the dance floor, and no one I wanted to hang out with was sitting at the bar.

There was, however, someone at Fred's who I'd been thinking about talking to. He was, in a way, even more scary than Fredi herself.

Donald. I had no idea what his last name was. He was this . . . guy. Old guy. Old Asian guy, skin weathered by years and scarred by old battles. He'd been in the White Night riots back in the seventies after the guy who assassinated Harvey Milk got off with a bullshit charge. There were rumors that Donald had been at Stonewall, though I thought that was probably a myth. He wasn't that old.

Or maybe he was.

Looking at him, you could see the old warrior in his face. But you could also see the gentleman, and sometime arbitrator of conflicts. He was at his usual table, with a man and woman I recognized as his friends (if by "friends" you meant "bodyguards"), and—my luck was good—Carlos.

Not a lot of people felt comfortable walking up and sitting down at Donald's table, but Carlos didn't think rules like that applied to him. During the two months between his twenty-first and Jaq's—when he was allowed in Club Fred's, but we weren't—he somehow made friends with Donald. And they'd been close ever since.

Even in the old days I wouldn't have invited myself to sit down at Donald's table.

"Hey there." I leaned down to kiss Carlos's cheek and nodded hello to Donald and his bodyguards.

"I was just telling Donald about the event you're planning. Sit, Zane."

I dragged over a chair and met Donald's eye. "Have you seen a lot of wakes at Club Fred's?"

"Some, over the years. None quite like what Carlos described. I assume you already asked her permission?" He smiled. "I'm sure she responded with all due grace and encouragement."

"She said yes—eventually."

I'd given her my exactly-one-page pitch, which she'd glanced at before shoving it in Tom's direction and saying: "Make it a Saturday, Jaffe. And I've been persuaded to comp it." Then she'd grunted and walked away. That had been the sum total of her involvement.

"I think it's about time we intentionally took stock of where we stand." Donald gestured to the room. "It's not something we've ever done well. Gay people. Or queer people. I love that word. It's like spitting in the faces of the people who used to fire it at me. We tend toward black and white, all or none. We are either running to outpace the devil, or we're whistling through the woods, pretending he's not at our back. I like the idea of being still for a moment to look at where we stand."

I wanted to thank him, but suddenly I wasn't sure I could speak. That was *exactly* what I wanted to do. I was calling it a wake, but what it really was had more to do with acceptance. More even than celebration.

He nodded. "It is a good instinct, Zane. Do you have a date yet?"

"The first Saturday in March."

"Very good. You will see me there. Or here, as the case may be."

Carlos squeezed my hand. "You know this is about to go totally out of your control, right?"

"I have lists."

"Uh-huh."

I sat with them for a while longer. Then they picked up a conversation they'd been having earlier, and I excused myself after only a few minutes. Time to head home. I walked to my car with my keys extended between my fingers, thinking of all the times I'd walked these dark side streets without even considering the possible dangers.

Maybe it was a loss. Or maybe it was a new recognition of what had always been true: no one was safe. Either way, we were left with acceptance. Donald was right—time to look around and see where we stood.

Aunt Florence came to breakfast again on Saturday morning and commandeered Dred after for a Serious Discussion.

At least, that's what we speculated, in low voices, from the kitchen. Where Emerson and I cleaned, while Obie entertained James by setting him in the middle of one of the raised beds and letting him eat all the plants he could grab.

We thought they were talking about big things—Florence wanted Dred to reconcile with her parents—but when they finally raised their voices, it was all about quilting.

"I'm not as good as you are, Auntie! Stop pretending that I am!"

"You always do this. You are just like your mother. You give up before you even start so you won't have to risk making a mistake."

That had an unfortunate ring of truth to it. I raised my eyebrows at Emerson, who shook his head.

Dred sounded miserable. "Why won't you let this go?"

Florence lowered her voice so we could no longer hear it.

"This family takes quilting very fucking seriously," Emerson whispered, brushing accumulated crumbs into the sink.

"So seriously they use it as a shorthand for everything." I tried to hear more, but now—nothing. Only the totally muddled sound of voices and James's clear, almost bell-like laughter from the garden. "Do you think James sounds like a bell when he laughs?"

"A bell?" He frowned. "No. Wait. What do you mean?"

"I don't know. Just that there's something so . . . pure about it. Like it's this pure tone."

"Huh. I guess there is something sort of elementally pleasing about the sound of him laughing. If that's what you mean."

We stared at each other for a long moment. He recovered first.

"Well, *I've* been meditating. I don't know what your excuse is. 'Bell-like.'"

"It *is*." Kind of. Maybe. Hell, I didn't even know what that meant. But it fit. "Anyway, what does 'elementally pleasing' mean?"

"Shut it."

I started to jump up to sit on the counter, then remembered Aunt Florence's face the last time I'd done that and decided against it, copping a lean instead. "So are you coming to the wake?"

"Yeah. You know you made that date for a weekend when she has James, right?"

"No—no, I checked that—" I had a calendar! I'd been careful!

"Yeah, except then he skipped the week before last, so now they're on a different schedule again. I'd say you better hope he fucks up in the next few weeks, but I don't think you have to hope. It's pretty much a given."

"Damn it." I'd fucking *planned* around that schedule. And now Dred wasn't going to be there? "What's his problem? James is a great kid. Who wouldn't want to have him for, like, the thirty-six hours or whatever Brian keeps him?"

"I guess it's probably scary. And also, I know it's not in style, but I'm not totally without sympathy for the guy. Obie liked him before, but now he acts like Brian's got a case of leprosy, and he doesn't want to breathe the same air. Mildred is, like, seethingly angry at him. Which I get, but doesn't make him coming over here any easier. And he clearly feels incredibly stupid for how he reacted to 'we're pregnant' with 'I'm leaving the country, don't bother calling.' Not that him feeling bad now justifies it, but I guess it seems like it's better than nothing." He shook his head. "But I've thought that before, and sometimes it's not really better than nothing. I think Mildred envies you, a little. Not having to think about stuff like that."

"Envies me for what?"

"For having a kid on your own. Instead of stumbling into having a kid and making it up as you go along."

"Oh. I guess I always think she's the cool one between us."

He blinked. "You have a steady job, a condo, money, a plan with a list and everything, and you're so driven you can just decide to throw a community-wide wake and make it happen."

"The only thing I can't do is get pregnant." The words were out of my mouth before I'd even really thought them, and for a second, I almost couldn't believe I'd spoken aloud.

But Emerson only met my eyes steadily. "Well, I can't cure MS. But I can sure as hell take better care of my body than I have in the past. You might not be able to get pregnant, but you can definitely start a family. There's more than one way to skin a cat, Zane."

"*Ew*. Why would anyone want to skin a cat?"

"No idea. But I've heard there's a number of methods, if you're interested."

"That's disgusting."

Obie and a giggling James were suddenly in the doorway. "Come outside, it's actually gorgeous out. I don't know when it suddenly turned to summer out here, but it's at least seventy, seventy-five."

"I hate heat." Emerson, contrary to his words, walked outside. "James, boy, what have you been eating? Grass?"

James replied, waving a fist with a few bits still clutched between his fingers.

"Wheatgrass? Ugh. Don't remind me. And don't put it in the juicer, it's vile."

They kept talking. When it didn't seem like Dred and Florence were going to be done any time soon, I followed.

I had an appointment in the Harbor District in the late afternoon, and stopped by QYP after to see how the guys were doing.

Cam's car was out front again.

"Hello?"

A brief scuffle of shoes led me right around the corner from the kitchen, where half-filled bookshelves lined the walls outside the utility closet. Keith and Cam were standing *suspiciously* far apart. And both of them were blushing.

"Let's pretend I didn't interrupt whatever I clearly interrupted, huh, boys?"

"Uh, yeah, let's do that." Keith brushed past me. "Hot chocolate?"

"Sounds good."

"Cam? And yes, we have almond milk here."

"Oh. Yes, please."

They had almond milk. For Cam. Aww.

"So we have a date for the wake." I let myself jump up on the drop-in center's counter, swinging my legs with no Aunt Florence to disapprove.

"I heard that from Ed." Keith assembled his hot chocolate makings. "And we'll be there, obviously."

I glanced at Cam. "You coming to the wake?"

"I meant him, too."

"I'm still asking the man himself."

Keith waved a hand. *I'll leave you to it.*

I raised my eyebrows at Cam, who shrugged. "I've already been warned that I can't schedule an event that night to get out of coming, so yes, I'll be there."

"Don't—not if you don't want to. That's sort of missing the point of the whole thing."

"It's not that. I apologize, Zane. I don't mean that Keith is literally dragging me against my will."

"Though I would," Keith mumbled in the direction of the saucepan.

Cam shot his back a slightly sour look. "I needed to be convinced, initially, that it was relevant to me. I've seen the changes at Club Fred's, but ultimately I'll continue to go there regardless of how people around me act." He paused, as if waiting for Keith to interject. "But maybe there's more power in the idea of the community coming together than I thought. I'm not sure. I'll be there, though. Threats have been made." His expression shifted, just a little.

Keith half turned, smirking. "I think you meant that rewards have been promised."

"It's the same thing around here."

"Ha, so true. Rewards, threats, what's the difference? Hot chocolate is served."

We took our mugs—mine and Keith's with cow's milk, Cam's with almond—to one of the tables.

"Merin already went home?" Sure, it was 7 p.m., but I wasn't so sure Merin had a home outside the center.

"He's in back with Josh, doing strong man things," Keith said.

Cam smiled. "They're lifting weights."

"Strong man things, like I said."

I pretended affront. "Hey, I lift weights. When I'm not potentially pregnant."

"Do you stop when you're all—" Keith did a hand-shake thing, presumably to indicate *possibly carrying a fertilized egg*.

"Yeah. It's mostly superstition, but yeah. Not that I'd be doing pregnant deadlifts, though you could probably find someone on the internet who did. But I back off on the heavy lifting just in case."

He visibly restrained himself from asking the next logical question, so I answered it anyway.

"Still in the two-week wait. I can test tomorrow morning."

"That's— Is that exciting, or not really?"

I started to shake my head, then stopped. "Sometimes I really think I'm pregnant by now. This time I don't have that certainty. It'll probably be negative." Even as I said it, though, I wondered. Maybe *not* thinking I was pregnant was a sign of pregnancy? If all the times I'd been sure meant I wasn't, maybe this time, being unsure meant I *was*.

It was crazy. But trying to get pregnant was a crazy-making thing.

Cam shifted in his seat. The only man I knew who wasn't actively awkward talking about me trying to get pregnant was Obie. "How long have you been trying?"

"This is cycle thirteen." God. It sounded longer every time I said it. Maybe I did have fertility issues. Maybe Jane somehow missed them.

"Damn." Keith played with his mug. "You don't want to adopt?"

"Oh, I'd totally adopt. I mean, some people don't want to adopt, and that's cool, but even if I get pregnant, I think I'd adopt if I wanted more kids."

"Huh. I never thought about that. You could do . . . both."

"Yeah."

"So what is it about being pregnant that makes you keep going this long? It's kind of a really long time, Zane."

I don't always explain it. It feels like there's a weird double standard where straight and queer people are concerned. My heterosexual

TTC friends get "just adopt" from their peers, but at least people seem to understand why they want to physically have a child. I lost a couple of friends for not adopting right off the bat. One of them thought it was our duty as queers to raise kids who didn't have other family (which was a neat inversion of the argument we used against people who said we couldn't have babies: why yes, but we're raising your babies, so it works!).

Most of the time, I don't explain it. But sitting in QYP drinking hot chocolate made me bold. Or reckless. Or something.

"It doesn't have to do with parenting, or with kids. It's going to sound kind of ridiculous, but pregnancy is . . . something I want to experience. Jaq and I took a trip to London when we graduated from high school. A week. And that's more what this is for me. An adventure."

Keith's brow furrowed. "You mean, separate from being a parent and having a kid?"

"Related to, but not identical, yes. Does that sound nuts?"

"Honestly, Zane, I get how reproduction works, but the whole thing sounds nuts to me. There are so many variables, so many places for it to go wrong, that I can't even fathom how the human race continues."

"Me neither," I said.

"Yeah, I bet."

My phone vibrated against my leg. A text from Dred. *You coming back tonight? You could stay over. The bed's big enough. NO PRESSURE.*

I took a larger sip of my hot chocolate and slid the phone back into my pocket. Did I need to reply? She had to know I'd say yes.

"Oh, secret text message." Keith nudged Cam. "Who do you think Zane's secret-texting?"

"I think Mildred's secret-texting her."

"Both of you can hush."

"Well, we *could*—"

"So." Cam raised an eyebrow. "Is it still fake-dating?"

"Not . . . exactly."

Keith grinned. "Ha! Finally! We were wondering when you were gonna figure out you weren't actually fake-dating."

"We were!"

"You weren't. You were pretend fake-dating to make up for the fact that you were actually dating, which is different."

"Oh yeah, buster? What makes you the expert?"

He crooked his thumb toward Cam. "This one thought Josh and I were just after him for his remarkable grasp of film history or something. It's adorable when you dense types figure out what's obvious to the rest of us all along."

"Is a punishment the same as a reward?" Cam murmured.

"You know that's right."

They smiled at each other, and I couldn't help smiling as well, even though it had nothing to do with me.

"Anyway, boys, I should be off." I downed the rest of my drink. "Thanks for the lovely hot chocolate, it's been swell."

"Are you running off to get laid?" The expression on Keith's face was probably supposed to be pouting. Though it looked a lot more like a grin. "So tacky!"

"No! Well. I don't think so. Hell, I have no fucking idea. But anyway, I'm leaving."

Keith saluted. "Have a *really good* night, Zane."

"You're getting a little too big for your britches, mister."

He laughed. "I really am. Ha."

Cam stood up and walked me to the door. "It worked out pretty well for me. The transition to actually dating after doing… something else."

"Yeah, I can see that." I kissed his cheek, on impulse, making him blush pink. "You have a good night too, Cam."

"I will."

CHAPTER 15

Only the light in the kitchen was on when I walked in. This time I locked the door behind me.

I found the kitchen empty and stood for a long moment, not quite sure what to do. Emerson might be in bed already. Dred might be putting James to bed. I was still debating making tea just for something to do, when I heard footsteps coming downstairs.

"Hey." Dred's voice. "Zane."

"I'm here."

"Hit the lights and come upstairs."

Yes, ma'am. I hit the lights and followed her to her room.

I loved Dred's room during the day. All buttery sunlight and warm wood. At night, with only one low lamp on, it was . . . even better. All darkness and layers of shadows with one sweet pool of light in the middle.

In this light, the variations-on-red quilt was darker, almost richer, its tones not muted so much as reaching deeper than they did in daylight.

"Did you stop by your place?" It was probably just an aural illusion that her voice sounded deeper and richer, too.

I froze. "Oh my god. No. I didn't. I drove straight here."

One side of her mouth quirked up. "You were so eager you forgot you needed a change of clothes?"

"I'm okay about the clothes, it's my toothbrush I'm missing."

"You're okay about clothes now, but you better hope Aunt Florence doesn't come over in the morning and see that you're wearing the same thing you were wearing today."

"I changed my clothes after I left here."

She glanced up and down at my outfit. "No way she believes you wore that to come over for breakfast."

"Point."

"Don't worry about a toothbrush. I have one for you. Or I have one in a package you can use."

"You bought me a toothbrush?"

"I bought you a toothbrush before we met, yeah. Watch out for the dust."

The farmhouse had been built in a time when people hadn't required a bathroom per bedroom; there was a full bath upstairs and a half bath downstairs. And the upstairs bathroom wasn't all that generous, but somehow they managed to share it. James's toys lined the tub, an elaborate shower caddy had shelves for each of them, and the sink was surprisingly clear of debris.

"I think your bathroom's cleaner than mine."

"Emerson's a little OCD. Plus, sometimes he needs shit to be out from underfoot and accessible, so we keep it that way. It's a huge improvement on before he moved in. For a while after James was born this was kind of a cesspit." She smiled, squeezing toothpaste on her toothbrush, then automatically putting some on the brush I'd unwrapped. "Obie was goofy as shit when Emerson started spending the night here. He was the slob between us, and he kept saying if Emerson knew how much of a slob he was, they'd break up."

I nudged her arm. "So this seems like a good time to mention I'm not as much of a neat freak as people think I am."

"Why? You moving in?"

Our eyes met in the mirror.

"You really don't have room." I started brushing my teeth to cover the sudden full-body desire to, yeah, move in. To do this every night and every morning.

We hadn't even had sex. Hell. We'd only kissed a few times.

Back this truck up. Stop thinking like this. It's hormones. Or nesting. Or who the fuck knows, but stop.

Hormones, right. Yeah. Probably. Anyway.

I finished brushing my teeth and went back to the bedroom. This would have been a good time to have . . . stuff. A bag. Clothes. Uh, pajamas. Because we hadn't even had sex yet. And she might not be interested. And I was standing here in the slacks and shirt I'd thrown on before my meeting.

I was supposed to be a planner, damn it. If I started spending nights at the farmhouse, I was gonna have to keep a go bag in my car at all times with a change of clothes. Thank god I always kept my basal body thermometer on me.

Tomorrow was twelve days after inseminating. I was supposed to test. But I didn't have to test. I could skip it. If you wanted the best results you had to test the first time you peed in the morning, when the hormone concentrations would be highest. And this close to ovulation, there was no point to testing later.

"What's up?" Her eyes narrowed. "Why does your face look like that?"

"Nothing."

"Nothing, huh?"

I relented. "Oh, it's luteal phase day twelve tomorrow. That's when I usually test."

"Hang on." She went to the closet and rummaged long enough to make me wonder if she'd gone to Narnia for whatever she was looking for. "Ha. I knew I had more of these."

The open box of pregnancy tests landed on the bed, spilling out one lonely test.

"Damn, woman, you're a full-service stop."

"It's part of my charm."

I wasn't going to tell her, but it really was part of her charm. "Thanks. You don't mind?"

"Seriously, keep me away from people with sperm. I don't have any sexual problems with them, but I can't be risking this shit again, Zane. I hope you like pregnancy more than I did."

My skin prickled. "I might not ever get pregnant."

Most people rush to assure the not-yet-pregnant lady that she'll get there eventually. It's as if the whole world sees pregnancy as an entitlement that anyone with a uterus just *gets*.

"True." Dred finished wrapping her hair in a scarf, tucked in the edges, and lay back on her bed. "You might not. Some people don't. Some people who don't want to, get pregnant anyway. There's pretty much no fairness in the world, so it could be that I got knocked up off a ripped condom and you can't get knocked up no matter how hard you try."

I fingered the test I'd pulled out of the box, wishing I had the courage to not test. If you weren't pregnant, you got your period. I wanted to be that patient. I wanted to accept.

"I really want to get pregnant," I admitted.

"But the thing I like about you is that if you don't, you'll find a way to have a family anyway, and you'll be happy with it. You won't spend your whole life wishing for something that couldn't happen. A lot of people do that and it's such a waste, you know?"

I set the test on the table beside the bed, then pulled out my digital basal body thermometer and put that next to it. My phone was at about fifty percent, so I turned it to airplane mode to keep it from wasting battery power overnight. Temping wasn't much good if I didn't have access to my spreadsheet.

"You want a shirt or something to sleep in? You know, before you do the walk of shame downstairs tomorrow morning."

"Are you teasing me?"

"Yeah. You got a problem with that?"

I leaned over the bed to kiss her. "Not so much, no. Do you want me to have a shirt to sleep in?"

She eyed me for a long moment, dark eyes unblinking. "I don't sleep naked. But it doesn't get that cold, and we keep the thermostat at fifty-five for James."

"Fifty-five can be chilly." I wanted to give her an out. Maybe she wanted me to have a shirt on. Maybe it felt like pressure if I didn't. Maybe I was making a big deal out of nothing.

"Do whatever makes you happy."

"Lend me a shirt."

She rolled her eyes and went to rummage in a drawer. "Here."

"Wow." It took me a minute to place the logo. "I didn't realize people still had Green Day shirts."

"Hey, you shut up. I love them. Obie had the biggest crush on Billie Joe Armstrong when we were in high school. Like, he'd casually propose we go hang out at this pizza place in El Sobrante just in case one of the band guys stopped by, because he heard a rumor that sometimes they did."

I laughed. "Okay, that's adorable. And Billie Joe is crush-worthy. I can see that." I shrugged my bra off and pulled the huge T over my head. "Let me guess: this was Obie's shirt?"

"Looks good on you. Though I might have totally screwed up. If we make out, we're gonna need to turn the lights off so I don't keep thinking about teenage Obe."

I shucked the rest of my clothes and kept on my undies, twirling for her with a flourish. "What do you think?"

"I think you should be in the bed already."

"Yes, ma'am."

"You call me 'ma'am' and we're gonna have to take this outside."

"Exhibitionism, Dred?"

She growled and tugged on the shirt until I toppled into her. "Get. In. The. Bed."

"Thanks for inviting me over."

She straightened out of her habitual slouch, nearly equalizing our heights. "I'm still unclear on why we didn't do this two months ago."

"Uh. Apparently I was, uh, pretending we were fake-dating. Or something. In my defense, it might be contagious, and if it is, I caught it from Cam. He apparently had a, like, different strain of it. Um."

"Is that right?"

"Yeah."

We kissed. The kind of kiss no one started and no one stopped. Like we were both being directed by the same force, and no one needed to be in charge for us to feel it.

"Come to bed, Z."

"Yes, ma—"

She covered my mouth with her hand. "Don't make me kick your ass out in the middle of the night."

I licked her palm. She squeaked and pulled away, then retaliated by shoving me over onto the bed. "You're disgusting!"

"Don't wake the baby!"

We rolled around for a few minutes, trying to pin each other, trying not to laugh too loudly. When I finally cried uncle—or panted it, really—she sat on my back and held me down, pulling the pillow so I wouldn't suffocate. "Tell me I win."

"You win. My heart's pounding. How can I be this out of shape?"

"Right? Don't you go to the gym and shit?"

I strained, trying to dislodge her. And promptly gave up. "If I die, you're gonna have a dead body in your bed. I'm just saying. It'll inconvenience you way more than it will me."

She laughed, muffling it against my neck. "That's a really good pitch. Not 'don't kill me because murder is bad' but 'don't kill me because murder is inconvenient.'"

"It is!" I groaned. "But if you wanted to give me a back rub, don't let me stop you."

"You wish." She rolled off. "I'm not super insecure."

"Uh-huh?" I opened one eye to stare across the quilt at her.

"But I'm still having a hard time imagining actually having sex. Or no, I can imagine it, but I can't imagine *doing* it. In real life."

"We don't have to."

"I know that. I'm not a jackass. But I want to have sex with you." Her jaw tightened and she looked away. "I want to, but my body is shut down in a way I'm not used to it being. I always had a racing libido, you know? Obie told me once it was a good thing I was pansexual, because I wanted to have more sex than one gender could provide."

"Like you'd exhaust the entire gender? Damn, Dred." I reached out, dragging my fingers along her throat, down over her shoulder. She was wearing a dark-blue cotton shirt, maybe one of those men's undershirts you'd see in packages. It wasn't the kind of shirt cut for people with narrow shoulders and large breasts, anyway. "You know I don't have any need for that, right?"

"You have no need to get laid? Really?"

"Tonight? None. Like none. Really."

She swallowed. "But I might. It's been such a long time. And I haven't been lonely—you can't really be lonely in this house—but maybe I've been physically lonely a little. For touching that's about me. Not someone else. And Bri and I were exclusive, so even before he left like a fool, I wasn't having as much sex as I wanted to be having."

"I thought you said he was good?" I teased, but gently.

"He *was*. It's such a bitch. Maybe because he was bi, so he didn't have a lot of those straight-boy hang-ups some guys have. I could propose anything, and he'd be excited about it." She shrugged, the motion rippling through her body. "So I had really great sex, but not enough of it. And then I had hardly any. And then I had none."

Oh. I slid closer and let my hand drift to her neck, cupping it from the back. "So we get physical. If there's anything you don't want to do right now, that doesn't mean we can't have sex, Dred."

The weight of her head leaning against mine was so welcome, so warm, that I inhaled the moment as if I could hold it inside me forever.

"We could have pretend fake-sex," I whispered in her ear.

"I'm pretty much done pretending and faking things, Z."

I wiggled until I was nearly beneath her. "Kiss me. Kiss me a lot."

"Yeah, okay."

That was the night I learned the texture of her skin, the way she smelled behind her ears, the vicious poke to my side when I'd get too close to her hair. (I laughed.) I kept my hands over her clothes, but I let them roam wherever I wanted, and Dred's breathy moans fueled more exploration than I would have risked otherwise. I mapped the shape of her legs, her sides, her back. I pulled her wrists to my lips so I could taste her and press kisses to the centers of her palms.

All about her, yeah, I could do that. With pleasure. With joy.

I cupped her breasts through fabric and she looked up at the ceiling, arching, giving me more than I asked for. Giving me everything she had. I kissed the skin above the collar of her shirt and rolled her nipples lightly while her fingers clawed deeply into my shoulders.

This moan was lower, longer, and felt a hell of a lot like a promise.

"Shit, shit, shit, keep doing that." One of her hands stopped bruising my shoulder and slipped under the waistband of her pants.

I switched nipples and re-upped my efforts at the hickey I was giving her, wishing I could still see what she was doing. My own body was overheated and eager, but I kept my legs pressed together while she panted.

Dred came, pulling me so hard against her I had to gasp for a last breath while she stiffened and whimpered in my arms.

"I can't believe that just worked." She sounded awed, breathless. Before I could say anything to that, she had me on my back. "Can I touch you?"

"Fuck yes— Oh my—"

I didn't have time. She was on me fast, fingers in my underwear, sliding into me.

"Oh Jesus, you're so fucking wet— Zane—"

I thrust up into her hand, unable to help myself, chasing down a rhythm I couldn't control. "I'm coming—"

She kissed me even harder than she fucked me, and I arched into her everywhere. Breathing was overrated.

The orgasm had been a little too fast, and I hadn't expected to have one; I hadn't primed my body the way I would have if I'd known this was how our night would end. My clit pulsed against the heel of her hand.

I shifted, reaching down to keep her hand where it was. "You mind?"

"You going again? Greedy bitch."

I laughed breathlessly, finding the right angle. Yeah, there. I rocked gently against her, letting the pressure build, focusing on the scent of her, how her fingers had been in her and were now in me, which was so fucking hot I couldn't stand it.

She growled into my ear. "I'm gonna count to twenty, and then I'm taking back my hand. You got twenty seconds, girl. Get off."

I groaned and buried my face in her neck. I wanted to protest the injustice of putting my orgasm on a clock, but more than that I wanted to come again. If the first orgasm was too fast, the second usually made up for it. But this was fast, stupidly fast; I wasn't even sure I could do it.

"Seven, eight, come on, Z. Show me how it's done. Give it to me, girl, you know you want to. Ten, eleven . . ."

I did. Desperately. I moaned and tried to spread myself wider, grinding myself harder into her hand. Yes, yes, yes. I almost had it! I was so fucking close!

"Seventeen—"

"Nooo, damn it—" I threw my head back and let it take me over, heedless now that I was using her hand as a sex toy. My legs shook and twitched and everything at the center of my body went liquid. I trembled and shattered and came until I was nothing but a pool of tingling postorgasmic goo.

Then I giggled. Because goo.

"You did it." She sounded impressed.

"I'm really good with goals."

"That's hot."

"*You're* hot. Dred. That was. I can't even."

"I am hot." My eyes were closed. I didn't realize she was in kissing distance until she was kissing me. "You're not so bad yourself, Z."

"I do my best."

"You sure do."

A click told me the lamp was now off. I still couldn't open my eyes. Or move.

"You are totally fucked-out now. Man. I'm gonna tell everyone that the best way to get you to slow down is to make you come twice."

"You should see me after three."

She laughed and snuggled closer. I managed, with effort, to get my arm around her.

"Good night," I murmured.

"Good night."

I have no idea how long it took me to fall asleep. Sixty seconds at the absolute outside, but I'd bet I was unconscious in half that time. And I slept hard that night, like I hadn't slept in months, maybe years.

CHAPTER 16

I knew I wasn't pregnant the second I temped. If you were carrying a collection of cells that wanted to be a baby, your body temperature stayed a little higher than usual. If you were about to get your period, it dropped.

Mine dropped.

I tested anyway. The human body was a strange and wondrous thing, and it didn't follow all the rules all the time. I set the test aside, peed until I was empty, and got my period. I waited out the test, just in case. One line. Negative.

Low temp, period, BFN. It's the "you're not pregnant" trifecta.

I'd been certain I wasn't. Convinced of it. Knew it absolutely. And yet.

I tried to keep my sniffles to myself, but I couldn't stay hidden in the upstairs bathroom when everyone else would need it. All the splashing water on my face and brushing my teeth in the world couldn't quite disguise that I'd cried. That I was still sort of crying in an impotent, teary-eyed way. Restrained weeping, to be done quietly, alone, preferably in bed.

Someone had gone downstairs earlier. Probably Emerson, judging by the steps, and that Obie came home around midnight. I didn't want to see Emerson. If I kept it down, I could probably slip back into bed and pretend everything was fine.

Dred didn't have thick shades over her windows, and one of them had direct eastern exposure. Light suffused the room around the edges of her curtains, flowing in almost as if it were a liquid, as if I could step in it and let myself be washed away.

"BFN, huh?"

I hadn't noticed she was awake. I'd tried not to look over.

She flipped back the blankets, shifting in my peripheral vision as I stared at the way the light hit the floorboards.

"I thought I was ready this time. I thought . . . I didn't even really think . . ." Impossible not to cry again.

"Get in bed, Z. Come on."

I got in the bed and let her hold me. She stroked my hair and didn't tell me that everything would be okay, that maybe it'd be next month, that I had to keep the faith.

All the stories I told myself to not feel this ache, this emptiness. The things I'd imagined someone else saying, as if it would help. Dred didn't even try.

When I'd finally calmed down, I lifted my head. "Sorry I got snot on your pillow."

"I'm gonna make you wash that, too." She kissed me. "If I could wish you my luck, I would. It sucks it's so hard."

"Yeah. Yeah, it really does." I sat up. "God, I'm a mess."

"Nah. Only a little bit of a mess. Hey, I have a wedding announcement shoot this morning, I forgot to tell you last night."

"I can't believe you're kicking me out when I'm already crying. You're so mean."

She smiled, teeth picking up light from the window. "Stay here. This time you've got someone to hold your hand, you know? So let me."

"I thought I could do this whole thing by myself. I wasn't supposed to need anyone."

"Yeah, I've walked that walk, and all it gets you is a lot of being scared and alone. I told Obie to go to work the night I gave birth to James because I didn't want to inconvenience him. Like I really thought, I don't know, I guess I thought when it seemed like the right time I'd drive my ass to the hospital and check myself in and call him when the whole deal was done."

"What, like . . . in the middle of contractions, you'd drive?" I thumped on her head. "That was silly."

"No more silly than you thinking you could cry about your BFN and I wouldn't know. Z, this shit is fucking *hard*. I was trying to do it by myself because I didn't think I deserved anyone helping me.

But you've done everything right, you know? Why are you punishing yourself?"

"I'm not. I don't mean to be. It's more that I . . . had a plan." Tears welled in my eyes again, even though I was trying so fucking hard not to give in. "I guess it never occurred to me that my plan wouldn't work. So now that it keeps failing, I feel like I dig myself in deeper and deeper, like I have to stick to the plan, I can't surrender, or it's just proving how stupid I was to ever think I could do this in the first place."

She ran her thumb over my lips. "It's not like that. You're not failing, you're *building*. And when you have your kid, Z, all of this is gonna make you more mindful, like Aunt Florence says. The harder you fight, the more meaning things have."

"You think?" I sounded so pathetic, so desperate.

"I *know*." She kissed me. "Let me take care of you a little bit today. I have this shoot, but they don't usually take that long, and we can work your quilt later."

"I would rather work on yours."

"My quilt doesn't exist."

"We should change that."

"Pushy ass."

I kissed her. "You don't like my ass?"

"It ain't the worst ass I've had, I guess."

I pretended to be affronted. "You're harsh. And my ass likes you so much!"

"Is that right?"

The baby monitor piped up. James's sleepy gurgles.

"The boy's up." I dared kiss her once more before she drew away.

"Yeah, we'll head downstairs. Emerson is probably up already." She paused in the doorway and raised her eyebrows. "You coming?"

"I don't have pants."

Dred laughed and walked down the hall.

I pulled on my good slacks and followed. If you were going to entertain your friends with a walk of shame, you might as well do it in suit slacks and an old Green Day concert shirt.

Unfortunately, Emerson had on his "we are not amused" face.

"You guys know there are other people in this house, right? I mean, you didn't have some kind of mutual aneurism that resulted in you *forgetting* you weren't actually alone last night?"

I winced. Dred put James in his seat and tugged it in Emerson's direction. "Tell Emerson me and Zane get to have fun if we want to, baby."

James obediently turned to Emerson and started talking.

"James, please inform your mother that some of us need our rest."

I started to apologize, until I saw him wink at James, who laughed.

"No laughing." Emerson waved his finger in James's face. "I need you to be firm with her, young man."

James giggled.

Emerson amped up his scolding in response to rising giggles, and I moved over to Dred's side.

"That's kind of amazing," I whispered.

"They're good for each other." She cracked a smile. "Thank god for James, or Emerson would have freaked out and broken up with Obie like seven times by now."

Emerson threw his hands up, dramatically, making James laugh again. "I'm like five feet away right now. I can *hear* you talking shit about me, Mildred."

"You sure about that?" She grabbed a jar of baby food peas and hooked a spoon out of the closest drawer, offering both of them to me. "You want to shove food in the kid's face? I should eat before I go take pictures of straight people about to set off on their perfect, happy lives."

"Sure." I went to sit on James's other side. He immediately turned away from Emerson and focused on me. Ha. Mental note: *James's affection can be bought with mashed peas.*

"How's the couple?" Emerson asked.

"Oh, fine. They're not nuts or anything. A little young, but this should only be the two of them, so it should go smoothly. It's when the parents get involved that everything really goes to hell."

I offered James a spoonful of mashed peas. He swiped it aside. "Hey!" The second time I slid it into his mouth before he could hit it.

Green oozed from between his lips. He grinned.

"That's so gross." I held up the jar in Dred's direction. "Hey, can I have a few of these? The jars, not the peas."

"Sure. Why?"

"Sperm."

Emerson choked on his cereal. "*What*?"

"Sperm. I need something for Tom to jerk off into." I shuddered. "I mean, you didn't think I was having sex with him, did you? That'd be sick. He's Carlos's husband. It'd be like banging my brother."

"Okay, just—" He shook his head. "Let's not talk about jerking off into baby food jars, okay? I'm so uncomfortable right now."

I pointed the spoon at him. "Hey. This is *procreative* jerking off into baby food jars. It's, like, blessed by baby Jesus or something."

Dred snickered.

"Let me get this right." Emerson narrowed his eyes. "Baby Jesus blesses gay men jerking off into baby food jars so lesbians can get pregnant."

I couldn't keep a straight face, but I tried. Then Dred repeated, in a choked voice, "Baby Jesus," and I lost it.

"This household is completely insane," Emerson muttered, going back to his cereal.

I realized, with an unsettling weight in my gut, that he'd just included me as part of the household. But I'd planned everything out, damn it, and being part of a household wasn't on my list. It wasn't what I wanted. Was it?

Emerson, still looking a little green, held out his bowl to Dred. "You want to get me another round of cereal to make up for totally ruining the innocence of baby food jars? To say nothing of keeping me awake with your disgusting lesbian antics last night."

She brandished a spoon covered in sweet potato mash at him. "Excuse me, *I* am not a lesbian. Just because I'm fucking a woman doesn't make me a dyke, you asshole."

James, picking up on her tone, said something that sounded suspiciously like, "Dyke, asshole."

I muffled a snort.

Emerson snorted. "Oh, nice, Mildred. The kid can't even talk yet, and you're teaching him slurs. What about daycare!"

"No one would know that's what he said. And anyway, can you imagine them talking to me about it? 'We think your son may be saying inappropriate things.' 'Oh? Like what?' 'Well . . .'"

"Actually, it might almost be worth it to teach him things they wouldn't want to repeat." Emerson touched James's arm to get his attention. "Say 'dyke,' James."

James started talking, but this time it was all consonant sounds and the occasional sibilant.

Dred laughed and carried the jar of sweet potatoes to the table. "What about 'dildo'? Baby, say 'dildo.' Can't imagine the ladies down at St. Pat's saying that to my face."

James crooked his head to the side and said something.

Even though it didn't sound anything like *dildo*, we cracked up.

Obie's laughter echoed from the stairwell. "Please tell me you guys aren't down here teaching James dirty words on a Sunday morning."

"It'd be better if we were doing it on some other morning?" Emerson lifted his face for a kiss.

"Maybe? Hey, Zane. Heard you spent the night." He smirked.

"I thought you were at work last night." I couldn't even muster embarrassment, really. The sex had been spectacular; feeling embarrassed now would be an insult to it.

"I meant 'heard' as in Emerson bitched and moaned about how he couldn't get any sleep until I, uh, distracted him."

Emerson got stiffly up from the table. "I did not move in here for the live sex shows."

"You're right." Obie passed him the cereal box and milk. "You know what would make everything better? If we moved downstairs."

"I'm not having this conversation again."

Dred laughed. "Oh, yeah, you are. You're having it until you agree." She grabbed another jar of food and brought it down to me.

"Thanks," I said. "And what conversation?"

"The one where Obie tries to convince Emerson it makes sense to remodel the workroom into a master bedroom for them."

"Huh." The workroom took up half the ground floor. "It would complicate resale value, but I think it's a great idea otherwise."

Emerson and Obie turned to each other at the same moment, as if each of them thought he'd won.

"Complicates resale value!" Emerson repeated triumphantly.

"It's a great idea!" Obie shot back.

Dred smiled at me. "Ha. That was good. You should tie them in knots all the time."

"Listen." Obie poured milk into his bowl, then Emerson's. "It makes much more sense for us to live downstairs. For one—"

"The crip will eventually suck at stairs."

"I was *going* to say, for one, then you won't have to hear Dred and Zane having sex."

This time we smiled at each other. Last night had been freaking incredible. This morning had been . . . pretty rough, but Dred made up for it.

"That point is provisionally accepted as a reasonable argument," Emerson mumbled. "People have no fucking respect."

"And two, I've been needing to remodel the workroom anyway, and there's more than enough space for us to have our bedroom there. Plus, that's about the only way I can justify putting in another bathroom, which would be awesome."

"But would complicate resale value!"

Obie rolled his eyes and leaned forward. "And, point three, there might not be enough room upstairs forever, you know."

"Huh."

Both of them looked over at us. I frowned. "Why not? Are you guys going to work on the upstairs? I was thinking, you could combine two of the bedrooms and make a huge master en suite, which would definitely be good for resale. But that's a big project if there's no relevant reason why you need to do it."

"We're not planning any work upstairs." Obie raised both eyebrows, looking between Dred and me. "But it seems like the two of you are . . . at least, that you might, at some point in the future, actually need all three bedrooms."

"Why?"

"Well," he said, sounding perfectly reasonable. "You are trying to get pregnant. Right?"

It hit me all at once. I was trying to get pregnant. Three bedrooms. One for James, one for Dred (and me), and one for Future Kid. With Obie and Emerson downstairs.

The warmth of the kitchen—the comfort of it—vanished, like a flame doused by a bucket of water.

"Uh, I just remembered— I gotta— I gotta go—" I pushed the jar across the table and half stumbled out of my chair. "Sorry, just, I have an appointment later. And I, you know. I can't really go like this." I laughed, only it wasn't real; it was high-pitched, nervous laughter.

I didn't mean to look at Dred, but somehow I caught the fleeting, horrible freeze in her expression, pain and surprise intertwined. Then she covered it all up with . . . nothing. Her face went blank.

Shit, shit, shit. I fumbled and patted James's head. "Uh, bye, James."

He waved a fist at me and chattered something as I retreated from the kitchen.

"Yeah, right back at you, kiddo."

Up the stairs, into Dred's room. *Dred's* room. Not *our* room. It was her room, in her house. I had my own place, damn it. I loved my condo.

I kept repeating that to myself as I gathered my clothes and switched shirts and found my bag.

"Don't forget your thermometer."

Shit. I turned toward the doorway. "I really do have to work. I sometimes work on the weekend."

Dred shrugged. "I sometimes work on the weekend, too. You shouldn't knock the Green Day shirt. You looked kind of cute as a teenage boy."

"Oh, I see how it is. That's your type, right? Teenage boy?" I was trying to tease, but it fell flat in the face of her unblinking gaze.

"Nope. You're my type." She gestured to where I was pulling my shoes on. "You. This. Running away. This is my type. You'd think I would learn, but I never do. Anyway, I'll see you around."

I listened to her footsteps down the hall, down the stairs, and tried not to start crying again.

I walked straight to my car, got in, and drove.

Halfway to Jaq's apartment I realized she probably wouldn't be there. And while it might have been fine to show up on your best friend's doorstep with a BFN hangover and demand comfort, it was less acceptable to do that at her girlfriend's place.

Plus, it was Sunday. They'd be on their way to Mass. Damn it.

I drove to Carlos and Tom's instead.

When we had all settled down after getting out of our various college programs, I'd started shopping for my condo. Jaq had lived in a series of apartments that improved, marginally, over the course of her career; six years into teaching she had an okay place in a relatively safe neighborhood.

Carlos had moved into the in-law unit behind the Moriartys. Jaq and I had been convinced he'd only moved there because, having been given the opportunity to live behind Sherlock Holmes's popular nemesis (he had a whole lecture on why that was canonically thin), he couldn't resist.

He and Tom had only been dating at the time, and he kept to himself. By the time Tom moved in, Mrs. Moriarty was calling them "roommates" and Mr. Moriarty was pretending he didn't have any idea what was going on. At one point he asked four-foot-eight, dark-haired Carlos if six-three, blond Tom was his big brother. Carlos said, "You can't tell he's younger than I am? Look at that baby face." Mr. Moriarty had gone out of his way to avoid them for months.

We'd assumed that after Mrs. Moriarty died that the old man was going to kick them out, until Tom admitted he'd been helping around the house and running errands for them. Without telling Carlos. Since he'd moved in.

I parked out front and walked through the side yard to get to the cottage in back, thinking about Mr. Moriarty alone in his house, surrounded by the life he'd lived with Mrs. Moriarty, but without her. I was crying again by the time I got to the front door of the cottage.

Carlos took one look at me and cursed under his breath. "Oh hell. Get your skinny ass in here."

I hiccupped. "Not skinny."

"You're plenty fucking skinny, Zane. Come on."

He led me to the sofa and dropped a blanket on my head. "Let me turn on the heat. Jesus. Coffee's not made, so suck it up."

"But"—sniffle—"you're brewing it, right?"

He growled.

Fifteen minutes later we were huddled under blankets with coffee while I sobbed that I'd never get pregnant and I'd die alone, like Mr. Moriarty, and then for some reason I started talking about Fredi, about how all she had was the bar and it couldn't be enough, I didn't know if it'd be enough for me if all I could show for my life was my stupid career.

Even as I was saying it, it sounded like a midlife crisis in a Lifetime movie.

Carlos let me run until I got to the part about my shriveled-up eggs, and then he put his coffee down and pasted his hand over my mouth. "If you keep talking, I'm gonna start laughing and then I'd look like a shitty friend."

He pulled away before I could bite his hand. "Jerk."

"You couldn't be a bigger stereotype right now, FYI. I can't help that it's funny."

I kicked him.

"You'll break my compromised-by-dwarfism bones!"

I kicked him again. And laughed. It was hard to take Carlos seriously when he tried to play the "compromised by dwarfism" card. His folks had a lot of flaws—like thinking he was going to hell for being gay—but they hadn't let him get away with ever cutting himself slack because he hadn't inherited their average heights.

"First of all, Mr. Moriarty had fifty-six years with the love of his life. If you're trying to feel sorry for him, or like he's unlucky because she bit the dust first, fuck that, Zane. Fifty-six *years* with her. Can you even imagine?"

I shook my head. "But doesn't that make it worse? That she died?"

"Yeah, if it wasn't for Tom being a way better son to them than their kids, we'd have probably found him dead in front of the TV before now. But that doesn't erase fifty-six years. And Fredi has all the companionship she wants. Do you really think she never takes anyone home from the bar?"

"Wait. No way. Fredi hooks up?" My mind boggled. Fredi, with her leather vests, and her impatience, and her permanent scowl. "Whoa."

"I can't divulge secrets of the marital bed, but I don't think you should feel sorry for Fredi, Zane. But obviously, you aren't. You're feeling sorry for yourself. So what's up?"

I set my coffee down on the table so I could better burrow into the couch. "I don't know."

"Liar."

Hell. I sighed. "I spent the night with Dred."

His eyes widened. He was actually surprised, not just pretending to be for reasons of mockery. "You did not."

"Yeah. I did."

"Oh, honey, it didn't work out?"

"No, it *did*. Everything worked out. Everything was fantastic." I buried my face in my arm and started crying again.

"Honey, here." Sounds. His mug on wood. Blankets rustling. Then Carlos, pulling me closer, wrapping his arm around my shoulders. "Are you in love with her?"

I pretended I hadn't heard the question, but it brought on a fresh wave of tears. In love with her? I couldn't be in love with Dred. I couldn't be in love with anyone! That wasn't my story. I wasn't one of those people who fell in love, who saw that in their future. And damn it, it wasn't on my list.

"Shh. Hush now. All your babbling is gonna wake up Tom, which would be rude, since you're drinking his portion of the coffee right now."

"Asshole," I mumbled.

"You're drinking his coffee and *I'm* the asshole?"

"No," I countered. "*You're* drinking his coffee, after generously offering yours to a friend in need."

"Oh, I think you know me well enough to know that no amount of tears gets between me and my morning caffeine."

I sat back so I wasn't leaning on him as much. "Sorry. Just, I got my period, I hate everything, and I don't understand why I feel this way."

"Well, shit, why didn't you lead with that? Of course you feel this way. You always hit bottom on BFN days." He pushed the coffee back into my hands. "The least you can do is not let it get cold, since you've already stolen it."

"You've got a hell of a bedside manner."

"I'm known throughout the land for my compassion and goodwill toward men."

"Gross. I don't want to hear about it."

Carlos rearranged himself to get more comfortable on the couch, not looking at me. "It's not a bad thing, you know. If you're in love with her."

"But— I can't— That's not—" I stared into my coffee, thinking about the way morning light fell on the floor of Dred's bedroom. "I'm thirty-five years old, Carlos. If I could fall in love, don't you think I'd know that by now?"

"You've always said that you couldn't. But repeating it over and over again doesn't exactly make it true. We never understood that. Me and Jaq. Why you always said it like it was a sure thing, like it was obvious. We thought maybe you were aromantic, except that wasn't quite right, either. You liked that side of things. You just . . . never let yourself go too far."

"I didn't want to." I could sense what he was talking about, even if my mind didn't really want to turn over all those memories to see what was under them. I'd felt that tug a few times, that pull toward the edge of the cliff. There'd been women who made me want to keep sliding, to fly out into that abyss to see if we could make it safely to the ground together. But I hadn't wanted it enough to do it. Only enough to look over at the unknown, confirming that there was nothing that intrigued me enough about mystery to tempt me away from certainty. "And it's not on my list."

"Then add it to your damn list." He paused, and I braced myself for more advice. "Plus, are you saying she's still good in the sack? Because I know she taught Jaq some things despite her youth—"

I elbowed him.

"Oof! You horrible woman."

"Don't talk about Jaq and Dred, oh my god, that was years ago!"

"I'm just saying, she was apparently quite astute with the lady parts back then, so—"

"Do *not* say 'lady parts,' it's transphobic!"

The bedroom door creaked open. "Zane?"

I grimaced. "Sorry, Tom! Go back to sleep!"

"No, I'm . . . I'm up." He groaned. "Everything okay?"

"She's fine. She's contemplating falling in love and drinking all your coffee."

"Falling in love?" Tom, over Carlos's head, was already making a second pot. "Oh, with Mildred?"

"I resent the fact that you all seem to think you know my heart before I do."

"Please." Carlos sat to the side so he could watch Tom, too. "Do you remember the denial I was in back in the day? You and Jaq couldn't stop yourselves from crowing about how interested I was in a certain ideal specimen of masculinity."

"Aw!" Tom called. Then: "You should introduce me to him. I have an appreciation for ideal specimens."

The expression on Carlos's face: fondness and love and affection and heat—

Oh god. What if I was in love with Dred? All these pictures flashed through my head: Dred laughing, holding James up really high so he'd giggle, poking Emerson while he cooked something, threatening Obie with a knitting needle and a glare on her face that promised retribution for a serious wrong.

The way she'd looked on top of me, touching herself, releasing everything she had.

I put my head down. "I'm so stupid."

"Honey, we could've told you that a long time ago."

"Carlos." Tom's presence was suddenly beside me. "Does Mildred . . . not feel the same?"

I leaned into him. "I don't *know.* I don't even know if I want to know. Maybe I don't want to know. Oh shit. I might not be in love with her. We're friends. Maybe we're just good friends, and the sex was amazing, and she makes me so happy—" I started crying again, which was stupid, and was probably mostly hormones, but I couldn't seem to stop.

Tom stroked my back. "Shouldn't it be a good thing if Mildred makes you happy?"

"You fail to understand how much Zane likes her lists. This one night, when we were in high school, Zane decided to learn everything she could about sex." Carlos cleared his throat. "To be clear, we were all very drunk at the time."

"You didn't."

"We may have. Not *everything.* But."

Tom's laughter settled over me, like a soothing warmth on my skin. "Where's the sex list? I want to see it."

"Burned, I hope."

"I remember it," I mumbled. I could picture it: binder paper, blue pen, my all-caps writing. "We did most of the stuff on the list, but it was a pretty short list."

"A list inspired by the lesbian zines of the nineties, with anything dick-related Zane could think of."

Tom's chest rose and fell: a huff of laughter. "And exactly how many dick-related things was that?"

"Handjob." Carlos held up one finger. "Blowjob. Vaginal penetration." Three fingers.

"That shows a disappointing lack of creativity," Tom teased.

"I wanted to add anal, but she wouldn't let me."

I flopped back, as dramatically as I could manage wrapped up in blankets, half-encased in Tom's arms. "I wasn't *that* drunk."

"And." He waggled his eyebrows. "Which of those did you guys do?"

I opened my mouth, but Carlos got in before I could speak.

"That's all we have time for. Tune in next week for another exciting installment of *Embarrassing Things We Did as Drunk Teenagers.* Cue applause."

"That's Carlos's way of saying he was too scared of girls to even let us touch him."

Tom grinned. "He's still scared of girls, you know."

Carlos's eyes narrowed. "You should be scared of me right now, husband."

"Shaking in my boots."

The two of them looking at each other *like that* was about to give me hives. "So, boys, my uterus is empty. How would you two like to make a human this month?"

Tom reached for my coffee. "I think we should do it. We read over all the papers, Zane. There's nothing in there we can't do, or haven't already done."

"Are you sure? I know it's a lot, and my midwife's a teensy bit nuts—"

"She's thorough," Carlos said. "Which is what we'd want. We half-ass drew up a parenting contract. You want to see it?"

"A *non*parenting contract," Tom corrected. "A 'we absolutely won't under any circumstances be parenting' contract." He cleared his throat. "And, um, just—just for peace of mind—I was wondering if we could see whatever relevant part of your will refers to who will get custody of the baby if anything ever happened to you?"

I blinked and pulled out my phone. "I hadn't even thought about that. Yeah, of course. I can email the draft of it to you right now. I'll have it notarized and everything the second I get pregnant."

"Or send it to us later. No rush."

"Uh. Well." I added both of them to a new email and attached a PDF of my unfinalized postpregnancy will, which I had in cloud storage. "There's kind of a timeline we're working on right now. Today's day one of my cycle, and I usually ovulate right around day twelve or thirteen. If we're going to try it this cycle . . . we should probably talk inseminations."

Tom shook his head. "We have to come up with a better word than that. When I think 'insemination,' I think about jerking a stallion off into an artificial vagina."

We stared at him.

He smirked. "I was a farm boy before you city folk corrupted me, you know."

Carlos pointed at me. "You. Agreed. Let's call it internal application of Tom's magic juice instead."

"Veto!"

He ignored me to point at Tom. "Don't ever say the phrase 'artificial vagina' in my presence again."

"What if someone asks me how to breed a horse?"

"Horses can't breed like everyone else?"

"Sometimes you breed them cross-country and have to ship the sperm."

I snorted. "I've been trying to breed myself cross-country with frozen sperm and no fucking luck. I hope horse breeders have it easier."

Carlos's face twisted. "Seriously, can we not talk about breeding? It's a little freaky."

I rolled my eyes. "Oh, unlike an 'internal application of Tom's magic juice'?"

"I happen to quite enjoy an internal—"

Tom and I both held up our hands.

"Stop, stop, god, ew, I don't want to know." I shook my head, a lot, in emphasis. "So anyway, I guess the question is, what're you doing at the end of next week?"

Tom, as eager as I was to switch gears, nodded. "I've been thinking about that. Is this the kind of thing we can schedule? Or do we wing it? I spent some time looking stuff up on message boards, but I got very confused very fast."

"I can tell when I'm ovulating. How about I give you a call and then you, uh, do your thing, and I'll come pick it up? I asked Dred for some jars, so I'll give those to you when I have them sterilized."

His eyes widened, but he was still smiling. "Right. Jars. Huh."

"Don't worry about it," Carlos advised. "I don't plan on you having much to do with that part of things."

I waved my hands around. "Too much fucking information! I don't need to know about that part, like you don't need to know about the needleless syringe and my cervix."

"I'm with Zane." Tom shrugged. "No offense to cervixes, but I'm not really interested."

"Thank you very much. Back to the point. How many times do you want to, uh, contribute?"

"Oh. I don't know. How many times do you want me to contribute?"

"Well." Was it greedy to ask for three? I'd never tried with more than one vial because they were so damn expensive, but three offered maximum coverage. I couldn't time this like I would frozen vials I was trying at home, with perfect intervals. Right. The real deal. I had to plan for when both of us were awake and Tom wasn't working.

Complications.

I pictured my calendar. "You still off on Sundays and Mondays?"

He nodded.

"Okay, that means we'll probably have to do it before you go to work."

"Actually, I sort of talked to Fredi about it. Because when I was doing research I thought about what would happen if you were ovulating when I was at work."

"You talked to *Fredi* about giving me sperm?" Fredi, quintessential butch, who thought I was a nuisance. "Oh my god."

"Sorry. I forgot you think she hates you. Anyway, she said it wouldn't be the first time someone came in her office, if I needed to use it on a break or something, so let me know if you need me to, you know, during my shift."

"Holy crap. The kid could have a Club Fred's origin story."

Carlos poked my arm. "Your eyes are glazing over in ridiculousness right now. Listen, honey, we want you to get knocked up so our lives can go back to normal. I can milk him as many times as you need, so you give us a number, and we'll do it."

I swallowed. He was making it kind of a joke, but it wasn't. And both of them knew it. "Three would be my ideal. I know that's a lot."

Tom laughed and handed me back my coffee. "Carlos is just going to treat it as a challenge. I'll be lucky if I don't have blue balls for days before."

"We're supercharging your sperm, baby."

"Oh sure." He leaned in to kiss my cheek. "Maybe it won't even work, but I'm glad we're going to try it. I don't want a kid or anything, but I really want you to have one, Zane. You'll be a great mom."

Which is when I dissolved into tears again.

Someday I'd be a great mom. God, that was such a powerful, terrifying thought.

CHAPTER 18

I texted back and forth with Dred for the rest of Sunday with totally invented questions about what I should do for the wake. She texted back with answers and suggestions. I finally got my shit together by the time I was going to bed to apologize for running out like a jerk.

Her answer? *That's most people's reaction to getting close to me. No worries.*

This was troubling on two levels. One: Mildred wasn't the type of person who said "no worries." I'd triggered some weird pop culture defense mechanism, leaving me feeling cold and somewhat bereft. Where was the derision that made me laugh? Where was the unrelenting accountability? I'd expected a threat to my life, or a barrage of insults. Not "No worries." What did that even mean in this context?

And second: did I really want her to lump me in with "most people"? I lay in my bed, considering the whole thing. Yeah, I'd been emotionally isolated from lovers, and maybe it was by choice like Carlos had said, but in panicking and dodging out, I'd completely ignored Dred. She hadn't had sex with anyone in almost a year, hadn't had sex since giving birth, finally did it (maybe on a whim, maybe after careful planning; with Dred I could never be sure), and the jerk she fucked ran out the next morning like it was the worst thing that had ever happened to her.

Basically I was a fucking monster.

I wasn't used to being a monster. Usually I was the nurturing type. I might not fall in love, but I always thought I had some depths worth plumbing, if you will. I'd held my friends while they cried.

I'd helped with moving, and wedding planning, and finding houses for the people I cared about.

Now I was "most people," running out on Dred. But no worries.

The worst part was that I couldn't think of a damn thing to say. I wanted to assure her I was over myself. But was I? I was damn tempted to blame hormones, except that was a shitty cop-out, and while hormones and yet another disappointing BFN definitely played a role in the massive amounts of crying I'd done all day, they weren't responsible for me wigging at the kitchen table while feeding James and talking shit with Emerson.

I finally sent back, *I'm prepared to beg your forgiveness in any way necessary. I'm sorry.* Then I pointedly did not stare at my phone, waiting for it to light up with a new message. Maybe she'd forgive me. Maybe she'd laugh. Maybe she'd tell me to fuck off.

Or none of the above.

Her eventual message had nothing to do with us at all. *Get your flyers out this week. It's time to get people talking. Let me know if you need help with anything.*

That was it. A last piece of advice for the wake, full stop.

I had another good cry, checked my phone just in case she sent anything else, and went to bed.

Dred wasn't the only one who was getting antsy about promotion. Keith left me a message mid-Monday-morning telling me he had some flyer ideas if I wanted to stop by the center. Steph had been out at meetings all day, so I left early and picked up donuts on my way to QYP.

Keith's eyes went big and round like a little kid's when he saw the Krispy Kreme box. "You are a god among humans, Zane. Merin! Josh! Brunch!"

Merin, face shrouded in his hood as usual, didn't look over from where he was painting one of the walls. "I'm not done with the—"

"Stop." Josh pulled the brush out of his hand. "Go eat something. Start with a banana."

"You're *not* my father."

Keith tensed, lips going white as he watched them.

"If I had a son, he'd probably be a stubborn jackass just like you. Go eat, Merin. I need a cup of coffee. We'll pick this up after a break."

Merin grumbled, but walked away. Toward the bathroom. Not to the kitchen.

Josh kissed my cheek in greeting and took Keith's hand. "It's impossible." His voice was low.

"I know."

I raised my eyebrows, and Josh glanced apologetically at me. "He keeps showing up within five minutes of us opening the door, on school days, saying he needs to wash up. Today we found him asleep on the floor of the bathroom with his hands still wet."

"There are just no resources for homeless trans youth," Keith murmured. "We can talk to him again about staying with us, but he'll say no."

"Maybe he will. But all we risk is rejection, and even rejecting us might still be better for him than if we let it go."

"True."

"Plus," Josh added, "I think once he graduates, it will be different. As long as he's in school he feels like a child. When he feels like a man, he might be more willing to accept our help."

Keith frowned. "How . . . does that even make sense?"

But I thought I might understand it a little. "Well, right now it's grown-ups trying to help a kid they feel sorry for. If he graduates and you offer him a place to live, and charge him rent, then that's a more equal thing."

"That's what I hope, anyway." Josh looked like he was about to say something else, but the door at the other end of the room opened, and we arranged ourselves casually in the kitchen, as if we hadn't been talking about Merin the whole time he was gone.

The guarded, dark look in his eyes made it clear he was under no illusions.

"Dred says it's time to paper La Vista with wake stuff." I shoved the box of donuts across the counter toward Merin. Subtly. Kind of.

Keith nodded. "Definitely. I have a few different types for you to look at, including one that I think would go well in places like the Rhein. Inconspicuous, not blasting a message. Just enough to get people interested. Are you putting a contact name and number down there? I took the liberty of setting you up an email address—hope that's okay."

"I hadn't even thought of all that. Yeah, that's perfect. And no, let's keep names off it. I want this to belong to everyone, if it can."

Merin grunted. "It can't."

"Well, yeah, but as much as possible—"

"No, I mean, you want people to get out of it exactly what you put into it. But they won't. People see what they want to see. Some of them are gonna go because they think it's sensational, or whatever. That they'll find out about this murderer. Some people will go for free food, or for drinks, or because they're bored. Most people won't be there because they wanna"—he waved an arm—"heal the community or whatever the hell."

"That's probably true. But maybe a few people will get something out of it."

"So all this trouble is worth it for like . . . a few people?" He shook his head. "That seems like a lot of shit to put up with for no return."

I thought about that and took another donut. Because it was definitely a two-donut day. "I guess that's not how I measure success, by how many people get something out of the wake. If the only person who feels better afterward is me, and no one feels worse, then I think I'd consider that successful."

"I feel better already." Keith wound an arm around Josh's waist. "I felt better when I was doing up the flyers, like—I don't know. It felt like doing something. Instead of just hoping eventually I'll stop jumping at shadows every time I'm outside in the dark."

Merin eyed him from under his hood. "Yeah, but that's you. You're making Cam go and it doesn't make him feel better. He wants to forget."

I added *Talk to Cam* to my mental list and tagged it *urgent*. I'd talked to him before, but he was with Keith at the time. Grabbing him alone was a better idea.

Josh broke off another half of a donut. "You think he can forget that night? I was passed out through most of it and I can't forget it for longer than a couple of hours at a stretch."

"I think he should be allowed to forget it if he wants to." Merin's voice was a little defensive, enough so I wondered what fight they were actually having, if it wasn't about Cameron.

"I think . . ." Keith pondered. "I guess I think part of loving a person is telling them the truth. I don't think Cam trying to act like nothing happened is a good idea. And I *can't* act like nothing happened. So you have to walk a balance between doing what you have to do, and respecting that that's not the same for everyone."

"You tell them even when they don't want to hear it?"

Josh brushed a hand over Merin's hood. "House policy around here. What, you didn't notice?"

"Hahaha, Josh." Merin grabbed a banana. "Can I go back to painting now?"

"If you eat that, you can."

Merin heaved a sigh and started peeling the banana on his way across the room.

"He's not supposed to be in school?" I asked when he was far enough away not to hear.

"Oh, he is." Josh's eyes followed Merin. "But when he stays out all night wandering around afraid to sleep, we make exceptions."

"Then we text Jaq, who does her best to smooth things over at the school."

I shook my head. "Sometimes I think the wake is just a very small piece of a very big picture, and I can't do a damn thing about any of it."

"It's the same here," Josh said. "We knew that going in. Only incremental changes really stick, and they're the most frustrating ones to work on, because you constantly feel like you're running in place."

"And some days are better than others," Keith added. "Anyway, let me go get the stuff I was playing with and you can see what you like."

I stayed another hour, tweaking and adjusting flyers. The copy store downtown was dead empty, so I got one stack of the main flyer, and a smaller stack of the more subtle one, which had a rainbow across the bottom but was otherwise free of all queer symbolism.

Time to track down my staple gun. Or, even better, borrow the one from work. But first: a few more meetings to earn my keep.

CHAPTER 19

I made it to the farmhouse shortly after five the following day. The sun was beginning to set, filling the whole house with orange-pink light.

At first I thought no one was home. Until I found Emerson sitting on the back porch.

"Hey," I said.

He looked up at me. Or . . . glowered up at me. "Who the fuck invited you here?"

"No one." I sat down, leaving a fair amount of space between us. "Is she pissed?"

"Pissed? What're you, new? Mildred's not pissed. She's not anything. She's acting like you using her and leaving her is exactly what she's worth, so well done there, Zane. Jesus." His fingers twitched, and he mumbled, "Sorry, Aunt Florence."

"I didn't *use* her." I hadn't. I'd definitely been a total asshole, but I hadn't *used* her, that was different.

"You fucked her and left like your ass was on fire the next morning."

"That was Obie's fault."

His eyes narrowed. "The hell are you talking about?"

"Listen. It's stupid. I know it's stupid." I leaned over my knees, playing with the way my fingers looked in the fading light. "But that whole thing about you guys moving downstairs because we might need the bedroom . . . I freaked."

"Are you *shitting me*? Because I've panicked about some really stupid shit, but that's a winner, there. And it's *Obie.* That's the way he thinks. He didn't mean anything by it."

"I know."

He surveyed me for a long moment, eyes still dark. "If I hadn't been meditating every fucking day all the time, I'd be really angry right now."

I cocked an eyebrow. "So this is you serene and sedate?"

"The difference isn't that I don't get pissed, it's that me being pissed doesn't affect my entire body." After a second he looked away, dropping some of the aggression. "Which is better. It passes faster that way. Anyway, you're a fucking dick, Zane. And you should be ashamed of yourself. And I hope you came here to grovel and she kicks your ass out because I can't fucking live this way."

"Self-absorbed, much?"

"Bitchy Mildred I can deal with. Depressed and putting-up-a-front Mildred is . . . disturbing. I didn't even know she could do that." He shuddered. "Obie says he thinks the front is for James, but I don't know. I think it's for herself. Anyway. You're an asshole."

"I know."

"You got scared and you ditched her. Like an asshole."

My fingers twisted around each other. "I know."

"Do you not get that she never lets anyone in? What about this are you missing?"

"I'm sorry! I told her I was sorry."

"Oh, well, jeez. In that case."

I sighed. "Can you not do sarcasm at me right now? Please? I know I fucked up. I'll fix it."

"Is that what you think?" He shook his head. "You don't know Mildred *at all.* She's not gonna let you fix it."

"But—" I stared at him, trying to understand. Of course I could fix it. "What do you mean?"

"I mean, there is no 'fixing' this. You get one fucking chance with her. You blow it, you're done." He shook his head again and stretched backward, grimacing. "She and I are a lot alike. We're not good with forgiveness and second chances. Why give someone the opportunity to hurt you twice? When Brian came back, he all but begged on his knees for her to at least try to be friends again and she shut him down."

"What I did was nowhere near as bad as what he did. I had a momentary crisis of faith, all right?"

"She let you in and you hurt her. You think she's gonna be seeing a lot of gradations there? Anyway, good luck. When you weren't being a dick, you were good for her. Damn it. I fucking *told* you not to hurt her."

"I didn't mean—"

"Hello! Mildred? Emerson?"

We uttered a chorus of "Oh my god."

"Out here, Aunt Florence!" Emerson called, pushing himself into a more upright seated position as quickly as he could manage.

"Well, hello. Nice to see you, Zane."

I stood to shake hands, but she held mine instead of shaking it. "Nice to see you too."

"Hmm." Aunt Florence's attention was specific and lancing; I wanted to shy away from her by merit of how closely she looked at me, and how exposed it made me feel.

"I've already read her the riot act," Emerson said. "You don't have to beat her up or anything."

She turned a look on him. "Excuse me, I do not beat people up."

"You kind of do. Just, without touching them."

"Thank you for your input, Emerson. I took the liberty of buying groceries, if you'd like to see."

He shifted his legs to a higher step and pulled himself up. "What'd you bring me?"

"Rutabagas."

"I don't even know what that is."

"Time to learn." Florence finally dropped my hand. "Are you staying for dinner?"

"I'm not sure."

"She wasn't invited, and Mildred's not home with James yet."

"Hmm," Aunt Florence said again. "Stay for dinner, Zane. Have you had rutabagas?"

"Is that the same thing as a turnip? I've had turnips."

I followed them into the house, feeling like an imposter. Bracing against Dred's arrival and discovery of me in her kitchen.

I didn't have to brace. She acted like nothing was amiss at all. Emerson must have texted her that I was here or something, or else how could she act like it didn't even matter?

He'd been right. She was completely shut down to me. I didn't get the side-eye jokes, or the pokes, and she didn't drop James in my lap or hand me a toy to distract him so she could do something else.

She treated me like a stranger. Someone she barely knew. She treated me with *politeness*.

It was the most alarming thing I'd ever seen her do.

I was about to take off after dinner when Aunt Florence directed Emerson to wipe the table.

"We wouldn't want anything to soil Mildred's quilt." She reached for James. "Let's see it, girl."

"Auntie—"

"You will not get me into that dark, haunted little room. Bring it out here in the light."

Dred sighed. "The sitting room isn't haunted."

"Sewing room," Emerson corrected. "And all of us won't fit in it. I want to see your quilt, too."

"It's not a quilt. It's a block."

My ears pricked up. "You finished a block? And you're not ripping it out?"

"It's one damn block. It's— No, I'm not ripping it out."

Aunt Florence snapped at her. "Quickly, please. Some of us are getting old standing here."

"You're making this a bigger deal than it is."

"*I* merely asked to see your quilt. *You* are the reason we're discussing it."

"Fine. But it's not that big a thing."

I sat back down on the bench seat, and was slightly shocked when Aunt Florence pushed James's booster seat next to me and plugged him into it.

"Here, idle hands. Play with this." She reached into her bag and pulled out a huge ring of keys, which James treated as if they were the greatest toys of all time.

Emerson sat on the other side of the booster, but Aunt Florence remained standing.

"It's one block," Dred mumbled, smoothing it out on the table.

"Holy shit." Emerson covered his mouth. "Sorry."

He was right. It was a "holy shit" kind of block. I didn't reach for it, but I could see it wasn't a normal block. It had layers. "Is that quilt as you go?"

"Yeah. I figured I wouldn't rip it out as much if I did it this way. And it's a lot easier to store finished blocks and piece them together later, instead of piecing together the entire quilt top, and batting, and backing." She fell back a half step when Aunt Florence moved closer to examine the block.

Her long, grayish fingers traced the strips of fabric Dred had laid out almost like a sunburst; from one corner each strip got wider toward the other end, giving an impression of movement. It was bordered in black, highlighting the brightness of the colors somehow, even though it seemed like that should have made them look dark.

"I got the idea from you, Z. When we were looking at your rainbow."

I felt honored that something I'd done had inspired her.

"These are personal scraps." Aunt Florence ran her fingers out to the edge of the sunburst.

Dred came closer again. "I always wanted to make a quilt like your crazy quilt. This is my pathetic attempt. Anyway, it's not that big a deal."

"This rose print is from a dress you had when you were a little girl. I don't recognize the orange, but isn't that yellow from one of your mother's prized tea towels?"

"Yeah." Dred smirked. "I stole it when I was fifteen. I thought it would kill her to not have a matched set."

"Oh, no doubt it did, rotten child. This blue looks distinctly like something Obadiah would buy."

"From the first tie he ever made."

Emerson leaned in. "The one he made for the boyfriend who didn't wear it?"

"That guy was a fucking tool."

"Mildred."

"He was, Auntie. You would have thought so, too."

James said something, loudly, that sounded like agreement.

"Exactly," Dred replied.

"Obie told me"—Emerson brushed his fingertips across the blue stripe—"that he made you the same tie and you wore it all the time."

She grinned. "It was magic, him making ties. And I was dating Jaq at the time, so I thought she'd, you know, think I was extra cool if I wore them."

Jaq loved a sexy woman in a tie. I smiled. "I bet she did."

"She definitely didn't have any complaints."

Aunt Florence cleared her throat. "And the green?"

Dred glanced at me. "Actually, that's pretty new. But I gave Zane a piece of it for her quilt and realized how much I liked it."

I swallowed. Our quilts would be bound by that green now, and probably no one would notice it, but I'd know. And she would.

"I can see its appeal," Florence said mildly. "And this purple?"

"I know that one." Emerson sat back. "That's from Obie's old curtains, isn't it? The weave or whatever looks the same. Though I thought they were black."

"They'd gone purple where the sun bleached them." Dred's hands smoothed down the block. "This is wrong side up, technically. Does it look off, Auntie?"

"Mmm. No. I don't think so." Florence shifted the entire block directly under the light. "No, and you found a very even piece of it."

Dred rolled her eyes. "That was my third try. If anyone wants a bunch of curtain scraps, I have them."

I almost said I did, but I was making a quilt with squares, not strips. Not sunbursts. Not anything as beautiful as this block, with all different colors and patterns that still somehow went together.

"What size will it be finished?" Aunt Florence asked, drawing it closer to herself to study the seams.

"Eighty-six by ninety-three, I think."

Florence nodded. "For a queen bed."

"Yeah. I think it might be time to retire my old quilt, Auntie."

"Long past time." Florence smiled at Emerson and me. "I made that for Mildred when she was just out of her crib. For years her mother called me every time she had to make the bed to tell me that doubling up the quilt on a child's bed was 'cruel and unusual.'"

"Mom loves drama."

"That reminds me. I brought you something, before I knew you'd stolen your mother's tea towel." Again, Aunt Florence reached into her deep bag. "Do you remember this?"

"Oh," Dred whispered, taking the . . . pillowcase? "Auntie, she'll *kill* you when she finds this gone."

"I found it at the very bottom of the linen cabinet. I'm certain she no longer uses it."

Dred spread it out, running dark fingers over white cotton, pressing it flat. "How long has it been in your purse?"

"Only a few hours. You see what I mean?"

"It's not ironed."

"Wait." I looked at Emerson, then back at Dred. "Your mom irons her pillowcases?"

"With lavender water. She says it helps her sleep. Auntie, I can't *use* this."

"My dear girl, you *must* use it. Unless you have your blocks planned out."

"No. No, but—but this— I can't cut this up."

"Better it be used and loved rather than at the bottom of the linen cabinet." Florence dragged her knuckles along the lace overlay at the opening of the pillowcase. "Her first grown-up sheets, before she and your father got married. 'Egyptian cotton, Flo,' she said to me. I thought it was all so hedonistic." She smiled. "Can you imagine how naïve I was? I was offended by how much she enjoyed her sheets. It's gone a bit yellow in places, Mildred. You'll want to find its true shade before you start working with it."

"I'm not sure— I don't know what I'd do with it."

Except watching the way she smoothed out the fabric, tugged at it to find its shape, made me think she knew *exactly* what to do with it.

"You'll work it out, I'm sure. Time for me to leave. James, I'll need my keys." Florence held her hand out, and James giggled. "Please, young man."

He giggled again and surrendered the keys, then immediately started playing with my sleeve.

"Damn." Emerson poked James's arm. "Seriously? You never give me anything I ask for. I say 'please.'"

"Yeah but you don't have Aunt Florence's tone." Dred carefully folded her panel in half, loosely, and placed the pillowcase on top of it.

Aunt Florence held up a hand. "Have a good night, you four. Think about what I said, Mildred."

"I'm not having dinner with them."

Aunt Florence gave Dred the same look she'd given James. "Just think about what I said."

"Fine, Auntie. I'll think about what you said."

"That's all I can ask." Florence swept out, and Dred sank into a chair.

Emerson went into the pantry for James's biscuits. "You gonna tell us what that was all about?"

"She wants me to reconcile with my parents. I told her it was under no circumstances gonna happen, but she hears 'no' and thinks it means 'please convince me.'"

"Huh. Here, James. Eat biscuits, not Zane's clothes. So Florence is trying to reconcile you against your will with your folks? That's hugely invasive." He shrugged his shoulders as if he was shrugging off the idea because it made him uncomfortable. "I wouldn't be able to deal with that."

"Apparently my mother's been 'thinking' about our estrangement and it 'weighs' on her." Dred snapped her fingers. "Not enough to call or come over or do anything at all that might change things. Apparently it's a vague weight on her shoulders and that's somehow my fault to fix."

I traded a glance with Emerson. "What about your dad?"

"Aunt Florence claims he's full of regrets and would see me tomorrow if I let him." She paused. "She said he wants to meet James. Mom hasn't expressed an interest in James at all. I'm like this blemish on her perfect record of being exactly what she was supposed to be. Poor mom. With her fat, pansexual, half-black daughter. And now I have a child out of wedlock."

I sucked in a breath and bit my lips so I wouldn't say anything. But I wanted to defend her from her own charges of imperfection. Dred was strong and incredible and funny and beautiful. And I definitely wanted to defend her from anyone who would dare be ashamed.

My teeth dug harder into my lips.

Emerson's smile was somewhat sick. "She and my folks could hang out. They think I moved away to the city to live a life of sin. They'd be freaked out if they knew I lived with a little kid, that you trusted me with him."

She reached across the table, and for a second they clasped hands. Two people who never went out of their way to touch, connecting over the perception of their wrongness in parents who should have only shown them acceptance.

Then they let go.

"I think I might be able to see Dad without killing him. He said a lot of fucked-up shit to me, but it was a long time ago, and he sent two hundred dollars when James was born. And a note that said 'Love, Dad.' That was it. Aunt Florence says he's repentant, which isn't really my business, but maybe—I don't know." She gestured toward James. "It'd be good for him to have a grandfather. Even if Dad and I never really get close, maybe he could be around for James."

We sat in silence but for James's crunching and occasional insistent question to which he didn't seem to require a response.

I stayed a while longer, trying to find a way to apologize to Dred. But even when Emerson went upstairs, she wouldn't let me. The second I said "Sorry" she held up her hand.

"Don't. It's okay. It's not part of your plan, I get it. I shouldn't have pushed the whole thing anyway, Zane. Don't worry about it."

"But—"

"Really. Let it go. And you can keep coming around to do your quilt and stuff." She offered me this small smile that looked like the kind of thing you did when you really wanted to cry. "We'll go back to fake-dating. We were better at that, anyway."

I wanted to know what that meant. I wanted to argue that the last thing we should do was go back to fake-dating. Instead I kissed James's head and said good night.

For a long moment I sat in my car, staring up at her bedroom windows. It was dark in there, just enough light coming in from the hallway for me to see vague shapes.

I'd slept there. Smelled it. Cried in her arms. Felt safe.

But I didn't even know this could be part of my plan. Maybe I want it to be.

Or maybe I didn't. I definitely couldn't go back to Dred until I was absolutely certain. And then I'd hope she'd give me a second chance.

CHAPTER 20

Jaq kicked my ass all over the gym on Wednesday and dragged me back to Hannah's after.

"You realize you live here, right?" I needled as I stumbled up the stairs after her. (Of course we weren't allowed to take the elevator.) "I mean, you might be in denial about it, but that's what it is."

"Oh, like you're one to talk about denial. Heard about your breakdown at Carlos's, kid."

"Bite me."

She laughed.

We finally made it into Hannah's elegant, lovely condo. I collapsed in a heap on her couch. "Your girlfriend missed her calling as a personal trainer!" I yelled.

Hannah appeared, like a wonderful post-gym fairy, with wine for us, a soda for Jaq, and a bowl of tortilla chips. "Tough day at the office, hon?"

"Actually, I negotiated leases for two different locations and sold a third this week. I'm on fire."

"Cheers to that." We clinked glasses. "Let me get the salsa and guacamole."

"Oh my *god*, guac. You are a goddess, Hannah."

"I know it."

Good guac is the food of the gods, but most people load it up with spices and shit. That's weak sauce. Hannah's guac, I have reason to know, is always good. Avocados, garlic, salt, lemon. That's all you need. Unless the avocados are underripe. That's the only reason to add more shit to your guac.

Hannah's avocados were *perfect.* I might have made a . . . sound. Possibly.

"Are you moaning right now?" Jaq threw herself into the other corner of the couch. "Gross, Zane. Keep your guac-based sex acts to yourself."

"It's not my fault that Hannah's guac brings all the girls to the yard. Oh my god, that's so good. It almost makes up for your sadistic treadmill routine."

"Almost?" Hannah snatched the bowl away. "Did you say 'almost'?"

"Totally. Totally makes up for Jaq's sadistic treadmill thing." My empty chip wavered in the air. "Please give me back the guac, I swear, I'll never say anything less than fully enamored of it again."

"Speaking of fully enamored," Jaq began.

"You shut your trap."

"Girls." Hannah refilled her wineglass. "I made a salad. I'm sure we can forage for carbohydrates after that, but I've eaten nothing but crap this week."

"Salad sounds great." It did. In the week leading up to ovulation I usually ate a lot of fruits and vegetables. It might have been intentional back in the early days, but now it was just another way of marking time, an internal calendar made up of inseminations and periods and everything in between.

Jaq relented and reached for the chips and guac. "So I did a horrible thing today. Kind of."

"A kind of horrible thing?" I asked.

"Kind of. I, uh, slipped with Merin's pronouns. In class. He'd said some jackass thing, and Sammy teased him, and I heard myself say 'Torture him on your own time, Sammy.'" She grimaced. "I've never done that before. I rehearse as they file in for Journalism. *She, she, she.*"

"What happened?"

She sighed and laid her head back. "Merin froze like he'd been shot. Sammy laughed and covered over the whole thing with a manufactured question about deadlines. Or something. But I can't stop thinking about the look on Merin's face. Like I'd stripped him naked in the middle of class. I feel horrible. And of course he won't let me apologize."

Hannah slid over to sit on the coffee table and take one of Jaq's feet in her hands. "Do you want to go back to using 'she' when you're at home? I think that made it easier."

"It did. But it also felt so wrong. No. Merin's—you know. I can't go back now. It's weird to me that I ever thought of him as 'her.' Babe, that feels so good."

"That's the point."

They traded looks.

I cleared my throat. "So he needs a place to live?"

"Yeah. He stays with Sammy for a few days, and at his girlfriend's parents' place. But he always goes back home when he worries he's overstayed his welcome, and that always ends with a huge fight and him walking out."

"He won't stay with Josh and Keith?"

She shrugged. "I think he feels like he already owes them too much. He might be willing to add their couch to his couch-surfing list, but he knows they'd let him move in permanently, and he won't do it."

Hannah began working on the other foot. "I hate feeling helpless. It's ridiculous that there's nothing we can even do to help. Short of funding an entire transgender shelter." She stopped. "Wait. Can we do something like that?"

Jaq offered a tired smile. "What, like you and me? I think it might be a bit more than we can afford."

"We need more rich queers."

"Right?" I got a third (or maybe twenty-third) chip. "I thought all queers were supposed to be rich. That's why I decided to be queer. For the money."

"And all the social advantages," Hannah added. "Like Club Fred's. Who could resist Fred's?"

Jaq took her feet back in favor of kissing her girlfriend. "Technically even nonqueers can get into Fred's."

Hannah and I performed gasps of mock-outrage.

"No way!" Hannah fanned herself. "They wouldn't dare!"

"Nonqueers," I said. "I'm trying to wrap my head around this idea. Who would choose not to be queer? Do they have some kind of webpage I can go to in order to better understand them?"

Jaq shook her head. "What would they even say? Must be so boring."

"Hey now." Hannah pointed at both of us. "You two be nice. Some of my best friends are not queer."

I leaned forward, trying to keep my face serious. "Will you ask them if they have a website?"

We dissolved into giggles.

Jaq clapped her hands. "Okay, okay, back to reality. There are actually some protections in place for transgender homeless people, though implementation is sketchy. Still, it's the Bay Area, so if you're gonna be trans and homeless, this is probably the place to live. But what do we do with these kids who are turning eighteen with no stability, no safety net?"

"We talk to Josh and Keith," I said.

Hannah nodded. "And I was actually serious. I can't bankroll a shelter, but there really *are* rich queer people. At least some of them would contribute if we could work out what it is we need."

"Scholarships." Jaq downed her cream soda. "Lots and lots of need-based scholarships."

"But." I hesitated. "Not everyone wants to go to college." Jaq was a teacher. We didn't always see eye-to-eye on education stuff.

"Well, setting aside the fact that a scholarship covering room and board would take care of a whole lot of problems at one time, and the fact that outcomes are still more promising for college graduates than non-college graduates, that's not actually what I meant."

I waited. Hannah nudged her with stockinged toes.

"Don't you think there should be a way we can fund... something, some kind of program, that would cover room and board, and prioritize job training, or apprenticeships, or hell, I don't know, internships."

Damn. "Sometimes I remember how smart you are."

She threw her chip at my face and got me in the neck.

Hannah, way less juvenile than Jaq and me, had unearthed a notebook and was hunting around on the table. "I need a pen. A scholarship for kids who want to go directly into a field, but it'd be a program, structured like college, with dorms, and a cafeteria. I love this idea."

Jaq glanced at me. "There might not be any demand for something like that—"

"Hush, Mama's writing."

I smothered my laughter in my elbow while Jaq glared at me. Glared *daggers* at me.

"I love everything about this idea," Hannah mumbled, still writing. "We have to talk to Josh and Keith. And Fredi. And the gentleman who always sits at the back."

"Donald," I said.

"Right. We have to talk to the people who might be able to find us some of those proverbial rich queers."

"You mean the old guard." I had a conflicted relationship with the people who came up when things were more militant and defined. I liked being part of a community that held a certain amount of fluidity as a core value. Sometimes sitting around with old queers made me feel like we were two different species of queer, nearly unrecognizable to each other.

"Hannah and I can interface with the old guard." Jaq straightened the lines on the button-down she'd changed into after the gym. "A butch and a femme, we're totally old guard. Right, babe?"

"You mean, except for the crate of sex toys?"

Jaq sputtered. "We wouldn't *tell* them about that!"

Hannah's pen didn't stop moving. "Mm-hmm. I think this might be workable, but we can't be the first people who've ever thought of it. I'll have to get on research."

"Ask Keith," I said. "He loves research."

"I will. Can you two get dinner going? I want to write all my thoughts down while they're fresh."

We retreated to the kitchen.

I raised my eyebrows. "So Hannah's kind of . . . driven."

"You have no idea. Here. Do something clever with"—she gestured to a bunch of greens—"whatever that is."

"I think it's . . . watercress?" I tried one of the leaves. "Is it weird that all greens taste like freshly cut lawn to me?"

Jaq wrinkled her nose. "Gross. How can you even eat them?"

"I guess I kind of don't mind eating grass." I dangled a bouquet of possibly-watercress in her face. "Yummy!"

"You're twelve years old."

"You know me so well."

"Focus!" Hannah called.

I sighed. "Yes, Mom!"

"Don't make me give you a time-out, Zane!"

"Awww."

"Hey." Jaq's voice was low. "If you need anything for this insemination, let me know, okay? You want to do another conception party? It's been a while since you shot up at home."

I shook my head. "I'm not doing anything. I'm not rearranging my schedule. I'm not skipping the gym."

Her eyes widened. "Seriously?"

"I can't do it anymore." I abandoned the salad and sat on the counter. "I can't stop my whole life twice a month: once to inseminate, and again because I'm so fucking depressed when I get my period. I can't, Jaqs. It's awful."

"I know."

"So I'm gonna stop doing that." My eyes pricked with tears. "Anyway. I talked to the boys. Basically Tom will give me as much spunk as I want."

Jaq cracked up, then covered her mouth like laughing was inappropriate at that juncture. "Sorry! Sorry, but Tom giving you spunk, oh damn, that's too fucking much."

"I know. What's weird is it's beginning to not feel that weird to me. Especially after all those years of being like, 'Whoa, unprotected sex, you could *die*.' And now I'm cavalierly gonna shoot up with unwashed sperm."

"Unwashed?"

"That's the term. There are different types—"

Her eyes started to glaze over.

I sighed. "Never mind. And anyway, he went and got tested for everything on earth, even before they talked to me."

"Aw. That's kind of sweet, actually. Like he didn't want to talk to you until he was totally sure it could work."

"Yeah."

"Plus, I think dying from unprotected sex was a whole lot more about, you know, getting punished for being irresponsible than it was about actual medical fact."

"Lesbian superpower." I held up my hand for a high five. One of our old rituals, dating way back to the first sex ed class we'd had in high school, when Jaq had raised her hand and asked the health teacher what the health risks of lesbian sex were.

The teacher had stammered and blushed and ended up getting a little angry at her inability to address the question. We'd laughed about it, but the undercurrent there was: *You don't matter. Your health is irrelevant. Your sex is irrelevant. Who you are is irrelevant.*

I thought about Merin sitting through that same class (though at least the current health teacher at LVHS was one of Jaq's friends, and probably would handle that shit better). If you were a trans teenager sitting in health class, what messages did you get from that? Other than the fact that you apparently didn't exist?

"Okay, bestie." Jaq returned to the salad-prep process. "Got it. Nothing out of the ordinary. I will hound your ass to the gym like usual. Noted."

"Hey, Jaq."

"Hey, what?"

I jumped down from the counter and wrapped her in a hug from behind. "I'm really glad we knew each other as kids. I don't know who I would have become without you."

She hugged my arms. "Me too. I think about that all the time. We were real fucking lucky, you know?"

"Yeah."

"Zane Jaffe! Unhand my woman!"

I gave Jaq a squeeze and disengaged. "You can lease her from me, but she's totally my best friend forever."

Hannah grinned. "As long as I get all the sexy parts of her."

"Ew. Gross. Don't talk about Jaq and sex in the same sentence. That's disgusting."

"Hey!" Jaq protested. "Sex with me is not disgusting!"

Hannah kissed her. "Damn right it's not, sugar."

Dinner was good. We talked more pie-in-the-sky dreams about what it'd look like to have a college that was focused on apprenticeships, and if kids like Merin would even be interested.

I recklessly volunteered to ask him. Jaq laughed at me. Hannah told me to take notes and send them to her.

I went home after, to my place, and as much as I still loved walking in, keeping the lights off, going directly to the bathroom to shower, leaving all the doors open, not bothering with clothes—I couldn't escape the idea that the night would have ended even better if I were in Dred's bed, with her, instead of my own, alone.

I got an email from Ed Friday morning, asking if I was free for lunch. I surveyed my to-do list and decided I was definitely free.

We met at Taco Junction and took our food around the corner so we could sit in the sun.

Transitioning had been good for Ed; he'd gone from being a masculine-leaning, lesbian-identified person who never looked comfortable, to being a man who looked comfortable in his skin in certain situations. Like now, sitting with me at a table eating lunch. He passed effortlessly these days, letting whiskers grow on his face, carrying himself differently than he had even six months ago.

"You look good," I said.

He cracked a smile. "Are you hitting on me right now? I'm flattered, but I have a girlfriend."

"Can you imagine Alisha in a cat fight? No, thank you. And I wasn't, babe. I'm only into girls."

His eyes flashed. "That, I'm not. And thanks, Zane. Appreciate it."

"Since I doubt you took me out to lunch so I could compliment you, what's up?"

"We have a thing." He rearranged his beans and rice and guac burrito as he talked. "It's— Actually, I have no idea how you're going to feel about this."

"Okay. Shoot."

He took a breath. "Joe Rodriguez—senior, not junior—wants to go to the wake."

It took me a few seconds to put the pieces together. "You mean . . . the guy's dad?"

"Yeah."

We looked at each other for a long minute. *I* had no idea how I felt about that. "Why?"

"I talked to him for a really long time last night. I think— Hell, Zane, I don't know. He's so broken right now. They were . . . shocked doesn't even come close. Devastated. They had no idea Joey could have ever been capable of the things he did. Maybe even more than that, the things he thought." He put the burrito down, with only a single bite out of it, and took a sip of his water. "They raised him right, you know? Going to church, getting good grades. Joe said they were so careful to raise him to be respectful of people, to know that even though he was light-skinned some people would never see past his last name, that he'd have to work harder than a white kid named Jones, but it'd be worth it. That hard work pays off."

I put my burrito down, too. "Oh god. Ed."

"I know."

"Not that I didn't think that it must be hard on the parents, but you always think—or you kind of hope—that maybe monsters like him come from bad experiences. That there's a reason they do horrible things."

"I tried to figure that out, at first. I was talking to Joe, and he's—" Ed swallowed. "He's my friend, you know? But at first I was treating him like the father of a killer. I wanted— I guess I kind of wanted him to tell me how he screwed it up. Then he started crying; this big, strong man, crying into his burger because his son . . ." He shook his head. "I can't even imagine it. And he said his wife is just numb. She doesn't smile, or laugh, and hardly talks. They were good parents. They tried to do everything right. And their son killed six people and almost killed three more."

"Is he— I mean, is he schizophrenic or something? Not that—obviously not that that would mean schizophrenic people are murderers—but maybe there's a—a brain chemistry thing—"

"He's a serial killer who thought he had to purify the gay community. They're trying to find a specialist who can diagnose him, get him help, but everyone they talk to—" He broke off. "Well, anyway, he probably wasn't supposed to tell me all that, and I definitely shouldn't be talking about it in public. But no, I don't think this is like he had a psychotic break and lost it." He glanced around, but we were the only ones on the sunny side of the building. "He hunted them, Zane. Like prey. And then he killed them."

I shivered despite the warmth of the sun. "So why does his dad want to go to the wake?"

"To grieve, I think. We lost friends. In a way, he lost his son, the son he thought he had. And he'll never get that back, no matter how long Joey lives."

"But—" It was our space. Wasn't it? Jokes aside, most of the time straight people didn't come to Club Fred's. Or if they did, they were *fluid* straight people. Not middle-aged men whose sons had terrorized us for months.

Or a middle-aged man with a gay son who'd hung out at Club Fred's for years. What had Dred said when I first proposed the wake? That we were just trying to feel better about partying with a murderer. How much harder was it for Mr. Rodriguez to feel better about raising one?

"The event is open," I temporized.

"He won't come unless it's okay. He doesn't want to intrude."

I bit off saying, *Well, it's pretty fucking intrusive*, and sat with it for a minute. All I'd wanted the whole time was to reinvent a safe space. Either we could do it or we couldn't; the presence of Mr. Rodriguez wasn't likely to tip the scales, I didn't think.

Still. I had to think about it.

"I can't give you my answer on it until I talk to Cam, Josh, and Keith. If they're comfortable with it, then I'm comfortable with it. But I'm not putting them in the position of facing the guy whose boy tried to kill them."

Ed nodded. "I would have talked to them before going back to him anyway, but it'd be better coming from you. Cam—you know. He'd say yes to me because Joe's my friend."

I picked up my burrito. "How's Mr. Rodriguez doing, really? I guess I hadn't really thought about going through your day wondering who's side-eyeing you thinking about how your kid grew up to be a murderer."

"He's coming to work. But he looks exhausted all the time, and whenever I knock on his office door he spooks, like he thinks someone's gonna—I don't even know. No one's said anything about it to him that I know of. I think he feels really guilty. And I can't even decide if I think maybe he should, like how do you raise this kid who kills people and not be at least partially responsible? Except I think maybe he's not. Which, hell, Zane, that might be worse. What if there's a certain kind of person who will always end up doing terrible things no matter how good their upbringing?"

"Stop it. Trying to get pregnant here. Do not want to talk about Future Kid being Future Killer."

"Sorry. Shit. But you know what I mean. I'm so into the power of will, but there's so much that I don't control. Which I should know better than anyone, but still."

I nodded. "Anyway, let me think about this. I'll get back to you, okay?"

"Sure. Thanks. And . . . sorry. I feel like I put you in a crummy position, but you're the only person who I could ask."

"Yeah, it was my idea. Well, Hannah's, but my job to put it into action. Speaking of Hannah, and Jaq, listen to this crazy idea they had the other night."

I told him about college-for-jobs. He told me about how things were going at the paper, and the newish half promotion he'd gotten to start updating the online version of the *Times-Record* more than once a day.

Joey Rodriguez, aka the La Vista Killer, had a dad, and his dad wanted to go to the wake I was planning for his victims and survivors. I could barely wrap my head around all the ways that could go wrong. But for some reason I really wanted to say yes. He might not even show up. But I didn't want be the one who closed the door on him.

CHAPTER 22

I wasn't sure if I was still welcome at breakfast on Saturday, but I decided to show up and see what happened. I was armed with a couple of topics I could bring up as fake reasons for why I was there, if I needed them, but they were obviously fake and wouldn't fool anyone.

No one asked. Of course.

It was so weird. On one level it was just like it usually was: I walked in, joined in the making of breakfast, messed with James's baby curls. Emerson shot me a look, but Dred waved hello, and Obie kissed my cheek.

"Here." The cutting board landed on the table in front of me. Dred pushed a produce bag across the counter. "Green onions."

"Got it."

Like that. That could have happened last week, or the week before. No big deal. Except there was some . . . distance between us. As if there used to be a bridge, and the bridge was gone, but the rest of the landscape was identical.

Everything seemed the same. Nothing had changed. And yet I knew there was no way back to how it had been between us. I could feel that as sure as I felt the knife graze too close to my knuckle because I wasn't paying attention.

"Ouch! Damn. I cut myself." I sucked on the cut.

Emerson swept the cutting board away. "Do *not* bleed on my green onions!"

"Your concern is noted. Jerk."

"No need for you to contaminate the food. You didn't bleed on the board, did you?"

"No, Emerson, I didn't bleed on the cutting board."

Obie leaned over from his seat across from me, where he was shoving food in James's mouth. "He's pissed at you on Dred's behalf. Isn't that sweet?"

I rolled my eyes. "Not so much, no."

"I don't need anyone to be pissed at anyone on my *anything*." Dred punched Emerson in the arm. "Especially your sorry ass."

"Fuck you. I've been meditating. I could choose not to be pissed at Zane, but I'm choosing to indulge myself."

"How's that different than you before you were meditating?"

"Before it didn't feel like a choice." Emerson shot me a smirk. "Now I'm pissed at Zane for fun."

"Thanks a lot." But it was hard not to smile at him. "So you're liking the meditation thing?"

"I'm not sure I'd say—"

"Yes," Obie interrupted.

"I was going to say—"

"You like it. I know you like it. You feel better after doing it. So wouldn't it be more, like, mindful if you admitted that you kind of like being mindful?"

Emerson turned away. "I'm so fucking Zen right now I'm ignoring everything you just said."

Obie grinned. "Whatever you say, dear."

"I know where you sleep."

"You better."

Dred cleared her throat. "Enough foreplay. Can we make omelets now?"

Breakfast was delicious as usual. The boys were taking James off to the fabric store after, still searching for the right material for Josh and Keith, who'd apparently commissioned a tie for Cam.

I nodded. "It's been weeks, hasn't it?" The first time he'd sent them fabric swatches had been the day after Carlos and Tom's wedding.

"Yeah," Obie said. "I think we're close. They'd let me make it already, but I can tell I haven't found the perfect thing yet, so I'm still looking."

"They're so cute, the three of them."

"And they're making a poly triad work, which is awesome." He scooped James up. "Let's go, papi. You too, Emerson."

"I'm coming, I'm coming. Bossy."

I stood on the porch, clutching my coffee like it was a hand stamp to get back in the house. They loaded James into the car and drove away, talking, looking like . . . a family.

"People always think they adopted him when the three of them go out."

I didn't jump a foot or anything. Coffee didn't slosh out of my cup and burn my hand because Dred scared the hell out of me. That would be a waste of coffee. Plus, that kind of thing only happened to jumpy people. Not me.

"Does that bother you?" I surreptitiously switched hands so the burning, dripping one could dangle at my side and someday cool off. Or possibly go numb.

"Hell no. I like that people see him as being part of a family. When it's just me and him, people think I'm a welfare queen. When one of the boys is with us, then we look like straight people with a kid." She shrugged.

I missed her shoulders. We'd only had sex once, and I missed the way her skin smelled up close. "You're not a welfare queen, Dred."

"Nope. I almost make enough to get us off food stamps." Sour smile. "I guess that's when I'll know we're hugely successful, right? When we hit the food stamps cap. I told Aunt Florence I was going to try to find a real job, and do you know what she said to me?"

"No."

"She told me it's almost wedding season and I'd be better off making quilts with Obie's scraps to sell in the online store. Or knitting hats and scarves. It's ridiculous. The worst plan I've ever heard. He's in daycare for five hours a day. I should be spending all of those hours doing something that gets us a steady paycheck."

"Okay." I sipped my coffee, watching her over the rim. "But what do you want to do?"

"I never want to go back to a normal job. Ever. My chest gets tight and I can't breathe when I even think about walking into the sign shop, and that wasn't a bad place to work. They'd take me back part-time. But it sounds like a nightmare, going back there again. Starting all over."

"Then I'm with Aunt Florence. Don't do it."

"Z, you make more in a month than I do in three months. Probably in six."

"So what? I like going to my office. I like my job. If I didn't, I'd find something else to do."

"Then you wouldn't be able to afford sperm."

"Hey, I've got it on tap now. Tom's gonna help me out."

She nodded, forehead smoothing out. "I'm really glad you decided to do it."

"We'll see how it goes." Now. Now was the moment. Now was the moment I could find a way back to where we'd been. "Dred, listen, just hear me out. I know I was an ass, but I swear, if we could try again—"

"When you figure out what you want—what you really want—I'll be here. But I'm not waiting for you. And I'm not holding my breath." She leaned against the doorframe. "You're all up in the air right now, and that makes sense to me. But, Zane, I can't be up in the air with you. If I'm gonna have someone in my life, they need to be in it for real, not for pretend. Not only when it's convenient for them."

I wanted to tell her that was me, that I was so fucking for real right now, that I'd never been pretending, not since the first.

Except.

I couldn't. Because when I looked into the future, I had no idea what was there anymore. My lists weren't working, nothing was the way I thought it'd be. How could I make any kind of commitment when I had no idea how I'd feel in a month? Let alone two, or six, or . . .

And what if there was a kid involved? Or what if there . . . wasn't?

"Sometimes I feel like everything in my life is on hold until I get pregnant. And then I think, you know, if I find out I need to do fertility treatments, then I'll do that. If that doesn't work, then I'll start the adoption process. And it's all this endless moving belt that I'm on and can't get off."

She looked at me for a long moment. I thought she'd say something—she'd tell me to leave her alone until I knew what I wanted, or she'd tell me never mind, she wasn't interested—but what she actually said was, "Sounds like you should be doing Emerson's meditations. Anyway, come in. Let's work on your quilt some more."

"What about yours?"

"I'll get you set up and start playing with another block, if it'll make you happy."

Kissing you would make me happy. But that was off-limits, so I didn't say it.

I lingered longer than I should have, but I couldn't seem to pull myself away from her. We worked in silence, except when I had a question. The unsteady stitching of the sewing machine in my inconsistent hands seemed to draw time out, extending it.

My stacks of squares had almost turned into columns, with quarter-inch seam allowances. After that, I'd have to learn how to piece the columns together, which seemed alternately like it'd be easy and like it was impossible.

Upside: I'd have to ask Dred for help. Real help. And she'd stand close, and show me things. I'd probably have to force myself to concentrate because I'd be thinking about what she said, about being in it for real. I wanted to be in it for real, but I didn't. I wanted to tell her I wasn't pretending, but how did I know, really? Maybe I still was. Or always was. Or never was.

Dred was sitting on the love seat, trying to plan another block for her quilt, laying out scraps, swapping them, playing them off against each other. I couldn't watch her because she'd know I wasn't working if the machine stopped running, but I liked that both of us could be in the same room, not talking, doing separate things.

Was this what being in love was? I could do the same thing with Jaq, or Carlos. But I wouldn't get the same electric charge from having them close by. I wouldn't anticipate the next time they glanced in my direction, or the next time I needed help so they'd come closer.

The day we met, Dred taught me how to knit. She sat close to me, touching my hands, changing the positions of my fingers until I was holding the needles so I could more freely move them. Ever since that moment I'd wanted her to teach me things.

Obie, Emerson, and James came back when I was nearly done with the final column of squares.

"Obadiah!" Dred called when the door opened.

"Mildred?" He pushed the accordion doors open with the hand not holding James. "What's up?"

"I need something from you. When's the last time you wore your bell-bottoms?"

He blinked. "Jeez. Years ago. Why?"

Dred reached over to adjust the lamp so it shone more fully on her lain-out pattern. "I need them. But I'd have to cut some off."

"Oh." He handed off James to Emerson and went to look at her design. "Right here, huh? They would be seriously perfect."

"And if you were okay with me cutting them up more than that, I kind of want the right knee for a different block."

"The right knee is more hole than denim."

"I know. I have an idea, to put something behind it so it'd flash through when you moved the quilt just right."

"Well. I guess . . . I'm not saving them for anything. I'll be right back."

"You don't have to—" Dred began.

"No, that's not why I'm doing it. I think it sounds kind of bitchin'. Plus, it'd be better for them to be on your quilt than gathering dust on my clothes rack."

"Wait, how dusty are we talking?"

He laughed and bounded up the stairs.

I turned my chair and quit pretending I was working. "So you're gonna use a pair of Obie's bell-bottoms in your quilt?"

"They're the first thing he ever made, back when we were teenagers. Hand sewn, because Aunt Florence hadn't shown us how to use the machine yet."

Emerson deposited James in his walker. "Wait. He's gonna let you cut those up? Oh damn."

"I think I'll use them three times, actually. I have an idea. And I want to get his careful little stitches in, too."

Footsteps on the stairs again.

"Don't talk about my stitches!" Obie, with ceremony, presented Dred with a very well-worn pair of jeans, cuffs belled-out with triangles of pink paisley fabric sewn in to widen them.

"Your stitches are adorable, look at them." The two of them bent their heads to study teenage-Obie's hard work. "So cute. These pants are the reason we became friends."

"We were already friends," Obie countered.

"We already knew each other. But when you started sewing in class, that's when we became friends."

He turned to us. "She means when I let her boss me around and tell me what to do is when we became friends."

Emerson choked on a laugh. "Oh man. You so have a type."

Dred pressed the jeans down on the rug, stretching them out, flattening them, running her hands all over them. When James toddled his walker over to look, she said, "Hey, baby. You want to help me pick which bits we're using for the quilt?"

He replied with a stream of babble.

"Uncle Obie used to look so damn cute in these jeans. I might get him to make you a pair for when you can walk."

Whatever James said then definitely sounded like agreement. She grinned up at him. "You're so happy. You get that from your dad, not me."

He cocked his head.

"Don't worry about it, James. Now look. This knee right here, we're gonna back with something really intense, so people want to see more." She outlined a rectangle with index fingers and thumbs, playing with the shapes. "But I think we'll keep the triangles down here, at least two of them. I'll cut them out of their seams. But I need a third one in situ so we can keep those stitches."

Obie, one arm loosely around Emerson's shoulders, shook his head. "Would you have ever imagined when we were sitting in Chemistry and you were telling me how to secure my stitches that someday you'd be telling your kid how you were gonna dismantle those pants for a quilt?"

"Nope. Didn't think either one of us was gonna live this long."

Obie's arm tightened. "I knew we would all along."

"That's why we call you Obi-Wan—"

"You better not or I'll cut you."

They laughed.

"Okay." Mildred locked the brakes on James's walker and reached for her scissors. "You ready? Once I start I can't go back."

"I'm ready. You're not even using a pattern right now?"

"This isn't the final. I'm just carving it out to see where it'll fit." She looked up. "Obe?"

"I'm ready."

She took a long breath. "Let's do this thing."

The first cuts were straight through the leg above and below the knee (which was an impressive shredded hole, from back in the day when we had to wear out our own clothes). Dred set aside the knee on the couch and began to turn the cuffs of the severed leg, searching for the piece she most wanted.

She seemed to study each triangle for ages, but James wasn't even impatient yet, so maybe it only felt that way to me.

"This one, I think. For the stitches." But before she picked up the scissors again, she looked at the left cuff. "Yeah. This one's perfect."

"Because it's the one I fucked up most, or the one I did best?"

"So not answering that."

Obie sighed. "Dred has this weird enjoyment of flaws. I don't get it. I want shit to be perfect, and she wants it to be . . . not quite right."

"Isn't that a quilting thing?" I asked. "Something about not wanting to offend God by creating perfection?"

Dred rolled her eyes without looking up from her work. "No one who's ever made a quilt thinks you have to do that shit on purpose. Everything handmade has errors. But yeah, this will remind me of watching Obie do it in class more than one of the better ones." Another long breath. "Okay."

She cut it more carefully than I'd ever seen her cut anything, allowing a lot of denim on the two long sides of the triangle, preserving every bit of Obie's stitching.

His face was rapt, watching, Emerson's arm around his waist.

"Is it weird?" I asked. "Watching Dred cut up the first thing you ever made?"

"No. No, actually it's—it's kind of liberating. I can get rid of them now, instead of staring at them for the next twenty years. They'll still be around in the quilt, so it doesn't feel like a loss. It's so clichéd."

"Makes sense, though." Emerson, also riveted, leaned closer to Obie. "Easier to let something go when you've incorporated it in other ways."

All three of us looked at him. James kept playing with his walker.

"What?"

Dred went back to work. "Mm-hmm."

"What 'Mm-hmm,' Mildred?"

"Nothing. Except I think maybe you're demonstrating personal growth right now, boy. Watch out for that."

"Shut the fuck up."

She grinned down at Obie's old jeans. "Last cuts. I'm just going to rip these out. If I cut them, they'll end up too small."

With painstaking effort she ripped out the stitches and set aside three pink paisley triangles with the other pieces. Then she bundled up the rest of the pants and looked at Obie.

"I can't do it." He shook his head. "Throw it away for me, okay?"

"Sure. Thanks. I really wanted them."

He leaned down to kiss her cheek. "Anytime you want to cut my clothes up and highlight how awful my early stitches were, you know I'm here for you."

"You're a good friend, Obe."

Emerson backed to the doorway and tugged Obie after him. "Come on, good friend. You need a nap. Which you might even get if I decide to let you sleep."

"Hey, I'm not making demands."

They went upstairs. I should have gone back to my column, but now that the machine wasn't betraying my every lapse in attention I made the most of it, watching Dred from the corner of my eye as she fitted her new pieces together. When James started to fuss, she put him on her lap with a pile of scraps from a different box and told him to start working on his quilt. He crammed bits of fabric in his face.

She glanced up before I could look away, both of us smiling at James's antics. The moment seemed to freeze, like the way you can see a drop of water balance on the brink of falling for an impossible length of time before finally going over.

James yelled something triumphant and shoved a fistful of scraps into his mouth.

Moment broken.

"That's not how you make a quilt, baby." She pulled the damp clump out and pressed it flat on her thigh. "I think these three look good together. Maybe—" Deft fingers rearranged them in a different order. "Like that?"

He picked up a few more scraps and layered them over the top.

"Oh, trying to get super experimental with it, huh? Okay. I hear that. How about this?" She picked another scrap, a long one, and put it perpendicularly across the others.

Apparently that was all kinds of wrong. James made a protesting sound and dropped the newest scrap over the edge of the couch.

Dred laughed. "No? Yeah, I agree, that didn't work. You gotta feel it out, James. Trust your instincts when it comes to quilts. And listen to your Uncle Obie, because he's way better at this than I am."

I turned back to the machine with a lump in my throat. I used to think about parenting a lot, in the years before I was trying to conceive. I had a ton of links and notes tagged with everything about parenting and child development. But until I'd started hanging out with Dred and James, I'd never really seen it up close. I tried not to think in terms of parenting because it just made not knowing how that would ever happen harder to take, but I pretended to rearrange my half-assembled squares and let myself wonder if I'd ever show a kid of mine how to quilt.

Still at least five days out from ovulation. I didn't really have an excuse to cry. Except having too many question marks and not enough control over their answers.

"C'mon, Z. You've been working on that awhile. Take him so I can put this stuff away and we'll do a picnic in the garden."

I surrendered my project and reached for James, who held his arms out for me. I didn't say anything, but it took me a few minutes to stop wiping my eyes.

CHAPTER 23

The flyers were in neat stacks in the backseat of my car. I drove to the Rhein early Sunday afternoon and brought a few of the more subtle ones up to the ticket booth. Cam wasn't there, but when I asked if he was around, the woman behind the glass gestured me inside and pointed across the lobby toward concessions.

The kid could dress. Today's outfit included an embroidered waistcoat and a shirt with French cuffs. He turned toward me, smiling. "Zane! It's good to see you. Did you come for the movie?"

I didn't even know what movie he was showing. "No, sorry. Now I feel like a tool. You want my five bucks anyway?"

"You really don't have to pay in order to drop by." His eyes slid down to the flyers. "Oh, I've already got one. Actually, three. With Keith's explicit directions on where to put each of them."

"I should have known." I had no idea how to start this conversation, except that I didn't want to have it in the lobby. "Hey, can we talk for a few minutes? If you have time. Or I can come back later."

"I have time. And if this is about the wake, I promise I am not attending against my will. I apologize for giving you that impression."

"I'm glad. But it's about something else."

Cam's expression shifted to cautious. "Ah. Okay. Well, I'm not needed here, so we can go upstairs." Slight lift on the last syllable.

"Thanks, Cam. That'd be good."

He waved to the folks at concessions and led me outside to the nondescript door on the far side of the ticket booth.

That Cam lived in an apartment directly next door to the theater shouldn't have surprised me—he was, in my mind, a figure practically synonymous with the Rhein—but it did.

"This is you, huh?" I said, totally unnecessarily.

"This is me."

Small dining area next to the door, living area beside the kitchen with a wall full of high windows overlooking the roofs of the next few buildings, and La Vista off to the sides.

"I bet this was a hell of a view before that parking structure went up, huh?"

"Actually, they apparently ripped down a department store to put in parking, and my grandfather said the parking structure was an improvement to downtown."

"Ouch."

"The owners were anti-Semites, I think, which was the cause of his animosity. Though that was in the late seventies, so it's only little bits of story I've gathered through the years." He gestured to his cute kitchen. "Can I get you something to drink? Sparkling water? Still water? Orange juice? I always have almond milk."

"Tap water would be great, thanks." I stood at the windows, sighting toward the Bay. Between the haze in the air and the freeway bisecting the view, I couldn't actually *see* the water. Only the absence of more buildings past a certain point. "This is a great place, Cam."

"It is. My grandparents lived here when I was a kid. Can you believe they actually raised my dad in this tiny place? I've seen pictures, but I can't really imagine it."

I'd bought a two-bedroom for the express purpose of having a room for Future Kid. "I can't imagine it. Where did he sleep?"

"In that corner. They built up a little cubby hole for him with a dresser and bookshelves, but there couldn't have been any privacy." He shook his head. "I'm glad my parents had a nice house in the suburbs. Though they probably bought more house than they needed because my dad remembered living here for all those years. Oh, sit. Please."

We took sides of his surprisingly comfortable red velvet couch, and I sipped my water before putting it on the coffee table. "I need to get your read on a wake-related thing."

The skin around his eyes tightened. "Okay. Though you should really ask Keith. He's a much better event planner than I am."

"I actually need to talk to him, and Josh, as well. I figured I'd head over to the center tomorrow."

He glanced at his watch. "They're due here relatively soon in any case. What's this about, Zane?"

"I talked to Ed yesterday. He's been talking to Mr. Rodriguez. The—the father. You know. Joey Rodriguez's father."

"They work together." His voice held no inflection.

"Right, yeah. They do. Um. So. Mr. Rodriguez has expressed an interest in going to the wake."

Cam sat back and crossed his legs. "Really? He's . . . going to go to Club Fred's for it? How strange."

"Ed thinks he's trying to reconcile the side of his son he knows with the side of his son—" I broke off.

"The side that I know? The side of his son that I met in this room?" He offered a small, forced smile. "Why are you talking to me about this? Presumably Mr. Rodriguez is as welcome at Club Fred's as anyone else."

"Not really."

"There's no reason anyone would know who he was."

"He's asking permission. Ed doesn't think he'll go unless we—unless I say it's all right."

"And you're asking us? Keith will say yes. Josh will go along with whatever Keith says."

I spread my hands. "Should I not have come here? If you don't want to see the guy, I'll tell him no, Cam. I'm more invested in your comfort than I am in providing him an outlet for his grief. If that's what it is."

He shook his head. "I feel bad for Mr. Rodriguez. And his family. The young man I saw here that night was not anyone I can imagine wanting to be related to." He stretched his legs and recrossed them. "Tell him yes. After you talk to Josh and Keith. But I'm not sure I can speak to him. I still—" Face turned to the windows, he swallowed. "I still have a hard time walking down the street at night when I'm by myself. I still think he might be right around the next corner. Or around the last one, coming up behind me." His fingers were curled into the upholstery of the couch like claws.

I didn't know what to say to that. "I'm sorry, Cam."

"I'm assured the nightmares and flashbacks ease off as time passes." That smile again, which made my guts clench. "I'm not entirely sure why Mr. Rodriguez wants to go to the wake, but I'm not entirely sure why it's so important to Keith that I go to it, either, and my lack of understanding isn't stopping me. I'm okay with it, Zane."

"Okay. Thanks, I guess. Though I—I'm still not totally convinced it's a good idea."

"There will be very few people there who get out of it everything you want them to, but Mr. Rodriguez might be one of them. If your idea is closure, or understanding, or a sense of what actually happened. Anyway. Do you want lunch? I can make something if you want to wait for Keith and Josh to get here."

"Is that all right? Would you rather I left?"

"No. Not at all. I'd much prefer it if you stayed."

I thought he was telling the truth, so I agreed. "When are you doing another film festival? That was fun."

"I'm planning on six Saturdays of Spencer Tracy in April and May."

We talked about Spencer Tracy, who'd apparently died days after shooting wrapped on *Guess Who's Coming to Dinner*. Cam was planning to show it last, but confessed he thought he'd probably cry when introducing it. We were still standing at the counter eating cheese sandwiches when Josh and Keith arrived, letting themselves in.

Keith made a beeline to Cameron and demanded to know what was going on. Since Cam hadn't had his phone out, it must have been some nuance of his expression Keith had keyed into. At least it saved me from bringing it up again. Cam explained about Mr. Rodriguez, and that he'd already given his permission.

His prediction was almost perfect: Keith immediately agreed. Josh studied Cam for a long moment before saying it was fine with him too.

I texted Ed when I got home to let him know. Then I returned to planning with my graph paper map of Fred's and construction paper tables. She'd given me leave to rearrange as long as I put everything back the way I'd found it. I was already scheduled to go in early the morning of the wake to clean, and I was angling for Tom to get me in at least once before then. One morning of cleaning wasn't going to do it for a place that hadn't seen a duster in a decade (at least).

I'd ovulate before the end of the week. If all went well, I'd inseminate at least once.

A week from this moment I could be pregnant.

I turned my mind away from the thought and back to the right placement of our table of remembrance. Which reminded me: I had to track down pictures. I added it to my list, trying to work out who I needed to talk to. I had pictures of Honey and Philpott and Felipe. Almost everyone had pictures of Mistah Olmes. I knew a few people who'd been close to Stephanie Hawkins. I wasn't sure how to track down a picture of Steven Costello, whom I'd bought a drink for on the night he died.

Abruptly, it was all too much. I reheated a cup of yesterday's decaf and curled up in my bed with a book. Screw my list, anyway.

I charted my cervical mucus, my basal body temp, and my cervical position. I'd used ovulation test strips for a while, but really, it all came down to this: I knew I was ovulating when my cervix was plump and hungry.

When I woke up Thursday morning, my cervix was spongy and open. My cervical mucus was all kinds of stretchy egg white consistency. I was ready. All systems *go*.

I texted Carlos, as per instructions. I'd dropped off sanitized baby food jars to them last week and he'd told me that he'd take care of Tom's end of things. I decided I didn't want to know what that meant.

He texted back, *Come over at ten and I'll have it ready for you. We take check and money order, sorry, no COD.*

I texted back that he was messed up and I wasn't giving him a cent.

Ten. Okay. I texted Steph that I'd be in at eleven because I needed to get jizzed up before work. She texted back a pile of poop.

If you don't have that kind of relationship with your boss, you're missing out.

It'd been months since I'd done my own insemination, so I got my needleless syringe out, and my hand wipes, and a vibrator, because I was old school and superstitiously thought an orgasm (which I couldn't do in Jane's office) might help my chance of conceiving. The internet informed me in no uncertain terms that it both did, absolutely, look at this study, and that it did not, even a little, look at *this* study.

Hell, it was an orgasm. I didn't need a study to tell me it was a good thing. Not that it had helped with the self-insems I'd done in the past, but even so, you couldn't go wrong with an orgasm.

I took a shower, got dressed, and drove to Carlos and Tom's place. I knocked and got a text in reply.

One moment, please.

Um. Okay. Sure. I stayed outside. Like, even if the door was unlocked, it was a small place, and did I really want to be on the other side of their bedroom door when they were . . . you know. Whatever they were doing. Right now. That was going to take them a moment and end with a baby food jar full of sperm.

Ew. I didn't even want to think about that.

I lingered outside, pretending to do things on my phone when really I was visualizing the whole process. I'd unscrew the jar, dip in the needleless syringe, pull up his spunk. Sure. No problem. I kind of vaguely remembered what spunk that hadn't been frozen in a million tiny batches looked like. I'd seen it before. It wasn't scary. Sure.

I forced myself past the spunk part.

I'd been feeling my cervix every day for two years; I could find it easily. I'd guide the syringe in, depress the plunger slowly, lie back. Get myself off because why not.

Right. Then I'd . . . clean up the stuff and go to work. Sure. Everything was cool.

Carlos opened the door, wearing a housecoat of some ancient vintage that he'd clearly hemmed everywhere to fit him. He handed me a jar.

"Oh my god, it's still warm."

He rolled his eyes. "Fresh from the source, as requested. When should we expect you to next come calling?"

"Um." I tucked the baby food jar carefully into my armpit to keep it at body temp. "Can we do late afternoon?"

"Four is the latest. Then he needs to go in to work."

"I'll see you at four."

Carlos's eyes glittered with mischief. "My poor husband. You owe him a drink, Zane."

"I owe him a lot more than a drink." I kissed his cheek. "Give him my love. I assume he's—"

"Tied up, at the moment."

"Ugh, TMI." I hesitated. "I— Just— I—"

He waved. "Go shoot up, you dirty dyke. *Tsk-tsk.* They should take your membership card for this. And your toaster oven."

"And on that note, I'm gonna go fill myself with your hubby's sperm. See ya."

"That has a seriously wrong ring to it, thanks a lot."

"Oh, I know."

I took my semen and drove home.

Inseminations loomed large in my head, but in actual fact they were the work of three minutes, if you knew what you were doing. But the *quantity* of fresh instead of frozen was miraculous. It felt like a ten-for-one deal. Judging by how many actual sperm there must be in a sample of this size, it was almost impossible to believe I wouldn't get pregnant from it. My vials from the cryobank were 0.5 ml. There was like . . . so much more in this baby food jar. So. Much. More.

I didn't remember there being this much, but I didn't have a lot of firsthand experience, if you will. Mostly it had been inside a condom or . . . something. It was all sort of foggy. I hadn't minded the actual sex part of having sex with men. It was the whole total lack of deep emotional resonance that convinced me I was most definitely gay.

Then it was done. Fini. Baby jar: empty. Orgasm: accomplished. I put my clothes on, and just like I'd pictured it, went to work and tried not to think about maybe being in the act of conception every aching second.

It was impossible.

Four o'clock rolled around fast. I was on my way back to Carlos's when my phone rang through the Bluetooth in my car.

Mildred flashed on the screen. I hit Answer. "Hey."

"You in your car?"

"Yep. Going to pick up semen."

Her laughter was a surprised burst. "Damn, Z."

"What? I tell the truth. What's up?"

"Nothing that interesting. You want to come over here after? I mean, I don't know if you have some sort of hippie lesbian skyclad fertility dance to do or something—"

"Okay, first of all, when we dance *skyclad*, we do it at night, so get that straight."

She laughed. God, I loved making her laugh.

"Second of all, just because I drive a hybrid doesn't make me a hippie. And third, sure, but I gotta shoot up. You want me to do that first?" I'd actually planned to park in the hills and inseminate overlooking the Bay, but I'd give that up for Dred's bed.

Whoa. Inseminating in Dred's bed. I suddenly felt . . . *aroused*. At the idea of lying in her bed, shooting Tom's sperm into my cervix. Which was weird.

"Hell yeah, come here. Can I watch? Is that creepy?"

My clit twitched. "Um. No. I mean yeah. If you want. It's not— It's kind of clinical."

"Z, for real, I bet it's hotter than the last time I had sex when I was pregnant. Like, I think she thought fisting was done with a punching motion."

"Okay, *ow*. Damn." I pulled up to the curb in front of Carlos's place. "I mean, sure, Dred. You want me to come over?"

"Hell yes. I'm gonna ask Obie to pick up James. I don't want to miss this."

"I'll, uh, be over in a few minutes."

"Yeah, see ya."

Right. This was totally normal. It was totally normal to inseminate in front of the woman I might be in love with while we definitely weren't dating. Or fake-dating. Or even pretending to fake-date.

I was dripping sweat when Carlos opened the door.

"Jesus! Did you jog here?"

"No. No, I—I think . . . um."

Tom emerged from the bedroom, dressed for work, and handed me my baby food jar before kissing me on the cheek. "Why do you look like you've just escaped a haunted house or something?"

"I do not!"

"You sort of do, yeah." He grinned. "If you want to stop by Fred's later, we can do this again. Did it go okay this morning?"

"Yeah, listen, do you have an enormous quantity of semen? Or is that the usual amount?"

He giggled. Truly. Six-four blond man. *Giggling*.

"It had been seventy-two hours, darlin'." Carlos handed me a bottle of water. "You should hydrate."

"Seventy-two— Oh my god. Did you torture Tom the whole three days? No, never mind, I don't want to—"

"He loves it." They kissed. "What's up with you?"

"Um. Dred just invited me over. To sort of . . . inseminate. In her bed. While she watches." I closed my eyes and waited for—

"*OH MY GOD*!"

I waited out their mingled laughter and interjections, trying to cradle the jar in between my arm and my body as fully as possible.

Carlos finally recovered enough to speak. "I can't even believe the two of you! Well, we don't want to keep you. Go show Mildred how it's done, honey."

"Shut your jerk face."

"You love my jerk face."

"Grudgingly. And only because you're grandfathered in from a time before I was choosy with my friends."

Tom laughed again. "Should you be so judgey right now? Shouldn't you be all open and accepting and welcoming or some metaphysical thing to prepare you for baby-making?"

I hit both of them at the same time and almost lost my precious jizz jar. "Damn it!"

"You're a danger to yourself and others." Carlos shoved me toward the door. "Go put on a show."

"Shut your—"

"Jerk face, I know." He shooed me away. "Go on now."

"I'm, uh, yeah. I'm gonna go do this now."

"Only you, Zane. The only person this could possibly happen to is you."

"It's not my fault!"

"Uh-huh. Bye!"

I waved and went back to my car.

And took a deep breath.

And drove to the farmhouse.

"I am so excited right now."

That's how Dred greeted me. At the door. Eyes alight.

"Um."

That's how I responded. Baby food jar of semen still squeezed tightly in my armpit.

"Come on." She grabbed my arm and pulled me in the direction of the stairs. "We'll be back, Emerson! Just gotta fill Zane up with sperm, you know how it goes!"

Something clattered in the kitchen. Then Emerson's voice: "Am I the only one who thinks this is a bit fucking weird right now?"

She laughed, dragging me into her bedroom. "Okay, so, how does this work? Tell me everything."

There was something irresistibly girlish about her anticipation, as if this were some new hairstyle I could demonstrate, or I'd bought boots she wanted to try on.

Innocent. Happy. Not all that much like Dred, really, except that she was lying on her side on her bed, just like she had the night I'd spent there, surveying me, waiting for me to do something grand. Like conceive a kid.

I put a towel down on the bed between us. I tumbled the syringe (in its sterile envelope; single use only), the wipes, and after a momentary hesitation, my little lipstick vibe, which I'd brought imagining I'd use it in my car.

Do other people not masturbate in their car after shooting a platonic friend's semen into their vag? Seems reasonable to me.

"Mmm." She grinned, a bit wickedly. "Z. You are so hot right now."

"Hey, don't say stuff like that when we're not—you know."

"The reason we're not is you."

"No, it isn't."

"Yes, it is. We'd be dating if you could decide what the hell you wanted out of life." Her hand made circles in the air. "Don't be shy. Show me how you do it."

I wasn't feeling shy. Dred, body all soft curves, lying there, watching me. Shy wasn't the problem.

"You're kind of a tease."

"Am not."

"Your very being here is a tease."

The smile deepened. "Am I turning you on, Z?"

"Oh, shut up."

To prove I wasn't turned on, or shy, I took my slacks and undies off. *Take that, smartass.*

Of course, then I was standing there. With no pants.

"Anyway, I gotta do this kind of fast." Brusque and businesslike, that was the ticket. I pulled the jar out of my pit and handed it to her. "Keep that warm."

"Okay." She stuck it in her shirt.

"Is it— Did you just put my semen between your breasts?"

Both of us giggled.

"Right, so, maybe I should rephrase."

"Yeah, baby, I got your semen right here. Hubba-hubba."

"Alternative insemination really brings out the goofy in you, doesn't it?"

"I didn't know until today, but I think it does. It's so . . . I don't know, it actually seems way more magical because it's nothing like the usual. Like it's so odd, that I guess I find it kind of charming. Plus, you won't end up saddled with a Brian, so there's that."

"True. No other parent here." Right. I could do this. I could totally do this. We'd had sex one time. I could totally spread my legs and feel around for my cervix on her bed. "So, uh, this gets—yeah. Well. Anyway. I'm going to do this now."

"Finally. Should I open your spunk jar?"

"Jizz jar, thank you very much."

"Jizz jar! Please tell me I can bring it down after and ask Emerson if he'll throw it in the dishwasher?"

"That's, uh— Yeah, okay, now that you said it we sort of have to." I climbed on the bed and pretended I was alone. Spread legs, achieve angle. I used my left hand on my cervix so my right could control the syringe. Easy as pie. "Will you unscrew my jizz jar, please?"

She giggled again.

I tilted the syringe to suck up as much as I could get (slightly less this time, I thought), then, hello awkward part, I inserted it into my vag and used my fingers to direct it to the right place.

"Holy. Shit. This is *amazing.*" Dred actually got closer, *closer*, like that wasn't weird.

"So now. Yeah. Here we go." I slowly, very slowly, depressed the plunger. I'd worried about drippage, but there hadn't been too much earlier. Slow and steady.

And done. I slooowly pulled the syringe out. Obviously there was a lot more than I was used to dealing with, but still. Waste not, want not.

I dropped the syringe in the jar, briefly considered and rejected the idea of trying for the dregs left on the sides, and finally relaxed back on the bed.

A wipe hovered in front of my face. I took it and mopped my hands. "Thanks."

"You still got one step left, if I'm reading this situation right."

"Nah. There's not enough evidence that orgasms actually help conception for me to go out of my way. I just wanted to make sure I could if I wanted to." I tilted my pelvis a little, encouraging all the swimmers to get in where they'd count. "This is when I always think of that sequence in *Look Who's Talking*. Remember? Kirstie Alley?"

"You saying Tom's sperm is getting around right now?"

"Hopefully they're going straight for their goal."

"So. Z."

I opened my eyes and looked at her. "Huh?"

"Not for nothing, but I could help you with the orgasm. Just in case it actually does aid conception."

"Uh, but . . . I thought we weren't having sex." Oh, brilliant, Zane. Was now really the time I wanted to be asking her to clarify stuff?

Then again, maybe it was.

"It wouldn't be sex so much as, you know, assisted-assisted reproduction. I'd be your assistance assistant."

I narrowed my eyes at her. "Is this turning you on? Oh my god, Dred, are you hot for making a baby in your bed right now?"

"Hey, this bed already made one baby. Why not go for two?" She picked up my vibe. "But you should come fast, so we don't leave Emerson hanging too long."

"I don't— Are you sure—"

The lipstick vibe wasn't my favorite—there was only so much one double-A battery could do—but in Dred's hands, with her manic grin backing it up, and considering that everything around me *smelled* like her—

I grabbed her hand and dragged it to my clit.

"Fuck yes." She shoved the towel and everything on it out of the way and moved in.

"I gotta stay on my back, you know, so gravity—"

"Shh, Z. Let me do a thing."

She did a thing, all right. She did me.

The second the vibrator touched my clit, I wanted to come, arching into it like it packed a much more serious punch than it did. With Dred driving, the vibe hummed and my body throbbed in answer, hips hungrily jerking up in search of more.

"Oh damn." She looked extremely satisfied with herself. "I can't believe you just had sex with a syringe full of semen."

I groaned. "*Not* sexy."

She laughed and claimed my leg in between hers. I spread myself open wider so I could shove up a little higher, but she wasn't having it.

"Naughty girl." The vibrator shifted away, making me pant in frustration. "Do you want to come, Z?"

"Come on! This orgasm is for fucking reproductive purposes!"

"Holy shit, we're having potentially procreative sex right now. Zane, we are fucking up the whole court case against gay marriage right here in my bed!"

I angled for the vibe and finally caught it right on the underside of my clit where I desperately needed it to stay. I locked on to her wrist so she couldn't pull away again. "Thought . . . you said . . . wasn't sex—"

"That was before I knew we were giving the anti-marriage bigots the finger. Now we're *totally* having sex. Hate sex with the radical right."

"Stop making me laugh!" I twisted and twitched, and for a second I thought it wasn't going to happen. Something about Dred made me confident and totally insecure all at the same time, like everyone thought I was queen of the world but I was really just a court jester. "Kiss me," I begged, desperate now. "Please, Dred. Please kiss me."

She didn't hesitate. She pinned me to the mattress with the vibrator to my clit and kissed me ruthlessly. I arched up everywhere we touched, and finally the vibrations did their job. Finally I could feel everything in me light up as a wave of pleasure crashed down, radiating from my clit all the way to my toes, to my ears.

I was shaking, still shaking, when she powered the vibe off. But she didn't move away.

"You're so beautiful." Her voice was a bit harsh, as if she'd been shouting. Or maybe as if she was trying to hide some other emotion beneath a layer of roughness.

I swallowed, blinking fast. "Thanks."

Jesus, her eyes, brown and deep, like I could see everything she'd ever seen just by looking into her eyes. Like I could show her everything of myself if only I dared to keep looking.

I bit my lip and fell back. "So thank you. For, um, assisting."

"You're welcome." She shifted until we were side by side. "Will you be okay? I mean, I guess it seems like it might be a little lonely after inseminating. You can stay for dinner."

"Yeah, thanks. I will. And not totally lonely, but yeah. There's a sense of . . . emptiness sometimes. It's too soon to feel anything, so I guess I feel a whole lot of nothing. But I think I'll stop by Club Fred's and pick up another donation, since I have the option. Maybe right around ten."

"If you want to come back here after, you can."

I turned my head, but she wasn't looking at me. "Uh. Okay."

"I mean if you want to spend the night. Sometimes it's nice not to be alone. That's all I'm saying."

Was she asking for me? Or for herself?

Fuck it, why did it matter?

"I'd like that." I thought about her arms around me.

"No kissing. That was for reproductive purposes only."

"Okay." I could deal with those terms. "So I guess we should go downstairs."

"Yeah. You think everything that's gonna swim up has already done it?"

"Pretty sure. We could wait another few minutes."

"Okay."

I wanted to take her hand. But I didn't.

The third insemination was a quickie at home, after which I didn't stay lying down for the usual fifteen minutes, because I had to pack an overnight bag and get back to the farmhouse.

Tom had handed the jar off to me with a cheeky smile, and Fredi had called over, "Wash your hands before you touch my bar!"

And weirdly, though it wasn't like we were advertising, a few of the usual suspects clearly knew what was going on. Jaq and Hannah kissed me and whispered, "Good luck." Alisha gave me a big hug and wished me good luck with my baking project, wink wink. Ed kissed my cheek.

It was a little like they were seeing me off on a great adventure. Not like I was just gonna go home, sperm up, and drive back to Dred's.

There was absolutely no kissing. But she held me all night long, and when I temped in the morning my temp had shot up, which meant ovulation had occurred.

Timing was spot-on. Everything else was up to the universe. Or fate. Or God. Or biology. I let Dred hold me longer than I should have, but at least in her arms I felt slightly less out of control.

Third Sunday of the month.

Andi and Jimmy's.

Not being a dope, I brought backup.

Andi took one look at Jaq and said, "Oh my god, Zane, what did you do?"

"Good to see you, too." Jaq pushed past her. "Jimmy! Feed me dead animals!"

Jimmy's laughter echoed from the kitchen at the back of the house.

Here I was. With Andi. Waiting.

Damn it. Jaq sucked at backup.

"Hey, big sis. You gonna let me in, or what?"

"Tell me you didn't. Tell me you didn't do such a stupid, irresponsible thing."

You'd think we had these overbearing, disapproving parents, but "hands off" was the only way to describe our folks. When I'd needed someone to agree to be Future Kid's family if I died, I'd gone to Jaq and her dad; when I told my parents I was planning to have a kid, they'd smiled and nodded and wished me good luck.

That was it.

But hey, who needed disapproving parents when they had Andi?

She glared at me. "Tell me you didn't have sex with Carlos's boyfriend because you're so desperate to have a baby that you lost your fucking mind."

I winced. Ouch. "You have no idea what you're talking about—"

"Because I'm not fucking *insane*. God, you're such a cliché right now. I can't even believe that you're *that* woman, after everything you've worked for."

Even though I'd braced for it, even though I'd known it was coming, I still felt my chest seize up. I opened my mouth, but I couldn't speak.

My backup returned, thank god. Jaq grabbed my arm and tugged me into the house. "Fuck, Andi, quit being a dick. One: they did not have sex. Two: Tom is Carlos's husband, not his boyfriend. Three: she didn't lose her mind, she thought it over, talked about it with her midwife, had a lot of conversations with Tom and Carlos, and made a decision. Just because it's not the one you would have made doesn't make it wrong."

Jimmy, loading the table with food, took a second to pour me a glass of wine.

I shook my head miserably. Wow, would wine be good right now. "Uh. No, thanks. I'm—"

"Got it." He put the glass in front of Andi's plate and reached for a sparkling water for me instead.

"Thanks, Jimmy."

"Sit, kid. Jaq, go get the potatoes."

"Aye-aye." She eyed me for a second, then apparently decided Andi couldn't do any more damage in the time it'd take her to go to the kitchen and come back.

"I can't believe you actually did this," my sister muttered. "I knew you were completely losing perspective, but this doesn't just affect you, Zane, it affects any kid you might have. Don't you get that?"

My hand drifted to my belly, where cells might or might not be dividing even now to the soundtrack of Andi's angry lecture. Tears dripped down my cheeks. I didn't even feel like I was crying. I was so tired of it all of a sudden. Tired of thinking about the whole thing, tired of talking about it. I didn't want to fight with my sister. I wanted . . . Hell. I wanted Dred. Even when we disagreed, she was never trying to convince me to change my mind.

Jaq slid into the chair next to mine. "Andi, back off."

"She doesn't understand—"

"Seriously, Zane's not a fuckin' idiot, and you're biased as hell. Hannah's a whole lot more familiar with case precedents for LGBT family law than you are, and we talked about the *actual* risks, as opposed to the psycho sister risks. Zane made a decision based on all the facts."

"A stupid, indefensible decision."

Jaq was about to go off, but Jimmy spoke first.

"Hey." He didn't raise his voice. Andi once told me that the thing she found most attractive about him was the way he lowered his voice when he was serious. He never got louder. It was probably how they'd managed to stay together so long.

Andi turned on him like she was about ready to strike out at whoever the hell pissed her off.

"That's our potential niece or nephew you're talking about." He spooned potatoes on our plates as if nothing was up. "It's not a risk we would have taken, but Jaq's right. It's not our decision."

It was so unprecedented to see him contradict her outright that I was actually physically uncomfortable, resisting the urge to shift in my chair.

"I can't believe you're taking Zane's side. We talked about this!"

"We did. But it's not our decision, Andi. And it seems like it's already been made, so there's nothing to fight about." He glanced up at me.

"I'll test next Thursday." I'd never waited fourteen days, and the truth was that I'd almost certainly get my period before then, but it felt like the only power I had was restraining myself from testing on day nine, and ten, and eleven, and collecting those BFNs.

"Good luck, Zanie." He raised his glass.

Jaq immediately raised hers. "To family."

"Family," Jimmy echoed.

It was worse than if they'd said nothing. *To family.* But what if I never had one? What if it never worked? I forced myself to act normal and raised my bottle of water. "Thanks. To family."

Andi sighed. "Fine. But I want to go on the record that I think this is a fucking bad idea." Still, she *thunk*ed her wineglass against my bottle. "Family."

We toasted, and drank, and everyone sat down, shuffling for the dishes they wanted.

"Anyway, if you need to sue him later—or countersue him when he sues you—we'll find the most coldhearted shark who exists to take your case."

Jaq snorted. "Man, the Jaffe family show their love in weird-ass ways."

Jimmy passed her the green beans. "I like that you say that as if you're not one of us. Oh, speaking of, I meant to call Richard. I'm starting to see vegetables in the garden section. Is it time for planting yet?"

"Yeah, you'll have to talk to him. He hasn't mentioned it to me, but I've been sort of, uh, distracted."

"Distracted how?" Andi asked.

I bypassed the green beans and started cutting my steak. Oh good. Now they'd get off my case. "She practically lives at Hannah's. Her apartment's like a storage container with a bathroom at this point."

Jaq elbowed me. "I came to your defense!"

"What? You don't want them to know you're cohabitating with your girlfriend?"

"We aren't!"

Eyebrows raised all around the table.

"Okay, all y'all can shut up. We aren't. I have a place."

Jimmy cleared his throat and did his questioning-a-witness voice. "How many nights do you spend there a week, Ms. Cummings?"

Jaq blushed dark red. "Shove it up your ass, Jimmy."

"Keep your apartment," Andi advised. "Very reasonable, Jaq. That's a decision I can get behind."

"Aw. Damn. Now I *know* I'm doing something wrong. Uh, no offense, Andi."

Andi got offended (again), Jimmy laughed, and I enjoyed my steak.

I'd managed to pretty much keep it together for the rest of dinner, but Jaq knew something was up.

She grabbed my hand as we walked to our cars. "Why don't you come back to the condo with me? Hannah's working late. We could raid the fridge and watch crappy movies. Wait, that sounded wrong. You could come over even if Hannah wasn't working late."

I rolled my eyes. "Nice try. And no, thanks. I think I'll head home and take a bath. You know, it's kind of my 'dinner at Andi's' self-care ritual."

She gave me a long, beseeching look. "Come on. That was harsher than usual. You really want to be alone in your house right now?"

Alone. Forever. Might as well be clear that this is what we're talking about.

For a second I almost gave in, just to get that look off her face. Except being alone had always been the counterbalance I needed, the perfect antidote to how exhausting it could be to spend so much time with people. So why wasn't I craving it now, when everything else felt so damn dire?

I didn't want to be with Jaq. I wanted to be with Dred. But I couldn't be that selfish asshole who only came around when I needed something from her, especially if the thing I needed was cuddling and I couldn't offer any kind of commitment along with it. I cared about her way too much for that.

"I'll be fine," I told Jaq, probably not all that convincingly.

"I'll call you tomorrow."

"Okay."

She shook her head. "Are you *sure*?"

I shoved her. "Get going. I have a date with a candlelit bath."

"That could be nice . . ."

I walked away before she could keep trying to help me.

For a few minutes after I got home, I thought I'd misjudged my imminent breakdown. Maybe I was just fine, no freak-out to be had. I gave myself over to the soothing ritual of running a bath, dropping in the right amount of bubbles, lighting candles. I tugged my towel down off the shower door and heaped it in the chair beside the tub.

Wait. Was I allowed to take a bath? I hesitated, scanning through my brain for any mental notes stored under *pregnancy* and *baths*. I probably wasn't pregnant, but if I was, I didn't want to boil the tiny clump of cells.

I ran some cold water in and swirled it around. Just in case.

All the preoccupation had been good. I wasn't even that close to crying now, which was both a relief and left me feeling vaguely bereft.

Maybe I should have gone to Jaq's after all. Except probably if I'd done that, I'd be a weepy mess by now.

Slippers, bathrobe, sparkling water. I slid into the water like it was welcoming me home.

Except I liked a steaming-hot bath. And this wasn't. It wasn't tepid, or anything. Still warm. But not scalding.

And I probably wasn't pregnant. The chances were low. Very low. Even with three insems.

Which made me just a woman with an empty womb, sitting in a bath that wasn't nearly hot enough.

Sorrow hit with breathtaking force, and I pressed wet hands to my mouth like I was trying to hold it in. I couldn't. In seconds I was sobbing, rough, broken sounds, bouncing back to me from the walls.

It was never going to work. And yes, of course I could still have a family, I told everyone that, and I was serious about it. I looked forward to adopting. I had an agency picked out. But it wasn't the same thing as getting pregnant, and damn it, I wanted that. Desperately.

I felt entitled to it, and I tried so hard to fight that part of my brain, the part that told me this was something I deserved. Infertility was mostly random. I wasn't more deserving of a healthy pregnancy than anyone else, and I knew from years on the message boards that my need for it was the same as every other TTC woman's need for it. All-encompassing and endless, like it was the only thing that mattered in the world.

I wanted to bargain with God, except I didn't strictly believe in God, and I certainly didn't believe some deity was sitting on a throne somewhere waiting to see what I'd offer up in return for a successful pregnancy. I wanted to say, *What more can I do? How can I prove I'm worthy? Why won't you let me have this?*

But my life was full of blessings already. I had a family. Jaq, Andi, Jimmy. Jaq's dad, my parents. Carlos and Tom. My friends. Club Fred's. The boys at QYP. All spaces where my family lived, where I could go to feel at home.

My mind drove effortlessly toward the next logical location, the most obvious and intuitive of them: the farmhouse. The kitchen, warm with cooking, filled with voices. Emerson, Obie, James. Dred.

The garden, the stairs, her bedroom, all golden light and her arms around me.

But I'd screwed up whatever chance I'd had of being part of that.

I leaned my head down on the rim of the tub in my empty condo and cried myself hoarse in a cold bath. Then I dragged myself to bed. Alone.

CHAPTER 26

It'd taken me thirteen cycles, but I'd finally figured out how to make the two-week wait survivable.

A big damn distraction.

I'd taken over two of the drop-in center's tables for wake prep, and most of that space was covered in pictures. I hadn't intended to make a scrapbook, but when I started asking people if they had photographs of the people we'd lost, I got a lot more than I'd expected. A lot were snapshots, and a lot were printed from home computers. Most were from the last five years, but some went way further back than that.

These weren't just the people who'd died because of Joey Rodriguez. These were all of our people, down the years. A few of them were of the NAMES Project Quilt panels instead of faces. A lot of them were pictures of couples or groups of people with their arms around each other.

And I had no earthly idea what to do with them, so I'd called in reinforcements.

Alisha and Dred stood at the head of the combined table and took it all in.

"Is that Donald?" Alisha touched an old picture of two young men with their shirts off, squinting into the lens.

"You mean because he's Asian?" Dred squinted at it. "I think I only met Donald once, I can't tell."

Alisha laughed. "No, like I actually think it looks like him. Not only because the guy's Asian."

"Yeah. Who do you think the other guy is? And Z, how'd you get a picture from Donald?"

"Carlos did. Or Fredi. Fredi actually handed me a shoebox full of pictures. I marked all the backs with an orange dot so I can return them to her." I had a whole spreadsheet of the codes I'd used to keep track of any picture that needed to be returned.

"This is really intense," Alisha said after another pause. "It's not exactly what you wanted, though, Zane."

"No. But I think it might be better. I mean, these are . . . our people." I touched one of the NAMES pictures and held it out to Dred. "How do you make a quilt with a signature in it?"

"A hell of a lot of painstaking work. Damn."

"So." Alisha shook her head. "I don't know, you guys. What do we do with all this? How do we honor our dead without making it all into a creepy shrine?"

"Exactly." The door opened and a dark figure slipped into the room. I was immediately on guard until they looked around.

Merin.

"Hey," I called. "You are exactly the person I wanted to see. Get your butt over here."

He looked like hell. And he was definitely supposed to be in school right now. I almost offered to text Jaq, but decided I'd leave that to Josh and Keith.

"How am I 'exactly the person you wanted to see'? That makes no sense."

I waved my arm over the pictures. "We're trying to work out what to do with all these pictures for the wake."

"What's the point of the pictures?"

"Remembrance, I guess."

Dred picked up another one. "No. Not remembrance. The point is that we are them and they are us."

"I'm not these fucking people." Merin took a half step back.

"You really are."

"The fuck? You don't know me."

Dred looked at Merin, up and down. "Please. I *was* you, all pissed off and alienated and thinking no one could understand me. Except I didn't shit on people who tried to help me as much as you do, so I guess I was you, but *smarter*."

"Fuck you, bitch."

She smiled. "Truth hurts, little boy."

Merin's mouth snapped shut.

"Anyway." Dred waved a hand. "That's your point, Z. We're all one big happy fucking family, even if we've never met, even if we despise each other. Even if we kill each other. Right? Even if we kill each other, we're still part of this godforsaken community."

I rolled my eyes. "Alisha, remind me not to have Dred make any speeches, okay?"

"I kind of liked it. You're lucky Ed's not here, or he'd be asking you to let him record that."

Dred shrugged. "I don't care much one way or the other. I've been dismissed and insulted and told I'm not queer enough, or not white enough, or I got a kid now so obviously I was straight all along. Fuck all that. I make people uncomfortable because I don't fit in some neat little box with a predetermined label? Good. I can't escape these fuckers any more than they can escape me."

"Great." I pretended to write something down. "Our motto is 'We're all stuck with each other, so deal with it.'"

Merin took another step back. "I don't want to be stuck with any of you."

Alisha grinned. "Oh, we're not all bad. I'm super nice!" She widened the grin until it took on a crazy edge.

"You're fucking nuts."

I laughed. "Okay, be nice to Merin. Merin, have you met Alisha and Dred?"

"I don't want to meet anyone. Where the hell are Keith and Josh?"

"Office."

He spun and stalked across the room, shaking his head the whole way. I thought he was muttering something that sounded like "crazy bitches," but that might have been wishful thinking.

I looked at my helpers. "Torturing the next generation of queers is fun, isn't it?"

Alisha nodded. "Torturing people is fun in general. You should see the shit we pull on Ed's grad student housemates. They're so gullible."

"Straight boys?"

"And hipsters. It's adorable. They have hipster names like 'J.P.'"

Dred started gathering up the pictures. "Boards. It's gotta be boards. Picture frames if you want to get fancy about it. Albums would get messy, and be too concentrated. But big boards, maybe three or four, would be perfect. Put them on easels, or hang them on the walls. Let people look to their hearts' content."

I pictured it in the front of Club Fred's, spread out.

"You'll definitely want frames," Alisha added. "People will be touchy. I think I'd make copies of everything that wasn't printed, and then you can just laminate them. I mean some of these pictures—" She reached for one before Dred could snag it. "Remember Mason? I forgot all about him."

I glanced over. "Damn, I did too. Suicide, right? Poor kid."

"Yeah, like ten years ago. We graduated the same year. He was so sweet."

"Uh, Zane?" Dred was staring down at a printout. "You should look at this one."

"Who is it?"

"Well, *that's* definitely Philpott."

I took the paper. I didn't recognize the women in the foreground with Philpott, but there was a familiar face behind them . . . wait. "Is that—?"

"If it is, don't put that up. It's too fucked up. Cut him out or something."

"Cut who out?" Alisha came around to peer over my shoulder. "Who are we— Oh. God."

"That's him, isn't it?" I didn't quite touch the picture.

"Joey Rodriguez. I'd know him pretty much anywhere. Ed does *a lot* of research. But what're you gonna do with this?"

"You can't post it," Dred countered. "I mean, seriously, you can't."

"But this"—Alisha tapped one of the women in the foreground—"is Sally something. She died like three days before Christmas. You know that accident on the off-ramp? There were like six cars involved, but I think she's the only person who died. You can't not post her and her girlfriend. I mean, this is probably the last picture of them. They didn't get together that long ago. And we don't have that many pictures of Philpott, either."

All three of us stared at the picture.

"Hell," I mumbled. Joey was just over their shoulders. He'd be impossible to carve out without completely destroying the picture.

The door to the back room opened and Keith emerged. "Hey, what did you guys do to Merin? He's traumatized. You must have— Whoa, why's everyone sad? All the dead people? Which I guess would be fitting."

Er. Fuck. Keith was one of three people who should *definitely* not see this picture. Four, if I counted Joey's dad.

I started to bury it under the rest of the pictures, but Alisha grabbed it back. "Maybe we can cut him out. We should at least try. Keith, do you have scissors?"

"Yeah. But why are we dicing up people's memories?"

Dred pressed the picture to Alisha's chest. "So you don't have to see them. Joey Rodriguez is in that one."

He stopped. One hand smoothed down his tie. "Uh. I guess—I guess that's not totally unexpected. If it was taken at Club Fred's."

"Right. We don't really want him to join the wall of our beloved dead, so we're cutting him out." Dred didn't move, keeping the paper tucked against Alisha.

"That makes sense." Keith hesitated. "Can I see it?"

Dred glanced at me. I shrugged.

Keith took the paper and put it on the table. He bit his lip. "I don't— Oh. God. And he's—he's standing there behind Philpott. That's so fucking twisted. He, uh, he said he'd had to work really hard to get close to him. That he almost got away. Philpott did. He sounded so offended by that." His Adam's apple worked up and down. "Yeah, cut that out. I don't want Cam looking at it."

"Or Ed." Alisha brushed her thumb across Philpott's face. "He had kind of an intellectual crush on Togg. Before he knew Togg was Philpott."

"It's so hard to see him." But Keith couldn't seem to stop staring.

The door, which we'd mostly closed against the chill, grated open. Cameron shook his overcoat off and hung it on the coatrack I thought they'd only gotten for him. "I'm here and I brought snacks. Thought you could use—" He stopped talking. "Keith?"

Keith flipped the picture. "Don't look at this. It'll wig you out."

Cam deposited two cloth grocery bags one table over and approached slowly. "Why?"

"Because it's him. Joey. In this picture." He hesitated. "With Philpott. Not *with* him, with him. Just, like, in the same picture. But I'm going to cut him out, okay? So don't look."

"Cut him out?" Cam's face hardened. "You can't."

"What do you mean? I have to. It's— He can't . . ." Keith's words trailed off as Cam took the picture from his fingers.

He stared down at it. I caught Dred's eyes and bit my lip. She offered the smallest shrug.

"I could just cut him out," Keith tried again.

"No. You can't cut out everything unpleasant and pretend it isn't there. He was there. If you truly want to honor what happened, you have no choice but to leave him in the picture, along with everyone else." He put the picture back on the table. "Is Josh in back?"

"Yeah."

"I'll go say hello. Feel free to dig into the food." Long strides carried him to the office door. He knocked once before opening it.

"You all right?" I asked.

"If Cam's all right, I'm all right." But Keith still couldn't seem to look away from the picture. "It's so weird to see him like this, like he's anyone else. In my head he's a villain, but he wasn't, really. He was just a very scary, very messed-up man. Anyway, I don't really want to be staring at this all night, so what else can I help with? Is it time for poster board yet?"

I nodded. "I think Alisha's right about making color copies of the actual pictures. But everything that was printed out we can trim up and start mounting."

Keith set us up with huge pieces of thin poster board and glue sticks, and we got to work. He also made a few phone calls to find a copy center that would laminate such big pieces and mount them for us so they'd stay standing on easels.

Dred was the one who trimmed the sides of the picture with Joey Rodriguez in it and glued it to a board. I'd thought about placing it somewhere at the bottom, along an edge maybe, but Dred had found a place for it in the middle, with all the other pictures, and no particular resonance.

Maybe it was better that way, after all.

I skated out of work early on Friday to go back to the center, where our picture boards were complete and amazing. "These turned out so much better than I thought they would."

Josh nodded. "They're really something else. Keith and I spent probably two hours last night looking for people we knew."

I glanced up. "Oh yeah?"

"Yeah. And yeah, we saw it. He said he wanted to cut Joey out but Cam wouldn't let him. Which is interesting."

"He got . . . intense. About it." I wasn't sure what else to say.

"Yeah, that's Cam when he feels strongly about a thing. Hey, you staying for dinner? He's bringing over food when he's off."

"Do I ever turn down food? Sure, if you're asking. Is Merin here? I have a question for him."

"He's in back."

"No hurry. Assuming he's here for dinner, too."

"He better be."

I looked up from my printed list of things to do. "How's all that going? He looked pretty tired the other day."

"Yeah, he's spent the last few days at his friend Sammy's house. Actually, I'm not sure if they're friends or enemies. Or frenemies. But Merin stays there every now and then." He shrugged. "Jaq told him if he wants to graduate, he's gotta buckle down and pass the last of his required classes, so he's basically stopped going to everything else."

"Is that all right?"

"Jaq says it's not ideal, but he'll still have a diploma at the end of it."

I thought about spring semester, senior year. It had been almost impossible to be in class, and I'd had a safe place to live. Of course, I'd also had motivation to get decent grades because I planned to start at the community college the next year.

No time like the present to feel Josh out a little. "So Hannah had this idea. College, but for jobs, not classes. Has she talked to you about it?"

He raised his eyebrows and pulled out a chair. "No, but I'm all ears."

By the time Cam arrived with food, Josh had a notebook out and was brainstorming. I took a picture of his scribbles and sent it to

Hannah, who texted back, *A man after my own heart. Are you at the center? Can we bring dinner?*

I, of course, invited her to bring dessert.

Keith and Merin came out from the back, Jaq and Hannah arrived with additional food and dessert, and the seven of us made a raucous table in QYP, eating and tossing ideas around.

"I love this whole thing!" Keith topped off everyone's sodas while gesturing with his free hand. "It's awesome! Like, it's all the advantages of having a college campus, but without the requirement that you have to be in school."

Hannah smiled her thanks for the soda. "But the funding. It's not nothing, starting a program of this scope. We could build it on a technical-school model, only emphasizing real-life experience instead of courses."

"With dorms," Jaq added.

Josh waved at the table. "And a cafeteria? That was the hardest thing about moving out of the LVCC dorms: trying to get food."

"Definitely." Hannah raised her glass to him. "Hon, you and I have to compare notes."

"We really do. Then we have to get Keith to write up a business plan. He has a gift."

"I totally would. I could sell this idea." Keith nudged Merin. "What do you think?"

"You're all a bunch of dumbass do-gooders." He didn't look up from his food.

I sighed. "Merin has us pegged."

"Hey," Hannah said. "I'm a do-gooder *with money*. You should be nicer to my people."

Merin rolled his eyes. "Maybe not everyone wants all that college-type shit. You geniuses ever think of that?"

Jaq threw a napkin at his head. "Don't make me send you to the principal's office."

Cam cleared his throat. "By the same token, there are kids who go to college who may not need the classes. I didn't mind LVCC, but I didn't need it. My job was a foregone conclusion. I took a few years of film studies classes for fun, but none of that has materially improved my career."

"I hadn't even *thought* of that." Keith's eyes were wide and thrilled. "That's a whole other angle to exploit!"

Merin sighted down the table. "You really wouldn't have gone to college?"

"There wasn't any reason to. Other than my parents thought the social aspects would be good for me."

"Were they?" Jaq asked.

Cam started to shake his head, then shrugged. "I don't know. They might have been. I mostly remember feeling awkward a lot. The thing you're talking about would have the same social aspect, but in place of classes, apprenticeships or jobs, right? So that would have been the same for me. It would have been a much better use for my parents' money."

Josh nodded. "Yeah, that's another thing. Not everyone can afford college. So what kind of program would you have in place for financial aid?"

"Good point." Jaq poked Hannah's arm. "The FAFSA is out the window."

"But we wouldn't be trying to pay professors or administrators. It's more about room and board."

Merin snorted. "It's a halfway house for assholes who couldn't get into college."

He'd meant it derisively, but the rest of us looked at each other like . . . yeah. *Exactly.*

"Or for people who didn't see the point of college," Cameron added. "Or for people who want to go directly to work after high school but don't necessarily want to live with their parents."

"More structure," I said. "Right?"

Hannah swirled her soda and considered it. "More structure than living in an apartment on your own, less than living at home. Merin, serious question."

He looked up, wary as hell. "What?"

For a long moment she surveyed him, still playing with her soda. "Say this existed. If QYP had a second level with a dormitory and a cafeteria, and you could live here and continue working— Is that something you'd do?"

"QYP is something else. Are you talking about for everyone, or for—" His sweeping hand took in all of us.

"Queer people," Keith said.

"Well, whatever you say, though I don't really get off on jumping for joy, because: labels. And anyway, you still have a money problem. My parents wouldn't pay for college. They sure as hell wouldn't pay for me to live here."

Hannah shook her head. "I'm a rich do-gooder. I'll foot the bill. If it was only queer people, say eighteen to twenty-four, and I was paying for it, would you live here?"

He shrugged and went back to his food.

"So that's our first big decision," Josh said. "Are we talking about something that's open to everyone, or are we focused on queer kids?"

Keith nodded. "And if we are, it's a different focus. It's about getting kids off the streets, not providing them an alternative to college."

"But . . ." Jaq sat back. "Why can't it be both? If all those homeless kids are queer like you said when you opened this place, why can't we make it about both of those things? Just because everyone else writes off homeless queer kids as if there's no way they'd ever pursue higher education, doesn't mean we have to."

Cam glanced down the table. "Merin, where do you see yourself in ten years?"

"Dead. Maybe. Or working some shitty job and hating my life."

"That's the long game." Cam looked at Jaq, Hannah, me. Josh and Keith. "The long game is you want to give queer adolescents, whatever they call themselves, whatever their resources, a better shot than that. How you frame it might matter for fundraising, but what you're really talking about is that buffer period between turning eighteen and being completely and totally responsible for everything in your life. Which is what college does for people who go."

Josh offered a rueful smile. "Or what having parents willing and able to support you past college does."

"Right," Keith said. "But it can't be dependent on parental income like financial aid at college is. My folks paid for LVCC, but they wouldn't have ever touched something like this."

I nodded. "And right out of high school isn't the only time you can go to college. Like Emerson's students at the community center—they're all adults, but they're there because they're already at jobs and want to get their GED, or they want to do their résumé or something."

Keith blinked. "Emerson teaches at the community center? My stepmom got her GED through there last year. I wonder if he knows her. That would be really weird."

Jaq reached around Hannah to shove my arm. "*Queers of La Vista*, right?"

"Yeah, Keith's stepmom can be our token straight lady."

"Ha." Keith laughed. "Actually, she'd like that. For real, I'd pick Marianne over both of my actual parents. At least she has a sense of humor. But I guess you can't choose your family."

"Well." I pointedly looked around. "I think we *do* choose our family."

"Cheers to that." Keith raised his glass.

For the second time in a week, Jaq and I toasted family. She pushed back from her chair and leaned over to kiss my cheek with tears in her eyes.

"Stop being a baby," I whispered.

"I like our family," she whispered back.

I touched my belly and thought about the farmhouse. "Me too." I pulled out my phone and texted, *May I spend the night? No funny business.*

Cam was telling us about the Spencer Tracy film festival when she texted back.

Hope you're not expecting me to change my sheets for you.

It was the perfect response, somehow. Irreverent and standoffish and funny all in one. I sent *See you soon* back and enjoyed the rest of the meal.

I didn't temp the next morning. My actual temps during the two-week wait weren't relevant, though it was good to stay in the habit. But I lay in Mildred's bed thinking about reaching for my bag, getting out my thermometer, and I just didn't feel like it. I must've been tired if I hadn't put it out on the side table.

Well. Or distracted. No kissing, but I apparently spent my life underestimating how glorious it was to crawl into bed beside someone and know their arms would wrap around me.

For hours.

And in the middle of the night, when I'd turned toward her and hugged her close, she'd pulled my arm in tightly. She'd been asleep. It would have meant something different if she'd let me hold her when she was awake. But it meant *something* regardless.

Even the next morning, I could still feel the way her hand had grasped my wrist and dragged it in against her body.

I thought we'd wake up together and go downstairs, but I was up early and she didn't show signs of gaining consciousness any time soon, so I finally got up.

Emerson was in the kitchen. Obie ragged him about not sleeping in when he could, but I thought he probably liked having time to himself. Which I was now interrupting, like a very bad houseguest.

"Good morning." He eyed me over his coffee cup and leaned back against the counter as if he'd only been downstairs long enough to pour his coffee, not to get comfortable.

I got myself a cup and leaned next to him, brushing against his arm. "I think I'm in love with Dred."

"You don't say." His voice was so deadpan that I was forced to elbow him.

"It's not funny."

"No. Actually, no, I agree. There is fucking nothing funny about being in love. It's exhausting, and complicated, and requires constant discussion and vigilance. Seriously, I don't know why anyone *enjoys* this." He sipped. "Except for the part that I don't ever want to live without him. Though even that just makes me afraid he'll die, or get sick of me, or I'll screw it up. Pretty much every part of this is deplorable, so I don't blame you for being in denial."

I thumped my head against his shoulder. "Was that your idea of a motivational speech?"

"Pretty much. Run like hell, Zane. Because you can't go back once you tell her."

"Oh my god." He smelled good. Clean and warm. And a little like the farmhouse. Or maybe after living here for a while the farmhouse took on people's scents. If I stood in the middle of the kitchen, maybe I could smell all of them: the baby-skin scent of James, Obie's vigorous windblown aroma, and of course Dred, whom I could sense everywhere around me, as if she disturbed all the energy in the house. If I paid very close attention, I could follow the path all the way back to her.

I groaned. "I'm so fucked."

He awkwardly patted my arm. "Yeah. Well. If it's any consolation, I'm pretty sure—"

Sudden footsteps on the stairs cut off his words.

Dred eyed both of us suspiciously. "There better be enough coffee for me."

Emerson waved toward the machine. "Do we look reckless enough to drink all the coffee?"

"I don't know yet. You look something." She grabbed her usual mug and shoved me out of the way. Only not. More shoved against me. Until our sides were pressed together from knees to shoulders.

I tried to control my breathing so it wouldn't seem like I was, you know, hyperventilating. Or turned on. Or anything crazy like that.

"Weird you guys stopped talking the second I came down here."

Emerson grunted. "You kill all the good conversations, Mildred. I've always said that. Anyway, you think pancakes today?"

"Do you mean real pancakes? Or those fucking French things you made last time you said pancakes?"

"Crepes. I only called them pancakes once! It was a fucking mistake."

They bantered, but the only thing I really paid attention to was the way that Mildred turned around and pressed against my side again.

She really did smell good.

I hadn't seen Dred's quilt blocks in a while. There were five now, and she said there would eventually be twelve, which sounded overwhelming to me. We'd cleared off the kitchen table so she could spread them out again. She and Obie were studying the blocks and playing with their positions when Aunt Florence showed up.

"You decided to applique some of them," she mused, touring around the nonbench sides of the table.

"I'm not sure mixing will work—"

Aunt Florence shook her head. "You'll make it work. I can already see it."

Dred didn't say anything.

"I brought you another scrap."

James tugged on my hand until I let him have it. He contentedly piled his collection of frozen mango pieces into my palm, then took them out.

"That mango's cold," I told him.

He grinned wide and held his arms out to me.

Back in quilt land, Dred and Aunt Florence were facing off. I couldn't tell if Dred was mad or just shocked. She was definitely something.

"You saw Dad?"

"Of course I saw your father. I allow him to take me to lunch once a week, which I think is generous." Florence smiled, and man, I wouldn't cross Aunt Florence for anything. She might have spent over a decade doing the Lord's work, but she hadn't internalized Jesus like some people did, as if the Christian God was simply love personified. Aunt Florence had clearly read the *whole* Bible, and she didn't mind a touch of ruthless with her religion.

"But . . ." Dred frowned. "He gave you this? Auntie, this is his robe."

"Of course he didn't. And yes. It is. The same robe he's had since shortly before Christmas 1979. I remember because I'm the one who bought it for him."

Obie and I looked at each other. His eyes were wide. Mine were definitely communicating a world of *Whoa, what now?*

"You did not. Auntie, I don't even want to know why you bought Dad a bathrobe."

Florence made a disgusted sound in her throat. "Please, Mildred, do not enlighten me as to whatever reasons you think it might be so." She touched the heap of fabric on the table, not smiling, but looking fond all the same. "Your parents were never as slick as they thought they were. After the fourth time your father sneaked out of the house before he thought I was awake, I bought him a bathrobe and pointedly hung it in the bathroom."

"Wait—you were okay with them spending the night together before they were married?"

Aunt Florence's gaze took in me, playing with James on the floor, then drifted back to Dred. "Even back then I did have some appreciation for the practical over the ideal, Mildred."

"But . . . I can't believe you *forgave* them. After catching them all kinds of sinning."

This time Aunt Florence's gaze was heavy on my skin. I looked away, but I couldn't miss the weight of her words. "Oh, Jesus is the one who forgives; the least I can do is offer a second chance to the people I love. Lord knows I'm a worldly sinner, too." She patted the heap of fabric. "Now, not all of this will be useful, but it did occur to me that you will need a border, and that this might serve."

"A border," Dred repeated. She shook herself. "But, Auntie—I can't steal Daddy's bathrobe and put it into a quilt."

"My dear girl, *you* didn't steal anything. This is a gift. I gave it once to him, and now I'm giving it to you."

"Yes, but he doesn't *know*—"

Florence cupped Dred's cheek in her hand, pale, translucent skin with spiderweb veins against the deep brown of Dred's. "Some people have enormous trouble letting go of the past. Isn't it kind of us to help them with that? Now, I'll leave it to you and Obadiah to determine whether you have enough, and how it looks. If it doesn't work, of course, it doesn't work. It's certainly faded in places. You may not be able to find appropriately long stretches where the color is consistent."

Obie finally unfroze and reached out to spread the robe over the table. "I love cotton. This held up pretty well, Aunt Florence."

"It wasn't cheap."

His eyes found mine again, but neither of us commented on that one.

"I see what you mean. It's gone from black to gray in places. Inconsistently. But I don't think that necessarily makes it a bad choice for the border." He nudged Dred. "You were going to make the border dark anyway, weren't you?"

"Yeah." She placed three of her blocks over the top of the robe and folded in the edges. "If we find the right order, the fading will just look like part of the design. You think?"

"Yeah. Put the darkest blocks against the lightest parts of the border."

They kept talking, and shifting things, and searching for the best stretches of the robe. Aunt Florence took a step back, watching them.

Then, slowly, she turned to me. And smiled. "Why don't we take James for a walk, Zane? I keep meaning to ask—is that short for something?"

I gulped. "Uh. Suzanne. But no one calls me that unless they're mad at me."

"Then I'll be an exception to the rule. Come, let's get James in something a little warmer."

I looked over at the table, trying to communicate with my eyes that someone needed to save me and, like, right now, but Dred and Obie were bent over doing fabric things. And Emerson was upstairs.

No one was going to save me from taking a walk with Aunt Florence.

"Er. Yeah. Okay. C'mon, James."

And so Aunt Florence, James, and I took a walk around the neighborhood on a Saturday. For fun. James looked around in a state of perpetual fascination, Aunt Florence told stories about all the people who'd lived in the area back when she was a kid, and I didn't even have to pretend to be interested.

Every now and then I thought about her, and Dred's folks, in their early twenties, living in the farmhouse before it had a huge garden in the back, before the neighborhood looked more tired than alive. Florence, lying in bed, listening to Dred's dad sneak out and rolling her eyes at the pretense.

When we got back to the house, Dred was laughing at something Obie had said, and any trace of denial still lingering in my psyche disappeared.

I was stupidly, completely, entirely in love.

Aunt Florence took James from me and patted my shoulder. "We should take walks together more often, Suzanne."

Oh my *god*. (Sorry, Aunt Florence.)

CHAPTER 28

Usually I temped on the tenth day after inseminating.

That was a lie. Usually I swore I'd temp on day ten. But I really started on day nine. Once on day eight. But only once.

If you spend enough time in the TTC message boards, you hear a lot of stuff. Like there's always someone who tested pregnant on day eight, and there's always someone else who didn't test pregnant until day twenty-five. There are always people who just *know* when they've conceived. And there are always people who just *know* every damn month. I was usually in that camp.

I'd hoped that trying this new thing with fresh sperm would switch things up enough to spare me the constant obsession. So I'd made a rule: no testing until fourteen days after insemination. Since my luteal phase is almost never fourteen days long, the likelihood was high that I'd get my period before then and end up not testing at all.

There was a rule.

Rules are always so much easier to keep in the five minutes after you make them. After that it's all uphill.

The only way I managed to keep myself from testing was by spending the night at Dred's and not bringing any pregnancy tests with me. I'd never tested during the day. People did, but I was into the rules, and the rules stated that hormone levels would be most concentrated in the first pee of the day, so that's what I used. If I missed it, I missed it.

So I missed it. On purpose. By staying at the farmhouse instead of my place. It was all very logical and rational.

I was increasingly aware of every gradation in her breathing, every soft hair on her arm, every nuance in her expression when she unwrapped the silk scarf from her hair in the morning and looked at it in her mirror.

I tried to hide the fact that I was watching her, that I was hungry for the curves of her body, the tones and cadences of her voice. I loved the way she scooped James into her arms and cradled him against her hip. I loved the way she held the paring knife when she was prepping vegetables for dinner.

It wasn't as easy as knowing I was in love with her and telling her, and living happily ever after. There were too many good arguments against telling her. Starting with: I didn't want to hurt her again. Ending with: I really, really didn't want to hurt her again.

Or maybe I was afraid of what it would mean, to tell her she had this power over me. That I was sometimes transfixed by the way her hands ran over her sewing machine. Dred had inherited a lot from Aunt Florence; she could be equally ruthless. Did I really want to open myself up to that?

Whatever it was, for the moment I was happy to spend all night cuddling in her bed, and all day more or less pretending we were just close friends.

I didn't test on day ten. I barely breathed all day, waiting to get my period. I didn't.

I didn't test on day eleven. I pressed my eyes to Dred's arm and took deep breaths until the very real desire to drive all the way to my apartment to pee passed. She brushed her fingers through my hair and didn't speak.

I didn't get my period.

Twelve days after inseminating, I woke up convinced I was bleeding. I carried the specific, heavy sense of dread to the bathroom.

I didn't give a shit about wasting the opportunity to test because I knew, absolutely, that I was about to get my period and it was over.

I wasn't bleeding. Every time I went to the bathroom all day, I knew this was the moment, this was the end of the cycle, the beginning of the next one.

It wasn't.

The thirteenth day was a Wednesday. Steph told me if I went to the bathroom any more frequently she was going to call for an emergency visit to my midwife because I sure as hell had a urinary tract infection.

I tried to only go once an hour after that. And I still didn't get my period.

We were in the final preparations stage of the wake. I collected Keith, Alisha, and Ed from QYP, and we went over to Club Fred's for an early sweep at cleaning before business picked up, which was Fredi's only concession to my pleas to let us clean.

I hadn't meant to say anything, maybe because it was bad luck or maybe because my friends were probably sick of hearing about how I might or might not be pregnant—again.

But I couldn't help it. And Tom asked, with bright eyes, what day it was.

"Thirteen. Um."

He blinked. I'd told them I wasn't testing soon, but that I usually got my period eleven or twelve days out.

"It doesn't mean anything," I said quickly.

Alisha, suddenly at my side, clapped her hands.

"*No,*" I snapped. "Stop it. We're not clapping. We're not doing anything. Except cleaning."

Tom surrendered the three small buckets of soapy water and rags that he'd made for us. "Okay. Yeah. Okay, so, anyway, Fredi said if you break anything, she's going to ban you for life. But don't worry, I have veto power."

"Good to know."

By the time I turned around Alisha had, of course, spread my not-news to Ed and Keith. The three of them deliberately avoided looking at me for about a minute.

Then:

"So how does it work?" Keith asked. "I mean, like, theoretically. Never having had a uterus, or eggs, or whatever."

Ed shrugged. "I actually do have all those things and I still don't get it. Like . . . when do you find out?"

Tomorrow morning. Twelve hours from now. Unless I get up really early.

"I'll test tomorrow."

"And it'll say you're pregnant or you aren't?"

"It will measure the concentration of human growth hormone in my pee. If there isn't anything, it'll come back negative, which doesn't mean I'm not pregnant, necessarily, it only means there isn't enough hormone to test positive."

"Well, what if there is enough? What does that mean?"

I couldn't think about it. Thirteen cycles. I'd never had that moment.

Alisha shoved both the boys. "Get to work, slackers. Let's try to be done before Fredi comes in and wants to babysit us touching all her precious things."

They turned away and I mouthed, *Thank you*. She kissed my cheek and handed me a bucket.

That night I was jittery and restless, unable to relax.

"Z." Dred's voice was thick with sleep. "Don't think I won't kick your ass out. There's a couch in the workroom."

"Sorry. I'm sorry."

Instead of kicking me out, she pulled me until my head was on her chest. And oh god, proximity to Dred's breasts, yeah, that was a really good distraction.

She giggled. "Are you burrowing into my ample bosom right now?"

Dred giggling. With her breasts against my cheek. Oh god.

"Incorrigible, Z. No funny business."

I sighed. "But—but I need a distraction—"

She giggled again. "You are not using my boobs as a distraction."

"Awww."

Distraction aside, it was soothing, being pressed against her like that. Feeling her breaths. Feeling her arms around me.

"I just got scared," I whispered.

"Yeah."

"What if—" No. I couldn't say it. Jinx.

"Shh. No what-ifs."

"But I just got so, so scared."

One of her hands rubbed the back of my neck, and in that moment it was the most sensuous thing I'd ever felt. I breathed into it, pressed into it, tried to feel the warmth of her hand all the way down into my bones.

"A lot of this shit is scary." Her voice was low and not totally stable. "A lot of it's fucking terrifying."

"I've never been scared like this before. I mean, you know, I thought I'd been scared before, but this is— I don't know what this is."

"It's different when you realize what it means." The fingers at my neck tightened for a breath. "But it makes things easier. When I used to get scared I'd let it stop me. I'd let it paralyze me, if it was bad. When we first started the business I stopped eating. Even though we still had income, it didn't matter. Suddenly there was this outside thing that I'd decided to do, and I had to do it all the time. No day off." She huffed a laugh into my hair. "And that was *nothing* compared to parenting."

"You and Emerson should go into business listening to people's deepest fears and confirming that they're justified. It's the opposite of soothing."

Another soft laugh. "Yeah. Assholes get off on that sort of thing. Anyway, I guess I was saying that parenting is so much worse, but it's also so much more simple in a different way. I have to just . . . do it. Whatever it is. Get out of bed. Occasionally shower. Go take pictures of another stupid winter wedding, where everyone's in big coats because it's freezing-ass cold. No matter how scared I am, I make sure James eats. No matter how scared I am, I pick him up when he's crying. I'm still terrified, but he focuses me."

I pressed my face to her, not teasing this time. Crying a little. I wanted that so much, and I was so damn petrified of it.

"It's okay. I know it's fucking scary, but no matter what happens in the morning, it's okay, Z."

I fell asleep in her arms.

This was it.

Me and the stick. Again. In a showdown.

"You and me, buddy," I told the inanimate stick that I'd peed on and put aside.

The stick, being inanimate, didn't reply.

Dred wasn't awake yet. No one was awake yet. It was light out, but barely. Shortly after 5 a.m.

I tried to breathe. I tried to read. I checked my email, realized I didn't care about any of it, and closed the app.

I looked at my list of things to do for the wake. Two more days. So much to do.

None of it mattered. The only thing I cared about right now was the fucking test. I stood and straightened the towels on the rack. I squared off the soap in the dish.

The fucking test wasn't responding. Did that mean it was negative? No. It had only been a minute.

I started rearranging the shampoo and conditioner and body wash bottles in the shower. Good plan. That had to take, what, like another minute? Easy. Each shelf belonged to someone. I'd just put the bottles in order. Shampoo, conditioner, body wash. Who didn't have conditioner? Emerson, probably.

My hand slipped and the entire rack somehow disengaged from the showerhead and crashed to the floor of the shower.

"Oh *shit*."

I held my breath, but the noise had been loud and the upstairs wasn't that big.

James's confused sputters got me moving.

"Hey, hey, hey," I whispered, stepping into his room. "Hey, baby, hey, it's okay. James, it's okay, it was just me, freaking out in the bathroom. No biggie. Don't cry, James, come on—"

His face screwed up, and he waved his arms and legs around. I knew that face. I knew what was coming.

"No— James—"

But it was too late. He hollered his rage at being woken up before he was ready. People all over La Vista were probably wondering who was killing the kid.

I grabbed him out of his crib, trying desperately to soothe him back to sleep before the police were called.

A hand on my shoulder. Obie. Looking half-dead.

James all but dove into his arms and rage-cried at him in a garble of words and half-shouted expletives. Probably. That was what it sounded like, anyway.

I knew he was telling on me.

Obie shushed him authoritatively, and James's complaints wore down to a more conversational recitation of my flaws. Obie offered me a tired smile and bounced James in his arms.

Dred's presence, in the doorway. "You trying to wake the house?"

I winced. "Sorry. I'm sorry. I got antsy and started organizing the bathroom and then sort of lost control of the shower caddy and . . . um. . ."

There was a slight twitch at the corners of her lips.

"Do not laugh at me!"

"I'm not, Z. Even though the thought of you at five in the morning reorganizing the shower is pretty funny."

"Shut up. I was anxious!"

Emerson's voice cut through Dred's laughter. "Um, guys?"

Obie shot an irritated glance toward the hallway. "Dude, everyone be quiet, he's almost back to sleep."

I sighed and followed Dred out the door. To where Emerson was standing, face pale, one hand braced on the wall outside the bathroom.

"Have you— Did you look at your thing? I'm not fucking touching it, because I'm pretty sure it's got pee on it, but—" He shook his head.

I scrambled into the bathroom and grabbed the stick, the fancy kind, with the digital display, not the lines. I'd decided I'd earned the fancy test by waiting this long.

"Well?" Dred pinched Emerson. "What'd it say?"

He shook his head, an insignificant motion in the top of my vision.

"Z?"

I held it out to her, willing her to see what I saw, watching her face. Maybe I was making it up. Maybe it was a trick of the light.

Except Emerson, behind her, was staring at me with the same stunned expression I could feel on my own face.

"Well, shit. You're fucking pregnant." And Dred smiled. The light from the bathroom reflected off her teeth. The scarf she wore to bed was coming untucked on one side, exposing her hair. "Congratulations, Z."

I closed my eyes. I couldn't be. I couldn't possibly be. Except even with my eyes closed I could picture the test, which had exactly one word on it: *Pregnant*.

She touched me, hands on my shoulders. "Z. You did it." Then she kissed me, and it was everything, it was all the yearning, all the hope and faith and joy I had carefully stoked for thirteen cycles.

I kissed her back, desperately holding her close, feeling every millimeter of her lips on mine, the light brush of her breath on my skin. "Oh my god," I whispered.

She laughed. "Yeah. Pretty much." She grabbed my hand and started tugging. "Emerson, you guys get James if he wakes up, okay?"

"I look like a fuckin' babysitter to you?"

"Yep."

He shook his head. "Hey, Zane."

"Hey, what?"

"You're gonna be a kick-ass mom. Even if you do pick really weird times to clean."

I swallowed. "Thanks."

Then Dred pulled me to the bedroom and I didn't really have time for a more elaborate response.

Dred's idea of celebrating my apparent fertility was to go down on me, endlessly, until I was begging in whispers for her to let me come. My entire body was a trembling nerve ending, keening at some frequency humans couldn't hear, all the relief and fear and excitement jacked up by Dred's lips and tongue and fingers until I had no thoughts, no awareness outside of my body.

I tried not to cry out—that would be a truly embarrassing way to wake up James *again*—but it was too much, and when the orgasm hit it wasn't pure pleasure. There was too much restraint behind it for it to be simple. It felt like all the months of waiting crashed down over me at the same time, a little bit painful, a little bit vicious, with a rough edge of uncontrolled hedonistic joy that crossed all my wires and wiped me out.

I couldn't stop twitching. My clit, my thighs, my fingers, the small muscles in my neck. I panted, trying to catch my breath, and she kissed me. "Yeah, I've been waiting to do that for way too long."

"I think you broke me," I mumbled.

"You needed it."

My entire body let out a breath. I swore I could feel myself deflate.

She kissed me again.

"Hey. Wait. We're kissing?" I tried to bring all of my brain cells together. "Are we kissing?"

"Now that I've fucked you into a stupor, it's time for us to talk, Z."

"Uh."

She smiled.

I squinted up at her. "Sometimes you look like Aunt Florence."

She stopped smiling.

I laughed.

"Don't bring up Aunt Florence right now!"

I would have zipped my lips if I'd had enough energy to move my arm. "Pretend I'm zipping my lips. I'll be good. Swear."

She brought her fingers to my lips. And zipped them.

Oh, *god*, come on, that was hot.

"You're gonna need a new list. Because you closed out the last one." She kissed my zipped lips and took a deep breath. "So the first thing on your new list is gonna be 'Marry Dred. In a small non-ceremony at the county clerk's, with no more than seventeen guests, and a very small reception, which will be catered by the San Marcos Grill, because we're classy like that.'"

I unzipped my lips, tried to think of something to say, and pulled out my phone.

"Z, seriously, what the—"

"Shh. I'm making a new list."

She shut up.

"But I'm not adding all the extra stuff. I have to be able to look at it and immediately know what's important." I saved my note and held it out to her. *Marry Dred*. "Good?"

A flicker of uncertainty crossed her face. "I thought you were going to argue it's too soon."

"Oh my god, did you just *pretend*-propose to me? Because no take-backs."

"No. And anyway, I heard what you said to Emerson the other day. I know you can't resist me. But I thought you'd at least try."

"You're a filthy eavesdropper!" I kissed her. "God, it's so good being able to kiss you. I'm going to kiss you all the time. Every day. All day long."

She groaned. "Come on—"

"No, you proposed. We're getting married." I paused. "Oh shit. Wait. We can't get married. Where will we live? You can't move out of the farmhouse. And I can't move in. There's no room. And there's, I mean, there might be—"

Her hand slid over my belly. "We have room. Obie's been working on Emerson to move downstairs for months. He's got a whole plan drawn up for the totally accessible bathroom he's gonna build, and how he'll section off the workroom and the bedroom. But you don't have to give up your place."

"I think if we're getting married, we're probably supposed to live together."

She smiled. "Z, we can do whatever the fuck we want."

"But . . . you really want to marry me?" I searched her face. "I mean seriously? It took me a stupidly long time just to realize I wanted to be with you."

"Yeah, that's kind of the point. You're a little slow, Z." She shifted up to kiss me, and stayed close. "Basically I can see into the future and

I know this is going to happen. You can take as long as you want to get used to it. But we're gonna raise kids in this house together, you and me. Can't you feel that's true?"

I closed my eyes against a wall of emotion.

"Can't you feel it, Zane?"

"Yeah. It feels really good." I swallowed three or four times. "The only time I'm not scared is when you're talking to me."

"I'm fuckin' magic like that."

I reached up to stroke her cheek. "I love you."

"I know."

We lay there awhile longer. We may or may not have been gazing adoringly into one another's eyes. At least until Emerson shouted, "Breakfast!" up the stairs, echoed almost immediately by James shouting something that sounded absolutely nothing like *breakfast*, but probably was meant to be.

I laughed. She kissed me. We got up and went down to breakfast.

CHAPTER 30

We set up the wake in the front of Club Fred's, farthest away from the dance floor. Despite Fredi's best attempts at stymying our cleaning crew (it would have taken two full days to *really* clean the bar), I swore it smelled better.

I confided this to Emerson as people started showing up, though most of them were just the regular Fred's crowd. He rolled his eyes. "Well. It does smell less like frat house the day after a kegger. I assume that was your goal?"

"Thanks for your support. Jerk."

He grinned.

"You know, when you smile like that you actually look your age. As opposed to ten years older than you are."

"I— You—" He couldn't seem to make his mouth form words.

"Chin up, champ." I patted his shoulder. "You smile more than you used to. The years are just melting away."

"You're older than I am!" He winced, as if hearing how weak the comeback was only after he'd said it. "Damn it."

I laughed and tapped Obie. "Your boyfriend needs your support."

He turned to Emerson, eyebrows raised.

"Zane called me old. Or no, she called me young. She said I'm young but I look old. God*damn it*."

"Babe. You look like you. No one's thinking about your age."

"So I *do* look old? Obie!"

I left them to it and took Obie's position propped against the wall next to Ed. Who was, as usual, scribbling in a notebook. "Tell me you're not working right now."

"I'm . . . not. Ish."

"Ed."

"I'm not! I, uh, wanted to get some notes down while I'm thinking about them."

"You were talking to Obie."

He relented, looking slightly abashed. "Okay, I might have been, uh, gathering quotes. But not *working*, I swear."

I kissed his cheek. "It's fine. Plus, I don't think anyone's actually here for the wake yet."

"You mean except for Jaq's dad?"

"Okay, yeah, that's funny. Between Jaq and Dad, I think Dred's probably seriously regretting demanding I marry her."

He laughed. "Yeah, I doubt that. I'm really happy for you guys."

"Thanks. Me too." I waved and started across the room. It still didn't feel real to me. It had been sixty hours since I'd made a new list on my phone, with only one item.

Were we really going to get married? Any doubt I had about the answer evaporated when I got close enough to hear the conversation currently going on between Dred and Jaq.

"We're not getting married in fucking March, so cram it."

"But you have to tie Zane down fast! She's flighty!"

"Not gonna happen."

"But you'll have the reception at Dad's house, right? Because he's always dreamed of—"

"Jaq, if you want to tie Zane down and have the reception at your dad's, then *you* marry her!"

Richard and Hannah, on the outskirts, cracked up. Jaq at least had the decency to blush. "Okay, gross."

Dred crossed her arms. Then she caught sight of me and the set lines in her face softened. "Inform your friend that she will not be planning our *simple service* at the county clerk's office. *Or* the reception."

"Jaq's a handful," I said. Hannah giggled. "Can you believe you had sex with her?"

"Oh my *god*!" Jaq put her hands over Richard's ears. "Mixed company!"

Dred sent me an unimpressed glare. "That was years ago."

"And I'm old enough to look out for myself, Jaqueline, thank you." Richard embraced me. "I like this one," he whispered.

"Me too." I kissed his cheek. "No offense, Dad, but we'll have whatever kind of reception we have at the farmhouse."

Jaq groaned.

He patted her arm. "I guess you'll have to make an honest woman out of Hannah."

Hannah laughed. "Oh, Richard. You know that'll never happen. Your girl's fickle."

"I am not *fickle*!" Jaq spun around, but Dred beat her to a response.

"This from the woman who was so afraid to introduce me to her best friend that she dumped me and pretended we'd never met. I think you might be fickle, Jaq."

"I'm happy you're fickle," I told her. "If you'd introduced Dred and me back then, we wouldn't be—uh—standing here now."

Dred smirked. "You can't say it. Ha."

"I so can."

"Then say it. *Without* looking at your list."

Damn. My hand was already on my phone. "We're getting married. There. I said it."

Dred raised a hand. "At the county clerk's, with no more than seventeen guests. *Not* in fucking March. If a reception's absolutely necessary, I guess we can have it at the house." She glanced around, nose wrinkled. "Better than here, anyway."

Jaq pointed at her. "Club Fred's is an institution!"

Dred laughed. "Babe, have a drink. You're embarrassing yourself."

"You did not just 'babe' me!" Jaq turned on Hannah, who was already shaking her head.

"I don't have an objection."

"But—" Suddenly she stopped talking long enough to hear the song coming over the sound system. And her eyes latched on me. "Oh my god, Zane—"

"Cher!"

We grabbed hands and started making for the dance floor.

"We'll be back!" I called.

After the whole crazy day—the whole crazy few weeks—dancing with Jaq to "Believe" was like a salve for everything that hadn't made sense. This moment was exactly what I needed.

She leaned in toward my ear at the end of the song. "Congratulations."

"You already said that!"

"Not about Dred." Her eyes darted down, then back up. "Congrats, kid. You earned it."

I pulled her in. "I'm not telling anyone, really. How'd you guess?"

"Because she said you had a new list. And I knew the only way you'd start a new list was if you finished the old one." She kissed me, eyes shining. "I'm so excited for you."

"I'm so excited for you. Auntie Jaq in the house!"

"Oh, you know that's right. You tell Carlos and Tom yet?"

I shook my head. "Tonight, if I get a chance." We started dancing our way back to the wake. "It's gonna be good, right? I keep getting these flashes of like abject terror."

"It's gonna be amazing. Marrying Dred, I don't know, but—"

I hit her.

"Okay, okay. I can kind of see the attraction there. If I squint."

"Jerk."

"Dork."

The picture boards were starting to gather small crowds. We skirted the edge and I smiled, catching little bits of conversations. "Oh, that's—" and "Remember that time when—" Exactly what we'd wanted them to do. Here and there someone was standing off to the side, fixated on a certain photo, not reminiscing as much as they were mourning, but even that was what we'd wanted.

A space for celebration, and also for grief.

She dragged me to the bar and pounded on the counter. "I'd like to buy a beer for the woman of the hour!"

"Um—" I caught Tom's eye. "No beer. Soda is fine." Everyone within earshot looked over, confused. I hadn't thought through this not-telling-people thing.

Jaq made a comical awkward face and tried to cover. "Right, yeah, my sister in soda solidarity! Two sodas, barkeep!" She lowered her voice. "Shit, sorry, forgot already."

Tom pushed two sodas across the bar and waved Jaq's money away. "How's . . . everything?"

"Good. Um." I couldn't look him in the eye and not tell him. "I'm off booze for the foreseeable future. FYI."

His face broke into the biggest grin I'd ever seen. "Got it."

Jaq shook her head. "Yeah, there's no such thing as a secret around here. There's just no way. *Queers of La Vista*, Zane. It's your soap opera. Anyway, where's your good-for-nothing husband, Tom?"

"He'll be here pretty soon."

"Send him over to the wake. I contributed a couple of pictures he's in."

"I hope you're wearing a cup."

She laughed. "I know. I thought about asking permission but decided this would be more fun."

We headed back to the knot of people with Richard in it. I glanced around, but Dred was talking to Josh and Keith at one of the photo boards.

"Well, kids, I think it's about time this old man went home." He kissed Hannah's cheek, then Jaq's, then mine. "I better be invited to your reception at the very least, missy."

I clasped a hand to my heart. "Dad! How can you say that? Of course you're invited."

"And your parents?"

"I haven't told them yet."

He sighed. Jaq muffled a laugh with her fist.

"What? They don't care. I mean, they *care*, but they won't care-care. You know what I mean!"

Richard gave me a hug. "I care-care, Zane. And I like her. A little rough around the edges, which makes her perfect for you."

I gave him a look. "I'm not entirely sure that was complimentary."

"No comment." Right as he was turning toward the door, it opened, letting in another old guy. Who looked way more fish-out-of-water than Richard. His eyes caught on the nearest photo board and he drifted to it, seeming a little lost.

I nudged Jaq. "You recognize that guy?"

She shook her head.

Ed wasn't anywhere I could see, which meant now I had the choice of approaching the guy—who might be Mr. Rodriguez—or letting him kind of... drift.

Richard touched my arm. "Let me talk to him." He walked over before I could answer, standing beside the other guy. I could just barely hear him say, "Do you have a friend in one of those pictures?"

I was desperate to hear the answer, if there was one, but I couldn't tell from behind them. I mean, the guy could be anyone. We'd promoted the party widely. Still, I had the weirdest conviction that he was Mr. Rodriguez.

I finally found Ed and gestured him over. "Hey, is that—"

"Joe. Yeah. Who's that with him?"

"Jaq's dad."

As we watched, Mr. Rodriguez turned to Richard and just sort of crumpled into him.

"Oh god," Ed breathed. "I should—"

"Let Dad handle it. It's okay." I caught Jaq's eye. "He knows from grief, Ed."

Ed visibly relaxed. "I just don't want anyone to—to say anything to him. I know he's— I know it's complicated, but he's so—"

"No one's going to say anything to him." I wouldn't let them.

Richard guided Mr. Rodriguez over to us, at least half holding him up. "Joe wanted to meet the organizer. Joe, this is Zane. Zane, Joe Rodriguez."

His eyes were bloodshot and damp, and he looked like he hadn't slept in days. I shook his hand. "Good to meet you, Mr. Rodriguez."

"Call me Joe. Please call me Joe." He nodded to Ed. "I hope you understand I mean no disrespect by coming here tonight. I guess I—I felt like I should—I wanted to apologize . . ." He trailed off. "I'm just so sorry."

"You don't owe us an apology. No one here expects that, Joe."

Richard's arm around his shoulders tightened. "Can I get you a drink?"

He huffed a watery laugh. "I'm sure neither one of us ever imagined buying a man a beer in a gay bar."

"Oh, I think of this place as the after-school hangout I wasn't invited to, but occasionally stop by anyway."

"Joey always kept this part of his life very detached from the part of his life he shared with us. We thought that was probably healthy, that eventually he'd meet someone, introduce us." His entire body seemed to shrink in on itself. "We never imagined— We could never have imagined—"

"Of course you didn't. Let me buy you a beer."

Joe nodded and permitted himself to be led away.

Club Fred's happened all around us, but for a long moment we just stood there: Jaq, Hannah, Ed, and I, watching Tom shake Richard's hand, listen for the introduction, then shake Joe's. How strange it must be for Tom, to serve the man whose son had been the reason he spent the weekend in jail months ago. But Tom pulled their beers and betrayed nothing else.

Ed broke the silence. "It's too bad Honey's not here. She'd really like this wake, Zane."

"Yeah. She liked any reason to get a bunch of people together, tell stories, and drink."

Judging that the old men at the bar were probably okay for the moment, we returned to the epicenter of the wake. We'd set out a table covered in pens, pencils, crayons, and note cards, inviting people to write whatever they wanted and stick them to a huge sheet of butcher paper on the wall, face out if they wanted others to read their card, or face in if it was private.

Ed grabbed a ballpoint pen. "Maybe I'll leave her a note." His voice was higher than usual. He cleared his throat.

"Me too," Jaq said. "She'd bitch my ass out if she knew I still haven't finished that blanket she helped me start."

Hannah kissed the side of her face. "I'm going to mingle, sugar."

"I'll see you around."

I wandered away. The pictures were drawing more and more people, including folks who just wanted to know what was going on, but got caught up in trying to find faces they recognized. I checked in with a few small groups, shaking hands, giving hugs, and eventually ended up where Josh and Keith were standing at a high table along the edge of the designated wake area.

"How're you guys doing?"

"We're good." Josh raised his chin in the direction of the bar. "That the father?"

"Mr. Rodriguez, yeah." I tried to see what they thought of that, but I couldn't get a damn thing out of their expressions. "You, uh, still good?"

"Cam's at the bar," Keith said.

I hadn't noticed him. He was two stools away from Richard, head down as usual.

"We can't decide if we should go sit with him or leave him alone. He might not want to talk."

Josh nodded. "More likely he's listening to everything they're saying."

"Did he want to avoid Mr. Rodriguez? I could—" Something. I didn't know what. I could do something, though. Probably. I couldn't really kick Mr. Rodriguez out. Maybe I could nudge Richard toward the door.

"Jesus." Keith gripped Josh's arm. "He's introducing himself."

This could go badly. I waved and made tracks across the room, approaching just in time to hear Richard say, "And this is Joe Rodriguez."

Cam reached his hand across to shake and settled on the closer stool. I hesitated before taking the one he'd vacated.

"Cameron Rheingold. Good to meet you both."

"Ah, so you're the Rheingold boy." Richard smiled. "I knew your parents, back when they went to St. Agnes, before you started school."

Cam nodded. "Nearly everyone knew my parents from somewhere."

Joe cleared his throat. "They used to give me a press pass discount, when I was younger and we couldn't really afford to go to the movies. I think they made that up just to cut me a break on the price, which at the time was three dollars. But for the three of us to go—" He broke off.

"I met your son. A few times." Cam's voice was perfectly even, but Joe's expression twisted as if he'd been stabbed.

"I recognized your name from the report. I'm so, so sorry. There are no—no words for how sorry I am that he—that you—"

Cam reached out for his hand again and held it, awkwardly, across the bar. "You didn't do the things he did. You can't apologize for them."

"I don't know what else to do."

"Me neither. Every day I wake up and I'm not sure if today's the day I don't get out of bed. But every day I do. That's all we can do,

Mr. Rodriguez. Keep moving, even when we don't know where we're going." He paused. "And I'm sorry, too."

Joe leaned his head over their clasped hands and started to cry. I wiped my own eyes and pressed against Cam's back.

"I'm so, so sorry," Cam whispered.

Keith and Josh approached carefully, and didn't fully come over until Cam looked at them. Then I moved away so Keith could wrap his arms around Cam. Josh settled for kissing his cheek and standing back.

"Z." Dred's voice, close to my ear. "Hey."

I turned and leaned into her. "Hey."

"If you're crying, we're breaking up. I don't do tears."

I muffled my tears—and my laughter—in her neck. She didn't let go.

Carlos held court at each picture board in turn, calling out names, inviting people to share their memories. He'd found a crate to stand on so he could shout from a higher vantage point.

I stood at the back with Jaq and Alisha, watching and laughing. And occasionally crying.

After a particularly illustrative description of a guy we'd gone to high school with (whom Carlos had never liked), Alisha said, "I think he missed his calling. Carlos should be an auctioneer. Or maybe a stand-up comedian, famous for his bitter tirades against members of the audience."

Jaq choked on her chili fry. "Shit, he'd be *perfect* at that. But I bet being a CPA pays better."

"Too bad." Alisha grinned. "I'd be his groupie. Like, I'd quit my job and follow Carlos around the country and cheer when he picked on people."

"Don't ever tell him that." I shook my head. "He might actually consider doing it if you tell him he has a built-in groupie."

She laughed. "Ed! Babe, come here!"

"What?" Ed shot her a suspicious look. "You're up to something."

"I'm not! Listen, if Carlos became a stand-up comedian, you'd quit the paper to be a groupie with me, right?" She planted both hands on his chest. "Right?"

"What . . . are we talking about right now?"

"I'm bored! We need to take a trip!"

Ed glanced at us, then up at Carlos. "But just you and me, right? I mean, I like Carlos, but I don't want to go on a vacation with him."

"Just us!"

Ed kissed her. "Name your month, as long as it's April or later, and I'll get time off work. But make it a surprise, okay? I don't want to know where we're going until we're packing."

"Screw that. I'll pack for you and let you know when we're already on the road."

He smiled and kissed the corner of her mouth. "Deal. Give me the dates. I'm gonna go try to get some more quotes for—" His gaze caught on me. "For, uh, the piece I am totally not writing right now."

Jaq snorted. "Way to cover your ass there, Ed."

"Gotta go."

Alisha clapped her hands together as he walked away. "We're going to *Mexico*. I'm so excited. He's always wanted to, and I think the vacation fund will have enough money in it by June. Oh my god, I'm *so* excited. I have to find a way to talk to his abuela without him knowing."

Jaq patted her shoulder. "Sounds like fun."

"Oh yeah. It's gonna be *fantastic*. I gotta start planning." Her eyes glazed over.

I traded looks with Jaq and both of us laughed.

"To each their own," she said. "Dance with me, Zane. You think we could get Fredi to play Madonna for us?"

"I think I'm not gonna ask her, but if you are, I want to watch."

She rolled her eyes. "Fuck it. Let's go dance."

"You think—" I gestured to the wake.

"It's fine. Everyone's fine. Come on."

I followed her to the dance floor, but right as we got there, the music cut out and Jaq laughed. In a suspicious manner.

"What?" I poked her. Harder than absolutely necessary.

"You'll see in a second." She laughed again.

Feedback hummed from the speakers, then stopped. Fredi could be heard in the background saying, "Oh Jesus fuck!"

People laughed.

She cleared her throat into the microphone and cursed again. "This is why I don't do fucking announcements. This is Fredi, as you all should know. If you haven't stopped by to look at the pictures at the front of the bar, you should. Because that's why people go to a fucking bar, to cry." She cleared her throat again.

I grinned at Jaq.

"Anyway, it's come to my attention that one of my most forgettable customers recently got engaged. Congratulations, Jaffe."

My mouth dropped open.

"Your poor wife-to-be. I really don't know what the hell she's thinking. Anyway, she wanted me to play the Beatles for you, but fuck that, this ain't a goddamn oldies bar. So she decided on this instead. Fucking congratulations. Jesus! Tom! How do I turn this fucking thing off?"

I turned, searching for Dred, but I didn't see her until Jaq physically pointed me in her direction.

She was leaning against a huge speaker, long skirt around her ankles, arms crossed. Watching me. Looking hot and like I was the best thing she'd seen all day.

For a second she managed to hold back her smile. Then her entire face sort of melted and reformed into . . . happiness.

I swallowed a lump in my throat and pulled her into the center of the dance floor as the club mix of Clean Bandit's "Rather Be" started up. "This is our song now."

She rolled her eyes. "Do we really need to be *that* couple? Who have a song? Really?"

"Oh yeah." I tugged her hands to my hips. "Hell yes." I caught sight of Emerson and Obie over her shoulder, dancing slower and closer than anyone else.

I wanted a little of that. I pressed myself in against Dred.

"Thought we were dancing," she murmured.

"We are. Just, you know, closely."

One of her hands slid around, grazing the side of my belly. "Fine. This can be our song."

"Because as long as we're both here, there's nowhere else you'd rather be?"

She sighed. "Yeah, Z. Because of that."

I leaned back and framed her face in my hands. "Jaq's right, you know. We should get married fast so I don't back out."

I expected an argument about the appropriate months for weddings, which I was prepared to counter with a reminder that we weren't having a big ceremony. But that's not what she said.

"We need time to make a new quilt."

"But we aren't done with our old quilts."

She shook her head, careful to not dislodge my hands. "Doesn't matter. We need a wedding quilt. Aunt Florence is already planning it."

I stopped swaying. "Wait. Seriously?"

"Yeah. And my dad wants to come to the county clerk's with us. Sorry."

"Wait. What? Is Aunt Florence planning our wedding?" I smirked. "How long have you been telling people you were going to marry me, Dred?"

"Shut up. And no. I wasn't. But some people . . . were not that surprised. Anyway, shut up. We have to finish our wedding quilt before we get married."

I pulled her back into a slow dance. "I kind of have an idea. But I don't know if you're gonna hate it."

"Probably. What?"

Maybe it was a terrible idea. It was either terrible or genius. I couldn't decide.

"Z, what?"

"What if we made more blocks for your quilt? But with stuff from like . . . my life too? Is that awful? I don't want to totally appropriate your Aunt Florence quilt—"

She kissed me, her entire body holding me still so that the only things moving were our lips. And her eyes, searching mine.

"Yes." Her chest was rising and falling fast. "Yes. Z. Yes, that's perfect. That is exactly what we're going to do. All the pieces of us in one quilt. Like all the pieces of the past coming together to make our future." She bit her lip.

I kissed her this time, and kept kissing her until she pulled away. Even though I knew she wouldn't bullshit about quilts, I still had to ask, "Are you sure?"

"Yeah. Completely sure. It's perfect."

We started dancing again. The song turned over, but we weren't really dancing to music, anyway.

I could picture it, if I tried. Our quilt. All of our blocks combined into one picture. One life. I could picture James chewing on the edge of that quilt. When I closed my eyes I could almost picture another baby, a younger baby, lying on it. Our family.

I shivered.

"You cold?" she murmured in my ear, arms tightening around my back.

"No. I'm totally and completely content in this moment. Is that crazy?"

She laughed. "Yeah. But crazy works for you, Z."

I leaned my head against hers, and we danced and danced and danced.

Explore more of the *Queers of La Vista* series:
riptidepublishing.com/titles/universe/queers-la-vista

Dear Reader,

Thank you for reading Kris Ripper's *As La Vista Turns*!

We know your time is precious and you have many, many entertainment options, so it means a lot that you've chosen to spend your time reading. We really hope you enjoyed it.

We'd be honored if you'd consider posting a review—good or bad—on sites like **Amazon, Barnes & Noble, Kobo, Goodreads, Twitter, Facebook, Tumblr,** and your blog or website. We'd also be honored if you told your friends and family about this book. Word of mouth is a book's lifeblood!

For more information on upcoming releases, author interviews, blog tours, contests, giveaways, and more, please sign up for our weekly, spam-free newsletter and visit us around the web:

Newsletter: tinyurl.com/RiptideSignup
Twitter: twitter.com/RiptideBooks
Facebook: facebook.com/RiptidePublishing
Goodreads: tinyurl.com/RiptideOnGoodreads
Tumblr: riptidepublishing.tumblr.com

Thank you so much for Reading the Rainbow!

RiptidePublishing.com

ACKNOWLEDGMENTS

As always, General Wendy took her red pen to this book, though it will be noted that one can never write enough Aunt Florence to satisfy her. Thanks for answering my urgent pleas for help. (Again.)

My quilting consultant was the delightful Jeanne, who once casually mentioned quilting in an email to me and had no idea that this offhand comment would spark my imagination. This is a cautionary tale: be careful what you say to your writer friends, lest they come back around six months later and demand to know everything there is to know about quilting.

A tip of the hat to anyone who guesses the historical romance on Cam's Kindle. Hint: if you follow me on Twitter, you will have seen me sing the praises of a particular series, and beg the author for more.

Keith gets his love of budgeting from me. I know that's random. But I really love budgeting.

Full Catastrophe Living is a real book, by Jon Kabat-Zinn. The app is also real. (Four weeks is as long as I've lasted, but someday . . . someday . . .)

There may have been a pizza place in El Sobrante (or possibly San Pablo) where the lads from Green Day were occasionally sighted. Not that I know anything about that. Or that I have any old concert shirts banging about. Um.

Regarding how you make a quilt with a signature in it, the artist had this to say: "Grief makes doing crazy, impossible things necessary and easy." You can find more about the NAMES Project AIDS Memorial Quilt here: aidsquilt.org. There are a lot of panels. At least one of them has a signature.

I owe a tremendous debt of gratitude to a lot of people for encouraging me to write this series when I wasn't sure anyone would want to read interconnected queer romance novels with a serial killer subplot.

First, I'm pretty sure this entire project can be traced back to the paper bags of mass market paperbacks traded between the members of my family throughout my childhood. Mingled romances and murder mysteries, ever-present in the trunks of cars, or falling over in entryways, long before I was old enough to actually read them. (If it wasn't for all the queer, my grandma would love this series.)

Another thing that weaseled its way into my brain is a podcast episode by EE Ottoman called "Six Things," about the things they would like to see in romance. The entire podcast is magnificent, but I was particularly inspired by a portion in the middle about seeing a broader representation of queer community in queer-centric romance.

In a sense, this series is my answer to that. My grateful thanks to EE for the nudge. The episode can be found here: acosmistmachine.com/2015/04/15/six-things.)

A few of the usual folks were more specific in their nudges. Thanks to Wendy, Judith, Roan Parrish, Alexis Hall, J.R. Gray, Ellen Dunn, and any number of other folks who raised their hands and said, "I'd read that!" More thanks to Sarah Lyons and May Peterson, who shepherded these books (and their author) through an often obscure publishing process, and to Alex Whitehall for ensuring I look way smarter than I actually am (and that I know how to use commas).

Most of this series was written at the Columbia College Library, where my fellow library-goers tolerated my mad seated-dancing to whatever Pandora happened to be playing in my ears. (I have somehow programmed the Pentatonix station to play a lot of Linkin Park. Yes, it's as awesome as it sounds.) And this list would not be complete without noting my delighted appreciation for the folks at my kid's preschool, who made sure she was safe and fed and happy while I scribbled as quickly as my little fingers would go. I couldn't have written five books in five months without knowing the kid was being well loved elsewhere.

I also want to clumsily say, here, at the end, that these books were fun to write, and they were also painful. They made me think of all the ways we are not safe, not even from each other. Far more than that, they made me search for the strength and courage and compassion that I have seen and experienced in my community.

We're still fighting. In some places we're still fighting for our lives every day.

These books are fiction, and they're meant to make you laugh, cringe, maybe even cry, because anything that makes you laugh should also be able to twist that part of you until you remember that shit hurts sometimes, too. But if I've done my job right, they should make you think a little, as well. About your communities, the intersections that make up your identity, and how we're all connected to each other. Real life ain't a soap opera, but you can be damn sure that you and I are connected, however tenuously.

Sometimes even when we don't want to be. Ahem. We may see Merin again one of these days. I'm not making any promises, but . . .

ALSO BY
KRIS RIPPER

Queers of La Vista
Gays of Our Lives
The Butch and the Beautiful
The Queer and the Restless
One Life to Lose

Scientific Method Universe
Catalysts
Unexpected Gifts
Take Three Breaths
Breaking Down
Roller Coasters
The Boyfriends Tie the Knot
The Honeymoon
Extremes
The New Born Year
Threshold of the Year
Surrender the Past
The Library, Volume 1

New Halliday
Fairy Tales
The Spinner, the Shepherd, and the Leading Man
The Real Life Build
Take the Leap

The Home Series
Going Home
Home Free
Close to Home
Home for the Holidays

Little Red and the Big Bad
Serial One
Serial Two

The Erotic Gym:
Training Mac
The Ghost in the Penthouse

For a complete book list, visit: krisripper.com

ABOUT THE AUTHOR

Kris Ripper lives in the great state of California and hails from the San Francisco Bay Area. Kris shares a converted garage with a toddler, can do two pull-ups in a row, and can write backwards. (No, really.) Kris is genderqueer and prefers the z-based pronouns because they're freaking sweet. Ze has been writing fiction since ze learned how to write, and boring zir stuffed animals with stories long before that.

Website: krisripper.com

Newsletter: krisripper.com/about/subscribe-what

Facebook: facebook.com/kris.ripper

Twitter: twitter.com/SmutTasticKris

YouTube: youtube.com/user/KrisRipper

Enjoy more stories like *As La Vista Turns* at RiptidePublishing.com!

Far From Home
ISBN: 978-1-62649-452-7

Stuck Landing
ISBN: 978-1-62649-329-2

Earn Bonus Bucks!

Earn 1 Bonus Buck for each dollar you spend. Find out how at RiptidePublishing.com/news/bonus-bucks.

Win Free Ebooks for a Year!

Pre-order coming soon titles directly through our site and you'll receive one entry into a drawing for a chance to win free books for a year! Get the details at RiptidePublishing.com/contests.

CPSIA information can be obtained
at www.ICGtesting.com
Printed in the USA
LVOW08s1036130317
527007LV00002B/14/P